ACROSS
THE NARROWS

ACROSS THE NARROWS

A NOVEL

MARTHA BURNS

atmosphere press

For my mother, Alice Anne del Castillo Jackson
(1928–2017)

*But she left us and broke the whole family, and the
sorrow was released and we saw its wings and saw
it fly a thousand ways into the hills...*

Marilynne Robinson, *Housekeeping*

PART I

CHAPTER 1

RUBY
1924

I was alone with the baby until my father arrived. The baby had not been expected for weeks, and she was my sixth, so I knew when things were not right. I was at Kings County Hospital in Flatbush, Brooklyn, on a late spring day in 1924. I watched as Papa pulled up the leather armchair to my bed and asked the nurse, who'd followed him in, to open the Venetian blinds.

"That tree there is full of busy birds," the nurse said. She squinted at the birds as if trying to figure out her next move and then left the room.

Now I squinted at the baby. Blonde curls swirled about her perfect ears. I could feel her weight even though the nurse had propped a pillow under her. I could feel the cramping too—it would go on like this in waves as if reminding me that this would pass, and I'd heal.

It just worked out that Papa was in Brooklyn that day: happenstance. Not that he would have seen it that way.

For a reason. That was his way of seeing the world.

He had come to town that day on the train to attend a luncheon at the Brooklyn Club. Surely, he would be called upon for both the invocation and the benediction. My mother was in Methodist Hospital in Mahwah, New Jersey, where my parents had retired. The nurse had called there, and after my mother explained exactly where to find Papa, Mother would have settled back down in her hospital bed and taken up her beloved detective fiction.

"Receive my love," Papa said as he lifted the bundle wrapped in the pale pink, ribbon-bound blanket out of my arms and kissed the baby's forehead. The midday sunlight fell on the two of them.

"Too late," I said. "She never even opened her eyes."

Papa nodded, which was something he was able to do with his whole body, as he said, "Precious child."

I'd never told him that I had not wanted another child. Hadn't wanted this baby. He would have said he didn't believe me.

But then the doctor appeared in the doorway, and the nurse came back into the room. Her starched white dress looked like it might crack with her movements, and her heavy shoes told me exactly where she had stopped her march across the room.

"Blue Baby," she said.

"Her name is Alice. My husband has always wanted to name a daughter Alice. We've agreed," I said.

Papa nodded and said, "So it shall be." The doctor looked befuddled, but he didn't need to understand.

"A heart defect. It robs the blood of oxygen," the doctor said, and when I looked up to stare at the man, he looked away and said, "Died for want of oxygen." He was finished with me. He'd come in to speak with my father.

"All for the want of a horseshoe nail," I said to put a stop to their chatter. It was something my mother was known to say to express her annoyance at one of us children, and then she would step back into her routine. Contentment was my mother's religion.

"You've called for Mr. del Palacio?" my father asked the nurse whose face was as pockmarked as my childhood brownstone home.

"Me? Well, yes, of course," she said.

"He's often waylaid leaving New York City," I said, realizing, as I said it, that I was making excuses for my husband. It was not something my mother had taught me, and I wondered if making excuses was the same as finding a reason.

"Might you go for a hairbrush for Mrs. del Palacio?" Papa asked the nurse. My hair was wild and damp on my forehead, but I refused to reach up and fuss with it.

And now the nurse looked at me and said, "Missus, you tuck your head under your wing." She may have winked. I was onto her now. She was steering me away from negative emotions—what with the asylum wing nearby and the ghosts wandering the halls pulling hair. My brothers had told me those stories to scare me when I was little, but that was long ago, and I was not a child.

The doctor bowed as the nurse left the room and started to follow her, but instead he turned on his heels, headed over to the armchair, put his hand on my father's shoulder, and said, "Dr. Farrar, we even tried putting her under a blue light. But from the moment of birth, she was in distress. She was many weeks early."

"For want of a nail," I said loudly now because it seemed they had forgotten me. My mother would not have abided such bad manners.

Just as a cramp was taking hold of me, Papa took one of his large hands from under the bundle and pressed it on the doctor's hand as if to assure him that he might leave safely. The cramp crested, and I slid down into the bedcovers.

When the doctor was out of the room, Papa began to unwrap the blanket. Someone had dressed the baby in a white gown with itty-bitty, heart-shaped mother of pearl buttons. It was meant as a kindness, but I've never been able to abide the stone since then.

Then, as if he were in a private conversation with God, my father said, "My soul is sad but faith sings."

I was used to such moments.

"Papa," I said. "When Juan gets here, tell him to remove the bassinet from our bedroom and give it away."

"I will, Ruby. Of course, I will do that."

He took my hand, and I never wanted to let go. Then, because I knew he'd believe me, I said, "No one will ever have one single thing to say about baby Alice."

"We will have to tell the story, Ruby."

He settled into his chair. Carefully, he rewrapped the blanket. I saw him rub the satin ribbon between his thumb and forefinger. He was preparing a story for me. He could tell the most marvelous bedtime stories to a sleepy little girl. Every winter when I had tonsillitis, he sat at my bedside and soothed me with his wonderfully gentle voice, but today I didn't want one of his tales. My baby was dead, and I had not wanted her.

I ignored him.

He looked away from me and studied the baby, and then said, "Hello, Juan." And then, in a voice he reserved for those who were grieving, he said, "My sympathies." I felt the ground shift as my husband, here to take control from my father, crossed the room. He was smaller than my father but took heavy steps. It should have been Papa who shook the ground, but he was not like that.

I turned to face the wall. Childish, I knew.

My father stood and said, "Let us express our thanks to God almighty for this child. Alice del Palacio."

"No, she is dead. I will not name her Alice," Juan said, and I turned to study him. His face revealed not even a hint of kindness.

Or sadness.

"Then we will call her Faith," I said.

Papa kissed the baby's forehead and held her up so that we all could study her. In the sunlight her hair took on a red glow, making me think that if she had lived her hair might have turned red one day like the great mane of red hair Papa had in my childhood. She had gently pouting lips. She showed no sign of distress, and unlike me, she was pretty.

With authority, Papa nodded to Juan that he should sit in the chair next to me and handed him the infant—our infant. Then Papa leaned over and kissed me on my forehead, and said, "We have a place for Faith at Green-Wood near baby

Richard." It sounded like a prayer, and I bent my head thinking he'd say amen. But he did not say that. He said, "Precious child," and he meant me.

I watched Papa cross the room, passing the nurse who had returned with a hairbrush that she waved at him, and he said, "She will be named Faith."

"I will let everyone know her name," the nurse said, holding up the brush as if to ask if she might help with my hair. I was sure then that she'd been the one to dress the baby, and knowing this made me smile. I saw disdain on my Colombian husband's finely sculptured face.

My husband being there, holding our baby, might have made the nurse think our marital craft was seaworthy. Juan and I had been featured in the newspaper often. Our wedding had been reported on page one of the *Brooklyn Eagle* society section—all so much hoopla about flowers and colors. But this nurse already knew more about me than any Park Slope busybody. She was right here in the room, seeing what she saw. I never wanted her to leave. I closed my eyes and let her brush my hair. It was only a minute maybe before I heard Papa come back into the room. I heard him whisper to Juan that he'd need to remove the bassinet.

"I've already thought of that," Juan said in his patrician tone. He used it to make certain people of lower classes knew he was of high birth.

"Yes, of course you have," my father said. "Blessed are those who mourn, for they shall be comforted," he added, but I was not sure he if he was speaking to me or to Juan. I opened my eyes and watched as my father took a step closer to the nurse, took her hand in his, and said, "The Lord gave us days without gloom. The Lord gave the birds a song." That sounded more like my father.

"Papa, please close the blinds," I said. And then, to annoy my husband who didn't bother with such niceties and hadn't thought to bring me sweets, I said, "You must stop and get

Mother some madeleines before you catch your train. And Papa, I'm sorry that you had to leave the Brooklyn Club before you gave the benediction."

"Ruby, I was meant to be here with you," he said.

I've remembered such things all my life, but I also remember that on that day he very much wanted to get back to the hospital in Mahwah in time to be with my mother. She was, after all, the love of his life.

I knew that by now Juan's mother would have left her home on Second Street in Park Slope to take charge of mine. She'd be ordering our new maid, Tessie, around and seeing to minuscule details—things that didn't matter. She was often there and had a room of her own on the third floor. She walked with a cane she did not yet need and used it to punctuate her sentences. The children were always wide-eyed around her, and even my littlest one, Clara, who was barely walking, knew how to scamper away and keep her distance from her grandmother.

The nurse took the infant from Juan, and with her eyes asked if I wanted to hold her again. I could not bear it. My baby looked nothing like my other children. She looked like my beautiful brother, Richard, who had died when he was still a baby. Maybe it was what death looked like.

I looked away from the nurse and she left with the infant and then returned and asked Juan to step out while she did what she called, "a little checking." I was bleeding, and I wanted to ask her if women who'd given birth six times sometimes bled to death. It would have been better to know. "The blood is normal and very red," she said before I could ask her about dying, and she gave me a spoonful of some sweet red syrup. "You aren't going to die, Mrs. Not with five children at home who must miss you."

A sob came up from the bottom of what Papa would call my soul. The nurse put her hand on my forehead until I got my breath. "My children are afraid of my husband's mother.

She is a cruel, secret adversary, and she is turning the children against me one by one. Like a thief in the night..."

I was beginning to sound deranged and so I stopped to gather my breath again.

"She is depriving them of childhood. Especially my son, Mateo. He's no longer mine. She tries to speak Spanish to him to exclude me."

I was feeling self-righteous and nasty, but the nurse, who still had her hand on my forehead, looked into my eyes and, intending to stop me, said, "Faith is a beautiful child. I am sure your others are as well. Beauties. And your mother called. She sounded very sad about the baby."

The nurse took my hand and held it in a way that made me explain that my mother was taking her time recovering from a double surgery. This time I was sure I saw the wink right before she said, "She told me that you will be receiving some flowers and madeleines. I am to watch for them."

"Oh goody," I said, but I was crying again, and she let me cry for what seemed like a long time. Then she checked my pulse by putting the tips of her index and second fingers softly on the underside of my wrist. We then looked at each other and she nodded.

She said she would go find my husband. I was so sorry then for her scarred face, but what could I say?

When she ushered Juan back into the room, he smelled of cigars and I wondered if he smelled blood.

Juan and I didn't talk at all in the hour or so he sat there. He could have taken my hand or asked if I needed anything. He did not assure me that our beautiful baby had died for a reason. We never touched. Not once; I would have remembered. When he got up to leave, I looked at him so harshly that he knew he had to say something.

"The children need me home now," he said.

I could not imagine for what. It was an excuse, and as the wave of the next round of cramps took control of my body, I looked right at him and said, "I am their mother. It is me they need."

He didn't reply. Instead, he checked his watch and fooled with his mustache. I knew he wanted a cigar because he always fidgeted that way before lighting one. I think he smoked all day long while he busied himself on Beaver Street in Manhattan in his world of men, leaving me with his mother and her judgment.

At that moment, when I was thinking about the world of men that did not include babies—dead or alive—I thought about the stray kitten Clara had found on our front porch the week before. Maybe it was the syrup making me think of kittens. Tessie, who had a kind heart, helped Clara feed the kitten daily in the mudroom at precisely four in the afternoon, but she would not dare to do that today with Juan's mother watching her every move.

"See that Clara's kitten is fed today at four," I said. Again, I saw disdain on his handsome face.

It had been a horrible mistake to call his attention to that kitten. Guilt, like the guilt a young child feels when they've done something heartless, ate at me for years.

Papa was young again in my syrup dream when I heard him say, "A long life is not the only reward." He was backing out of the bedroom he shared with my mother. He was on tiptoes. He began to whistle a little senseless tune.

"Stop that," my mother called out. "I am not lighthearted."

"Oh, Ruby," Papa said softly when he spotted me standing on the stepstool at the hand basin outside their bedroom. I'd been watching him in the mirror while he spoke to my mother, who was buried beneath her red silk puff.

"Let's have you ring the dinner bell, Ruby. Gather your brothers," Papa said as he pulled the folding doors to their bedroom closed behind him and bent to take my hand to walk me down the front stairs of our brownstone on President Street. I smelled the white funeral flowers that had stood proud in their tall vases just after baby Richard died but were drooping now. I faked a choke and felt Papa's hand on my back, patting gently. He was on to me.

Now I used caution to open my eyes. I spotted the lilies that my mother had sent making the hospital room unbearably sweet with their heavy fragrance. They had been carefully arranged in a pink pot the shape of a cradle. It seemed cruel. Then out of my fog I realized it was my nurse making her rounds who was singing Papa's little tune as if it weren't the middle of the night—as if all her charges at the Kings County Hospital were content, snugly tucked away under soft blankets.

"Hello, Missus," she said as she walked up to my hospital bed. The light from the hallway made her white uniform iridescent. She fluffed my hair and said, "Your father taught me a verse today, and I made it into a song. Imagine that." I heard her stirring around the room later, and I think she must have come in to remove the vase of flowers because the next day they were gone.

CHAPTER 2

RUBY
1924

Three weeks later, my mother was still too weak to travel from Mahwah, New Jersey, to Brooklyn for Faith's burial, and Juan's parents had gone right ahead with their plans and sailed to Colombia. My brothers were scattered here and there and were busy men, or so my mother often reminded me, and so it was just the three of us burying Faith at Green-Wood that summer day.

It was just as well. My mother-in-law had been judging me since the day I came home from the hospital with no infant. That woman judged in silence but complained aloud about how the task of running my household had puffed up her ankles. They had never been fine-boned.

My children were in the early days of their summer holiday and once their grandmother left on her worldly travels, they had relaxed. They knew that the baby I had been carrying had died, but they felt no guilt in living and why should they? And they did not grieve either; mostly, they looked after one another. Of course, there were maids. There were always Colombian maids, grateful to be sent to New York for a new life. Juan left early each day, crossing the Brooklyn Bridge to attend to business in Manhattan, and returned home late. So, I'd settled into my recovery, and with no infant to mark the time of each day, my mind was settling too.

Papa put me between him and Juan as we walked through the gates at the northern entrance to Green-Wood Cemetery, and Papa said, "We have a blue-sky day."

He had presided at many funerals here. My brother Richard was buried here. His grave marker said that he had not lived to the age of buttons and buttonholes. We Farrars were nothing if not a sentimental family. I looked at Juan, saw his gold cufflinks flashing in the sunlight, and knew that there would be no kindness between us today.

"Did you spot the parakeets, Ruby?" Papa asked as if I were his small child.

"Where?" I asked, interested because even at thirty years old I was his child still.

"There, in the spires of the gate." He pointed so far up that I was looking mostly at sky. He was right; the sky was a violet blue. I saw the nests too. They were large, delicate structures made of small, pointed sticks, as if the birds were imitating the exact style of the Gothic gate.

"Monk parakeets are social creatures and smart," Papa said.

"Unsightly," Juan said. "And feral. In Cartagena, they are rightly considered pests."

Juan had a firm hold of my upper arm. He squeezed, and I said, "Juan does not like birds." It was the evilest thing I could think to say just then about my husband.

And then, yanking my arm free, I said, "You mean these colorful birds that have escaped captivity are feral?"

One of the birds screeched, a loud and throaty cry, and Papa said, "That one there must have a twenty-inch wingspan."

It would have been a terribly long walk to the open grave, and we would have needed a map, and so Papa had arranged for a carriage. It was black. I decided then that I'd bring the children here. People did that, and I'd tell them about Faith and the seven thousand trees spread over hundreds of acres here at the cemetery. I'd explain that Faith, a pretty little thing, had not been strong enough to live and that I was sad, very sad she'd died. And I'd show them the nests the parakeets had built in the gates.

The white coffin waited for us at the small grave. It was draped in a cloth of pink Killarney roses. My mother had seen to that from her hospital bed.

When I was married in the parlor of my childhood home on President Street, Mother had filled the room with those fragrant pink roses, but it was not the roses on my wedding day but rather the pungent smell of the lilies that had made my nose itch and my eyes water with memories of my baby brother.

"Do not scratch your nose with those gloves on," was the sum total of the advice my mother gave me on my wedding day. For that, I had not forgiven her.

A wedding, I'd wanted to tell my mother a few years later, is not a marriage. I wanted to make her responsible for the disappointments I had caused Papa, because I had disappointed him with my loveless marriage. I shook my head, looked at the small grave, and tried to think about Faith in the delicate white gown.

Green-Wood was a garden and so on that day as we three stood at the grave, Papa spoke of gardens. "God made the world, but did not finish it," he said. "He only did that part no other person could do. Then God made Adam and told him to complete the work. From that time on, men and women have been at work making the world into a garden."

"Like Paris?" I said because I knew that this cemetery had been designed after a Parisian Cemetery and because for some reason my mother had taught my brothers and me how to dream about Paris. Juan, who'd not said a word at the grave of our baby, said, "Like Cartagena." He was proud that way.

Standing at the grave that June day as the coffin was lowered, I heard the whir of wings and looked up at the green underbellies of a flock of those spirited birds. They'd followed us and were chattering to each other. I heard another carriage come slowly up the lane toward us and I thought perhaps one of my brothers had arrived to be with me at the baby's burial, but I could see that there was only a driver, and then I heard the woman who was wandering amongst the graves.

"My carriage awaits," she said, pointing. She was too young, and the day was too hot for all the layers of black she was wearing. I too was in a black dress, and so she might have felt we shared something. "Another Farrar baby?" she said just as my father took my arm and wound it through his.

"No, a del Palacio," I said after several seconds because I had to think about it. But Juan was not listening this time for the slight, and it didn't matter anyway.

"What's her name?"

"Faith," my father said, and I saw Juan glare at the woman as if he were telling her to move along. Her carriage had pulled up alongside ours, and the horses were stomping and snorting, and the woman waved at the horses gaily as if to say, "Don't be silly."

"I walk here often. My babies are buried over that hill. I'll come by and check on Faith when I visit mine."

"What a beautiful thing love is, stronger than anything, even death," Papa said.

The woman held her delicate hand to her mouth, indicating we should all be quiet. A large emerald ring on her left hand caught the light as she looked up for the birds, waved, and said, "Goodbye." And then this woman in her fine black satin walked away with a lightness in her step.

To distract me from the grave where now two cemetery workers were politely waiting for us to leave, Papa pointed to a spot under a cherry tree that held only a few white blossoms, and said, "Your brother Richard is buried right over there," and then he took my gloved hand and walked me toward Richard's grave.

"Papa," I said, "it was the swans at Prospect Park that made Richard sick. I know that you knew that. I know Mother told you. And now Faith is dead." His eyes narrowed, and suddenly I didn't recognize him. He bent his head as if he needed time to think.

My mother and I had gone to Prospect Park with my little brother and our maid Annie to see the new snow-white swans. Papa had said they were mute swans.

Everyone in Brooklyn had heard about the pair of swans. They'd been a gift to the city to adorn Prospect Park. I couldn't imagine who'd give swans as a gift, but I was a child and wanted to see them come floating across the lake. We had not expected them to be wandering along the bank, and before Annie could gather baby Richard up from where she had sat him in the grass, the swans were at him.

Now, as Papa gripped my hand tighter, I said, "Papa, they fought us with their wings. Mother beat at them with her umbrella, and they ran."

I waited for him to say something, but we kept walking, leaving Juan behind at Faith's open grave.

"Papa, those backing-away, black-footed swans should not have been beautiful to me, but they were. I never told Mother that I was showing Richard their nest, and how I stepped back on their eggs. It was an accident."

When we reached Richard's grave, my father said, "Ruby, your baby brother was a sick little child. The swans had nothing to do with him dying. I think he must have loved seeing those perfect little eggs, don't you?"

I looked back at my husband and watched as he lit a fat brown cigar and then held his head back to blow smoke at the parakeets.

I shook my head at him in disgust and shouted, "Stop it." And then I turned back to my father and made no apology.

I never once heard Papa whistle again after that afternoon when I was four years old and my mother was grieving for her dead child. I remember it was late summer because the four-o'clocks were in bloom and Papa had promised me that after our lunch there would be time to see those flowers open up in our backdoor garden.

After lunch that day, he said, "Way too much quiet in this

house," and led me to his study. He took a seat behind his large desk and pointed to the guest chair. And once I was settled on the stack of books he kept handy as a booster, he began to explain that my mother was heartsick about her baby boy dying. "The simple fact is, she's sad."

I had built up three or four days of self-satisfied annoyance at the chaos that had taken over our house. After all, there were things my mother was supposed to do. I felt nasty, and I couldn't think of one single way to be sad for her.

Papa got up from his swivel chair and said, "Come along."

We stepped up and out onto the roof. He took his seat in the rocker, and seeing that I was clear of the rungs, he began to rock.

"Mother's garden sparkles at four-o'clock," he said, and I finally gave into a smile for him. We both knew that my mother never stepped out into the garden.

He pointed at the flowers that were beginning to open and said, "Did you know that rubies can sometimes be that exact color of pink?"

I looked straight at him because often he teased me, and I could tell it was a tease if his nose wrinkled up a bit. But it wasn't a tease, and he said, "Sometimes, if you're sad, you need to just learn something interesting."

"Hmmm, interesting," I said.

He kept rocking.

"Now, perhaps you should dash down to the garden and pull me some weeds," he said. And so, I uncurled my legs and slipped back into his study, took the back stairs at an unladylike clip, and dashed through the kitchen and into the garden. There were indeed weeds, and some were too painful to touch. I pulled on Annie's gardening gloves and tiptoed out far enough to look up and see Papa. He had his eyes closed, and it was years before I realized that he too was simply sad.

I could hear the woman's carriage moving away. I didn't know why I had never bothered all those years of growing up to visit Richard's grave, why my mother had not brought me here to Green-Wood.

But I was a lazy little girl, that I remember. On that afternoon when my father sent me out to pull weeds, I pulled out only two long-rooted weeds, dropped Annie's gloves on the flagstone walkway, and made a dash for the door. I knew Annie would retrieve the gloves, and besides my mother was in her bedroom and never leaving it again as far as I could tell.

But I had been wrong about my mother. When I went back into the kitchen, I found her there sitting in her kitchen rocker. Her hair was messy and not as black as usual. It looked as if she'd been dusted with ash and her sad eyes were puffy. She said, "You and I will eat supper here in the kitchen with Annie. We carry on. Go back and pick us some flowers for our table and throw those weeds in the bin. And pick up Annie's gloves, Lady Vere de Vere."

Annie was packing up leftovers that Papa would take with him to church that evening. He'd head over later with the younger two of my brothers, Jimmy and Eddie, for the six o'clock Young People's dinner. Girls were not allowed.

When we sat down for our dinner, I heard Papa calling my brothers, and then he stepped into the kitchen. Annie handed him the basket of food and he turned to my mother and said, "Meet me at the eagle." It was something they'd started saying to one another when they visited Wanamaker's in Philadelphia long before I was born. My brothers and I had heard that story many times. We knew all about the eagle and its thousands of bronze feathers. But it had nothing to do with me, so that evening I had ignored him.

Now my father put his hand on the small of my back to steer me over to Faith's grave. I saw that Juan was holding three of the pink roses at his side as if he did not know what he should do with them.

As we crossed the lawn, Papa said, "Do you remember the blue and white striped ribbon that your mother strung with silver bells for Richard's last Christmas?"

I nodded because I did remember, and I remembered that when my mother came into my room that night after dinner with Annie in our kitchen, I told her I was sad. I think her reply was simply, "That is fine."

The next day, I had forgotten about sadness and after breakfast I noticed that the dreadful lilies were gone. When Papa had left for his busy day, my mother said, "Papa tells me you never finished pulling weeds in my garden. Scoot." I'd put my hands on my hips in a priss, thinking I might make her laugh. But she walked away and said, "A horse, a horse, my kingdom for a horse."

When Papa and I joined Juan at the grave, he handed my father and me each a rose. After we tossed them into the grave, I took my husband's hand and said, "Those roses are naturally thornless. That is why my mother chose them for our wedding." It was a little thing, but I've always remembered it.

CHAPTER 3

RUBY
1925

A year later, at precisely two o'clock, Juan and I paraded our family into my in-laws' parlor at 621 Second Street in Park Slope, Brooklyn. There had been many afternoons like this one, but this afternoon stuck in my memory because I had carried in our six-week-old infant who was to be my last child. At the distance of so many years, I can see that I was never part of this merchant family. But even then, I was learning that motherhood could be short lived in some families.

Another new Colombian maid led us into the parlor. This one was untamed and had sparks in her eyes. She took baby Alice from my arms and placed her in the bassinet that was dressed in unbleached Holland linen gone yellow, the color of my mother-in-law's teeth. I gritted mine as I waited at the end of Nana's reception line. It was her right as the matriarch.

Mateo went first. The children were expected to kiss their grandmother, but she was no hugger. As her turn came, Clara, who was one to throw herself into a stranger's arms, stood back as if waiting for something. "Go ahead," I said to her. "Mind Nana's hair now." I had allowed Clara to wear the romantic tutu I'd sewn for her using the fabric from a chiffon dress I'd worn as a tiny flower girl. I had a vivid memory of that wedding. I knew it was a fancy affair and very exclusive, and all these years later I am sure that it was for a senator named La Roche. It amuses me what sticks in my memory, but of course I'd been much admired that day in my green chiffon.

I watched now as Clara was waiting to be admired, mistaken in her thinking that she was pleasing to this stuffy old woman.

I wasn't expected to kiss Nana, and so I turned to take Clara's hand and helped her sit on the sofa where our three daughters had taken their places. They each had brought a book. I envied them. I watched Mateo take his spot in the window seat where he was allowed, now that he was ten, to play with a selection of Juan's toy soldiers. He would have much preferred to read, but there was an order to things and if we each kept to Nana's petty rules, there would be no arguments when we returned home after dinner, and I could go to my desk in our bedroom and write something down. In the days after delivering this baby, a sentence was sometimes all I could manage. Still, I longed to put things down in writing.

Juan sat in the pink chair next to his mother. He dangled his fine hands over the ends of the arms of the chair. The chair was meant for a man and perched on wheels so that it would not get mired down in the deep Spanish rugs the del Palacios collected on trips to Spain. That too, I decided, was a silly thing to choose to remember, but in a long life, memories are not of our choosing.

I counted seconds, waiting to see if the matriarch would ask to hold her new grandchild. Of course, she had taken up residence in our home to spy on me when I brought Alice home from the hospital, but left when the July heat got to her. She'd been no help and I'd been happy to see her go.

"I will need a chair placed next to the bassinet," I said to the maid who was not introduced and would not be. This one didn't check with her mistress before she took action. That would be her undoing.

I felt moisture gather between my two full breasts. They were rock hard. I'd be icing them this evening after the children were put to bed. I would have thought I should be over this by now.

Holding her hand up to shield her mouth as if she was

about to speak about something forbidden, my mother-in-law said, "You need to leave the room to nurse the infant." My oldest daughter looked up in alarm. It seemed that both my daughter and her grandmother were looking at the same spot on my breast as if I might disrobe right there.

"I will nurse her when she is hungry," I said and felt my milk let down. The chair the maid had pulled up for me was upholstered in black velvet, and I would leave a spot if this sparring went on. Juan stood and walked toward the bassinet to signal to me that he was taking matters into his own hands. But without meeting my eyes, he turned toward the door to the study where we could hear his father shouting into the phone in Spanish. A business meeting was in session and the sweet smell of Juan's father's aged cigar told us that the meeting had been in progress for some time now. The man was hiding out.

Juan pulled at his mustache and his mother said so loudly that her own husband was sure to have heard, "Juan, do not interrupt." My husband obeyed his mother. I decided I would do nothing to make nice, and watched as Juan, who was a slight man, took big steps over to the window seat to speak to our son. If he had expected me to save him from his mother, he'd chosen poorly.

"It seems Grandpapa has been waylaid in his own home," I said to my daughters as I stood and patted the pocket on the front of my dress. My mother-in-law and I had discussed pockets recently when she was staying in my home—making the children and our maid Tessie nervous. She found the pockets on my new housedresses common and had said they were something peasants would stitch onto the front of their aprons just to make life easier. This was from a woman who had no problem with me popping out one child after another like some Colombian peasant. I regretted that I had not stashed a small book or cigarettes into my pocket. Yes, cigarettes would have been the better idea.

I could smell the Spanish rice cooking.

"The children will be hungry soon," I said and met the matriarch's eye and then looked past her. I had upset the cart because children never came first in this home. I was certain that the black velvet chair was more precious to her than the children in the room. I narrowly avoided pointing this out when Juan's mother grabbed her cane and pointed it at her son while she spoke in halting Spanish—not loudly this time—but she didn't stab the floor; she saved that for my home. The three older girls, in white Sunday afternoon dresses, snugged closer together, but I caught them looking over the tops of their books.

I understood a great deal of the Spanish Nana spoke and could speak some myself. And so, I said in perfect Spanish, "Yes, eleven years we have been married. You are not the only mother in this room." I saw my future and braced myself. The woman brought her cane down on the floor and the maid, no doubt answering the call of that cane, scurried into the room and this time addressed her mistress with a silent bow. Juan nearly knocked the young woman over getting back to his seat. Mateo pulled the floor-length lace curtains closed, so that he was cocooned in the window seat. The room went silent, and we all waited to see what Nana would do next. I wished for the baby to cry and cause an uproar, and I wished for Juan's father to appear and turn this all around. I knew that would not happen. He practiced avoidance, and the business world he shared with his two sons provided that.

Everyone sat silently in the late summer heat while I lifted the baby out of the bassinet. The maid did a skip over to me and gestured that she would take the infant, but I held Alice tight against my breast and softly sang a parlor song someone had sung for me when I was a child, "Beautiful dreamer, wake unto me." As I remember it now, I see that I was performing, something maybe that I had learned from my brothers. Had there been mermaids chanting? But I had no adoring audience.

Clara, who had taken her place in the lap of one of her sisters, jumped to her feet and grabbed my leg, and I was thankful for a reason to stop my silliness.

Clara was not going to let go, not even when her grandmother scolded her for misbehaving and ordered her to go and sit with her sisters.

"Come along, little pink rose of your mother's heart," I said as I took Clara's tiny hand and gave it to the maid and said, "Where shall we go? Shall we all hide like tiny little mice in Nana's kitchen?" Then we sashayed across the parlor. Juan went to stand, maybe to stop me—maybe to draw me toward him, maybe to admire our baby as my father would have done, but his mother waved her flat, gloved hand at him and once again he obeyed.

I kissed Alice's forehead and followed the maid out of the room.

Surely it was my hard breasts that were making my brain hot. Waiting too long to nurse a child could make a woman mean.

"Get me a cigarette," I said to the maid. It was out of my mouth before I had even stepped into the sitting room off the guest bedroom. I'd been here many times. There was a fringed shawl draped over the back of the hard-backed sofa—a concession to comfort. I'd never told my mother-in-law that I loved this room. She could have locked me in here. A place to be quiet and write and I'd be just fine—happy even, I thought, but if only I had a cigarette. "Please," I whispered now. "I will not get you in trouble. Clara will not tell a soul, will you?" The maid held Clara in her arms now and Clara buried her face in the young woman's neck as if she belonged to her. I promised myself I would do something kind for the maid and for my little daughter, too. French perfume for the maid, I decided, and a kitten for Clara. Juan would not take notice; he was so rarely home.

I stepped backwards and dropped down into the sofa. I

balanced the baby in my lap and began working the buttons on my blouse. The maid watched and then left the room with my daughter, who said, "Don't be sad, Mama." I've always remembered that and to this day I remember her voice. Husky.

I counted the buttons and tried to relax, especially my teeth, which I had been holding in a clamp. "You'll pay for that sour face," my mother used to say when I got myself into what she called a "Girl Snit." And she was right, I would wake up the day after one of those episodes of self-righteous meanness and my mouth and even my neck would ache. I held Alice to my breast, and she latched. At six weeks old, she still took my breath away when she began to nurse. Both my feet lifted off the ground and I tried to hold my thoughts still.

"It will get easier," my mother had said when Mateo was days old. I wasn't sure then what she meant—thinking, maybe hopefully, that she meant life in general. I knew now that she'd only been speaking of nursing. It was draining but easier now and sometimes left me feeling content. I quickly moved Alice to start on my other breast and felt the relief that came from a softening. Alice felt it too and her tiny hand began to knead, and I thought of the kitten Clara had found the year before. It had needed so much love. One night Juan found the kitten in his study. There was a bare spot in the rug where the kitten had pulled threads. Juan banished the creature from our home, speaking so harshly that the kitten never returned. It had terrified the children. Yes, I would find Clara a new kitten. Juan wouldn't know.

Both my feet were resting on the rug now, my face was relaxed, and I felt a rush of well-being. I would have told my mother she was right, but it was too late. She and my father were dead, having died weeks apart. A week after Papa died, my mother said that she'd never considered outliving him and that she didn't have a plan for that part.

My brother Jimmy was with her when she died in her own bed. She'd had Agatha Christie's book *Murder on the Links* at her bedside that fall and winter. When I asked her to tell me about it, she'd said that Agatha warned that two people rarely saw the same thing. Jimmy reported that in the minutes before she died, my mother kept whispering, "Meet me at the eagle." Of course, it was Papa she loved most dearly, and losing him had robbed her of the will to live.

An orphan is what I became the Christmas of 1924, and I dug into my grief as if it was I who had been personally robbed. Jimmy was no better. "I cannot manage that I will never see them again," he said to me at our mother's service. I don't recall much about that Christmas. Someone had arranged for a Christmas tree and gifts for the children, Tessie perhaps. I hope I arranged for sweets.

Clara and the maid came back into the sitting room. Clara sat on the floor, arranged her skirt into a perfect circle around her, and held up a small stuffed sock toy to show me. The maid held two lit cigarettes.

I didn't even know her name.

"We'll smoke together," she said, "and if Missus smells smoke, blame me."

I held the baby tight in the bend of my left arm and lifted the cigarette high over my face. As I exhaled, I repeated a piece of scripture my father had taught me to say when it got hot in August. "Blessed are the peacemakers," I said as I tipped the point of my cigarette at her and added, "I'm Ruby."

"I'm Alice," she said, and we both laughed. Her eyes sparkled as she said, "It is a popular name in Colombia." Her English was pretty good, like Tessie's, and I wondered if Nana knew. I should have warned her to stick to Spanish in this household.

"My husband had a nanny named Alice," I said with what I knew was a tone of conspiracy. "He has a photo of her holding his hand on a beach in Colombia. He keeps it hidden away. His mother wouldn't approve if she knew he had kept it."

"Sit," I said and nodded to the other end of the sofa, which was English and ample, but she wouldn't. We both smoked. Clara was making small talk with the toy, which could have been a fox or a monkey. I wanted to tell this young woman about the maid who had helped raise me and how I had loved her. But I'd been so spoiled and really Annie had loved my brothers best, and besides it did not matter.

Instead, I said, "So, tell me. Do my children look Colombian?" I saw the sparks in her eyes flare. She firmly shook her head and finished her cigarette. She snubbed it out in an ashtray that stood next to the sofa and pushed it closer to me. I was taking my time with my cigarette.

"Not your new baby. Not with her blue eyes." Then she motioned to Clara and said, "Let's take a walk." I could see that Clara was very happy to leave with her.

Clara fluffed her fairy skirt. I had added a top layer of black tulle, which had pleased Clara and me too. I said, "Sail away, but return to me." I leaned back into the sofa, closed my eyes, and arranged for myself a dream of my choosing. This time, I thought, I will dream a beautiful dream of my brother Dales. He'd always approved of me. Of course, no woman had yet seduced him away. Dark eyed with dark wavy hair, Dales was too pretty for a wife.

A little metal duck had arrived in the mail earlier that week, made of strands of copper like all the other five with a hook for hanging the stuff of childhood. Alice's name was woven in copper thread. When Dales sent the first one for my son, I hadn't understood that he had made the pretty little thing himself.

"Your brother is now making playthings?" Juan had said dismissively.

"Got your ducks in order?" was something my mother was known to ask each of my brothers when they'd one-by-one made the decision to leave home. Odd, I thought as I tried to stop thinking and let the dreaming take over, that Dales, the most mischievous of my brothers, would remember something so sweet. And then the dream did take over and my mother was back in her bed, nursing her sadness after my oldest brother left home. And then there she was up again, in her chair in the kitchen ordering Annie to pay attention. In my dream she kept rocking and saying, "Gone is gone, done is done." I went to her and asked her if she'd be sad when I left home. But she ignored me.

I opened my eyes then and studied the door to the bedroom where Juan and I had slept the night of our wedding so that early the next day the del Palacios could take us to catch our early train. We'd undressed here in the sitting room—left clothes right here on the floor—not waiting to use the small dressing room to undress. Juan's brother, Carlos, and my sister-in-law, Margie, had come from Mountain Lakes in New Jersey for the wedding, and they had been in another bedroom tucked away upstairs. If they heard us, they had not said.

Alice stirred, and I helped her unlatch, and when I felt the fullness of her weight, I knew that she would not wake anytime soon. I lowered her to the sofa, made a bed of the shawl, gathered myself together, and thought again about those proper wedding clothes spilled across the sitting room. I'd left my wedding gown at my parents' home where I'd changed into my wedding suit. I watched my mother arrange the gown on my childhood bed as if to put it on display. I had worn it such a short time.

The gown had been the color of new snow. It was heavy satin with a long court train that fell from my shoulders. It had been an ordeal to stand tall in that gown. It was the lilies of the valley that I carried that had made my eyes water and my nose itch. Juan's mother tripped over her swollen feet getting to the basket of flowers the minister from the Republic of Colombia had sent.

"Carry these, Ruby. It will show respect for our family. A fine tribute," Nana said as she handed me the basket, which would have made me look the part of Mary with her little lamb.

My mother had turned her back to the woman and said to me, "A tisket, a tasket."

"Lilies it is," I said, trying for a lighthearted tone because I knew I had a long wedding day ahead of me. A quiet ceremony had been the plan, but the del Palacios balked. "Society people," my mother said with each concession she made. At least I'd be out of this bridal getup when we sat down for dinner at the del Palacio home with twenty people I did not know, my parents uninvited to the lavish dinner at the house on Second Street.

"Ordeal," I had said to my mother who was trying to secure the veil into my rather thin hair.

That certainly was not the dream of my choice. I stood and wandered around the room. On the bookshelf was a collection of framed photos. One of them was of Juan and me and his brother and sister-in-law at the bar where we went after our wedding dinner. I took it back to the sofa with me. One minute I was studying the person I had been and the next I was standing behind the bar of the Third Rail with my new husband, breathing in air free of flowers.

We four young people were posing, playing the part of free spirits. From the costume racks, Margie and I had chosen feathered hats and heavy coats with beaver collars to wear over our summer suits. Juan leaned in for the photo with his glass raised in good cheer.

It was the thing to do—going to the Third Rail on your wedding night and having your photo made. A perfect send-off for a honeymoon. Niagara Falls was our destination. More fresh air, I told myself as we four gave up our costumes and took our seats at the center table. Juan was flush with good humor.

"We will have to step in here once a month for a year to cash in our tab," Carlos said. He too was full of cheer. Each time he poured from the jug on our table, he'd nod at the patrons—all male and all drunk. I could see myself in four different mirrors and could see Juan at all sorts of angles. I liked having him to myself without other women around—without his mother.

Margie didn't count. She did not compete for anyone's attention. Juan's good looks were wasted on her. She loved bums and her husband equally, and I liked being with her.

I saw Juan spot himself in one of the mirrors. He was checking his tie and then he winked at himself when he caught me watching him. He never studied me. No one would have called me beautiful, not even in my wedding suit with my bowtie pin of diamonds and rubies that Juan gave me as a wedding gift. Something his mother surely had chosen. I no longer own that pin. I gave it to my niece, Jimmy's daughter, and never looked back.

"Time for a toast," a wrinkled man across the smoky room said as he stood and began to sing. It was an Irish tune, sweet I thought until he crossed the room, coming right for me. He puckered his dry lips, and Carlos reached across the table and batted him away. Juan was beaming. His pretty eyes, which were much prettier than mine, sparkled. It was as if Juan was proud of me for the first time that day. The man turned to me and said, "Mother, may I?"

"You're drunk out of luck," Juan said, and the man backed away.

Carlos said softly, "You two have an early train to catch tomorrow."

I snapped my eyes open. I hadn't been dreaming—not really—just reliving, and I thought of the sex that had followed.

Juan and I had almost waited for our wedding night—we'd been so rarely alone. We'd outdone ourselves that first time and our wedding night too in the bedroom off the sitting room. But the door to the bedroom was always closed now. I should have carried Alice in there and slept the afternoon away, beside her on the bed, waiting for Juan to find us, looking for the sparkle in his eye.

I heard Juan's footsteps. They always told a story. When we'd first married and lived in a small brownstone near his parents' home, I'd listen for his morning footsteps and could read them—the harsher the steps, the more anxious I'd become. He had a way of setting off my whole day before he left for his business world.

I put the framed photo, which had spiked edges, into my front pocket. I would have to be careful not to hold my daughter against my stomach until I got it home and hid it away.

"You've found us," I said with a lighthearted lilt to my voice as he came into the sitting room.

"Collect yourself. For God's sake, everyone is waiting on dinner for you."

"I was waylaid by our blue-eyed baby," I said. I thought I saw something in his face soften and so I sang the nursery rhyme my mother had sung to me. "I wrote a letter to my love and on the way, I dropped it, I dropped it..." His eyes might have sparkled, but it passed.

"You have been smoking," he said.

"Why yes, I shared a cigarette with Alice."

I could see he wanted to slap me. He straightened his vest.

I gathered up the baby and held her against my chest. The maid appeared and opened her arms. I passed the baby to her and said, "Thank you, Alice. You are a dear."

I've always known that I got that girl in trouble, because the next week she was gone, and when I asked, I was told nothing. I had no idea where the discarded maids went. A Colombian sourpuss named Louise was there to manage things at the del Palacio home. Louise scared the children badly, and I knew I had made a horrible mistake with Alice—just another one on a long list of my selfish stunts that took so long to regret.

That Sunday afternoon after dinner, Juan had been presented by his father with a business issue—an opportunity to prove himself yet again. A merchant maestro, Juan's father was. His plush office on Beaver Street, off Wall Street, was his universe.

That was where he presided. When I think of him now, I'm not sure he was such a bad sort. At lunch that day, he had cooed at Alice and had asked to hold her, and I recall that he had admired Clara's costume. It was a sweet thing to recall, that and a pink chair designed especially for a man.

This business issue, whatever it was for I was not to know those details, took Juan to his study as soon as we arrived home on Argyle Road.

"Tell the maid I'll have my coffee in my study," he told me before leaving me to orchestrate our arrival home. He didn't have to tell me that he'd need quiet, would not want my company. How much I'd learned in our eleven years of marriage. There had been a time we would have had our after-dinner coffee together, maybe kissed each of our very pretty children before they went up to bed. But had that ever been us? It was my parents who made a world together, not the two of us.

I was in our bedroom nursing Alice yet again when I heard Juan at the foot of the stairs. He called to the children to come down to tell him goodnight. It was his routine. But I knew that the children were in the kitchen—a plan hatched by Tessie for the dog days of summer, having told the children as we came in through the back door that night that ice cream sodas awaited them when they were ready for bed.

I left matters alone.

"My watch tells me it is bedtime in Brooklyn," Juan said in a voice too loud for children. I knew he expected that they would come scurrying. And they always did, for it was his house and his rules. I stood with the baby still latched to my swollen breast and went to the bedroom door.

It was not my concern, but Juan did not tolerate commotion and I worried for Tessie. A month earlier, when I was first home with Alice, I'd pitched a fit when I suspected that my mother-in-law was itching to replace Tessie. That worry had started a nasty brew in the pit of my stomach and soured my milk for several days.

I heard the kitchen door swing open. Our house gave away so many clues. I could bet it was Clara who'd been sent out as a decoy.

Juan said, "Little Miss, it is bedtime."

"Papa," she said in her husky voice, "You know I cannot tell time. But I know that two and two are four."

The rest I didn't hear because he'd followed her back into the kitchen. The door swung on its hinges and scraped to a stop. He was in there now with his flock of children and probably didn't even realize that in there Tessie was presiding.

I took the baby from my breast and went down the stairs quietly—flattering myself that my husband might be listening for my steps—thinking that later that night I'd present him with the photo I'd pilfered from his mother's sitting room. Then I saw that I had surprised him coming out of the kitchen. His face held a purposeful look; he'd been so deliciously handsome when I first fell for him. His expression turned to judgment when he saw me.

How cruel to have kindness for the children and not me. But my dress was probably askew because of the way I was holding the baby, and my hair, so thin after this last birth, was hanging in my eyes. But those things were only part of the judgment on his face.

And before I could stop my mind long enough to think what the look on my face might have been, he said, "Kitchens are for staff, not for my children." He blew a mouthful of smoke in my direction. I batted it away from the baby. My mind was muddled. I simply didn't know what I was thinking. All I wanted was to sit at my desk and write, and I would smoke if I chose to. That much was clear to me as I stood there staring him down. And so, that is what I shouted at him. It was like spitting when I said, "I will smoke when I want to." And then I passed by him and as I stepped into the kitchen, I shouted, "My kitchen."

The children were wide eyed at the shouting but then pretended, the way children do, that they were very busy making their sodas. My mother had purchased the soda glasses, each one a different color, at Wanamaker's in Philadelphia where she credited herself with discovering the treat. Each of her grandchildren had a glass of their own. They would make a wonderful collection were they to be gathered together on a sideboard.

"Mother," my oldest daughter said and waited for me to really look at her. It was a demanding tone she took. "I've topped my soda with Nana's dulce de leche." I watched the thick syrup float and thought she'd be the peacemaker.

"Lovely," I said and handed the baby to Tessie, who believed that babies should be put down to sleep amid ordinary life.

"Baby Alice will remember the sound of her brother's and sisters' voices forever," she'd said when I brought Alice home. And now the shouting. That too they'd remember.

Alice was still sleeping when I carried her up to our bedroom and placed her on her side in the bassinet. As I laid her down, she looked right at me and then settled into something that looked like determination.

After my mother died, I had wanted to name the baby I was carrying for her. Ella was a sweet name that would have fit this child. An impossibility, I knew, but still I said aloud to Alice, "Would have, should have." Then I watched her study me until she gave into sleep. I went to my desk. It was a schoolgirl affair; something I had brought from home and my childhood dictionary stood on the corner of the desk. I sat and tried to think up my brother Eddie's voice. He was my writing subject in this chapter.

Eddie was ordained in the Episcopal Church. It'd meant a lot to Papa, of course, to have a son who was ordained. Soon thereafter, Eddie's wife had taken him to live amongst her family in Florida as if he were a man on a leash. I had this strong feeling I would never see him again. The dictionary was a distraction I could not resist, and I leafed through to find "ordained," thinking all along that it was something that surely felt like goodness being poured over you. I was in need of that, I knew, but women weren't ordained and so I closed the dictionary before finding the word. We women took vows that were often of silence. I felt resentment climb up my legs.

I wanted to snap the pencil that I'd propped behind my ear into two pieces, but I had no time for tantrums or the ice pack that Tessie had delivered for my breasts. I licked the pencil and wrote a full page without stopping. But it was not about Eddie. My mother had taken control of my pen. Later, as I reread that page, I decided it was the candy-colored soda glasses that had taken hold of me, and I was pleased with the page.

Juan came in very late that night. He put his hand on my forehead, and something was exchanged between us in that moment. It was years though before I thought about that moment again and wondered if I'd shown indifference. I had been so soundly sleeping.

When I woke for Alice's predawn nursing, I decided I'd take her down to the sitting room. After I nursed her, I'd write down what had come to me in the night, something about my mother and our trips to Asbury Park where my father did summer relief work for local pastors. A whole scene had flown into my head as I slept, and so I took paper and the pencil from my desk.

Before I sat to nurse, I stood at the window thinking I might spot the Dog Star that rises in August at the same time as the sun. Papa had shown my mother and me that star when we'd stayed that first summer at the New Jersey shore. My parents called it the County by the Sea. For three summers, my parents and I took the New York Railroad to Asbury Park and together we all stayed in a small cottage with a screened-in porch. It was a good place to begin a story, I thought, and maybe a good way to begin a day, maybe one without regrets. I looked at Alice and thought about the merry-go-round on the boardwalk. I held that in my mind and tried to think of a way to describe sea air.

"Mother's milk," I said to Alice as I settled into the leather chair—a gift from Juan's brother. The chair was made of Colombian leather and moaned with our combined weight. "It's never enough," I said to the baby as she looked at me and pulled the nipple into her hungry mouth. She had my mother's Paris blue eyes. My mother was sure enough haunting me now. I had another page written in my head before I took Alice from my breast. We both slept there in the chair until Tessie found us.

Before I knew my mind, I said to Tessie, "It would be so peaceful if we could take the children to the seaside. We could lease a large cottage with a porch. Shall we? Juan could take the train down when he can get away."

Tessie nodded and held her arms out to take Alice.

"Juan and I could walk Clara and Alice on the boardwalk, and he will see how people admire our children."

I heard Juan's footsteps and Tessie handed me Alice, who stared at me. Tessie stepped away to see what all my husband needed for his day.

I went to the window and looked at the morning sky. "Too late," I said, and pulled the baby close.

CHAPTER 4

RUBY
1927

Alice stood at the bedroom door. Her tangled hair hung in her eyes. She was a tender-headed child who wouldn't hold still for brushing, but otherwise not difficult. My older children were in school, and Tessie had taken Clara to nursery school. Mateo was recently back from a three-month stay in Colombia and was adjusting to having a mother once again. He was twelve now and too old for toy soldiers or mothering. I'd asked him many times for details of his summer with his father's family, but it seemed as if he considered it a private matter not to be shared with me. I knew I was not going to ever see Juan's beloved home country—ashamed of me, maybe—and so I stopped asking.

I was still in bed, my head heavy with the vapors Tessie kept brewing for the head cold that had put me to bed. After the house had quieted, she'd steamed the bathroom and helped me walk across the hall to "breathe in." Today I was to have a final dress fitting for my gown for the celebratory dinner at the Commodore Hotel on Forty-Second Street in New York City.

Juan had balanced on his tiptoes when he arrived home from the office with the invitation to the "WE" banquet celebration for Charles A. Lindbergh. Juan's parents were in Colombia. We were most likely stand-ins for his parents, I knew, and Juan knew, but I had not seen him cheerful in a long time and so I smiled broadly.

"We will be seated with the Colombian Envoy," Juan announced, as if more pleased with that than the chance to hear the aviator speak about his flight in the Spirit of St. Louis. Then he added, "You will need a new gown."

I tried for glee. "Something with plumage perhaps," I proposed and fluttered my fingers at him as if I were holding a long cigarette.

His parents would never make it back in time to preside over the evening. But too much good luck was not to be trusted, and so I didn't suggest they rush. But then I got sick.

My gown was all but finished—a creation from a Butterick pattern from their Paris collection. My mother-in-law sent her dressmaker to me. "Pronto," is what she wrote in her telegram to the nervous dressmaker, or so the woman explained. My gown was the color of an overripe avocado. I'd apparently grown to the age of wearing vegetable colors. But I'd been sick a week now and didn't much care about colors anymore.

"Your eyes are sunken," Juan said on the third day I stayed in bed.

If I hadn't truly wanted to see the waterfall in the lobby and all the ballgowns, I would not have done Tessie's breathing exercises and would not have allowed her to put the raw egg under my bed. Juan did not know about the egg cure.

"La limpia," Tessie said when she checked the raw egg each morning.

I was to be cleansed by those eggs.

Tessie came up the stairs and stood behind Alice. "The dressmaker will need to take in the dress, Missus." Tessie was not one to nag, but the way she pointed at the dressing gown told me that she wanted me to get up and put it on.

I felt as if I was bruised from so much time in bed and yet I said, "I'll get up if I can go back to bed the minute she leaves."

Tessie pointed again at the dressing gown and announced that the dressmaker was downstairs waiting. She told Alice to scoot like a bunny under the bed and pull out the basket of sand that held the egg. Alice said, "The nest?" and then crawled under the bed on all fours as I put my feet on the floor. Even my feet hurt.

"You didn't bring anything with bows or flounces," I said to the dressmaker, who I knew was here in part as Nana's spy. I almost felt sorry for the woman except she was also a groveler. I could not pity anyone who groveled.

"We certainly are going to a lot of trouble so that I can be in a flock of women picking away at each other's gowns," I said, hoping to lighten the mood in my bedroom, which smelled of cloves. Tessie took Alice's hand and walked her over to my desk where she motioned for her to sit.

The seamstress took shallow breaths as she laid the dress out on the bed that Tessie had straightened. The dress was green tulle with an overlay of black silver lace that gave it the avocado color. I'd won on the uneven hemline and the dropped waist—but then we'd all be in dropped waists. Thinking about my mother-in-law in a dropped waist gown with her fat tummy gave me a case of the giggles. Alice gave a little giggle when she heard me start in.

The woman held the dress up and swished it around for us to admire the back where it dropped into a deep V and from there a line of buttons the size of small marbles stopped at the dropped waist.

"Did we agree on buttons?" I asked and walked over to inspect them close-up. I could feel my face redden. "No to buttons and no to mother-of-pearl." I shuddered.

"They are quite French," the dressmaker said.

"I doubt that. Besides, they look gooey. No bows, no flounces, and no mother-of-pearl." The room went silent, and it was up to me to change that. "Besides, how can anyone sit on marbles?" I said, and Alice looked relieved, and I felt sorry that I had alarmed her with my brattiness.

I turned to the dressmaker and said, "The dinner will be torture enough."

"Whatever you please, Mrs. del Palacio."

"Anything but mother-of-pearl," I tried to say nicely this time.

"I have metal push buttons. Very flat," the woman said, and I knew she would report this to my mother-in-law—perhaps in another telegram.

But Tessie laughed and Alice dashed across the room and jumped into my arms, which I didn't realize were open.

"Wonderful," I said and passed Alice to Tessie. I let the dressing gown drop to the floor. The seamstress looked away demurely, and I slipped the ballgown on over my head.

"Tender button, yes, that will work," I said, because sometimes I didn't know what possessed me.

"Mama is beautiful," Alice said when the dressmaker finished pinning me in, and I realized that this was Alice's one and only childhood, and so I twirled for her and suddenly I was three feet tall, wearing the red and white striped, polished cotton summer dress some dear old Quaker aunt of my mother's sent me for my third birthday. There was a three-inch ruffle at the hem, and I twirled when my father walked into our parlor and saw me.

Something of that girlishness was still in me in the summer of 1913 when I'd been fitted for my first formal gown. I was nineteen. It was the girlishness at work that summer.

I was home from the Quaker world of Bryn Mawr, where I'd been sent to grow up. In truth, I'd been banished from the freedom I'd found in my Foundation Year at King's College in Nova Scotia. How I'd loved the sea and thought then I'd always live near water. It was a lively place. I was watched over by my brothers Jimmy and Eddie and they included me in some of their hijinks. In comparison, Bryn Mawr felt like a tomb—a nest of girls. If growing up was what my mother had in mind for me, King's College was the place. When I complained to my brother Eddie that Bryn Mawr was out in the hills, he said, "Come on, Ruby, Bryn Mawr literally means 'large hill,' so what did you expect?" Then he comforted me by saying it was a better place to become a writer, because I'd made the mistake of telling him that I fancied myself talented with words. From then on, he'd plagued me with pen names he'd invented for me. But by then, he'd become a divinity student and was under the influence of the girl he'd marry, and I no longer trusted him.

He and Jimmy had jobs to go to that summer and so I spent most of my time alone in our big home on President Street. I was trapped in my childhood bedroom with nothing much to do, and I was no child.

"Mind your reputation," my mother cautioned when I'd leave for my daily walks. She knew I was heading for someplace, a public place to read and smoke. She was so very sure of me. Nothing I did surprised her.

Juan's family home on Second Street was often closed up and word was that they traveled back and forth to South America—worldly sorts. My three older brothers had moved away from Brooklyn by the time the del Palacios arrived, but Jimmy and Eddie's gang knew of Juan and his brother Carlos. Most Brooklyn boys were in a gang in those days and the President Street Gang was always at odds with the Gowanus Gang, but the del Palacio boys—who were not boys by then but rather men—expressed no interest in being a part of a gang.

"I thought you had to be from Europe to call yourself European," Eddie said one day at Sunday dinner. It was the first thing I ever heard anyone say about Juan.

And since then, I'd seen Juan and Carlos walking about. We all knew that they were men in a hurry. But in the summer of 1913, it was I who was idle, and so I decided to take Second Street to Prospect Park, planning to enter the park at Fourth Street. From there it was a straight line to the Long Meadow. I was looking for anything to happen, and it did. Juan skipped down the five steps of his family home just as I approached.

As I got to the foot of those steps, I nodded. Then I heard my own mother's voice, "Do not be so easily flattered, Ruby. It is unbecoming."

Juan stopped on the last step, and balancing on the very edge, he checked his watch, which was on his wrist. "Miss Farrar," he said. And then I heard the carriage come up the street behind me, and I knew it wasn't me he'd dashed out to greet but rather a horse-drawn carriage. All my life, I've regretted that I nodded first. He waited for me to pass and then I heard him do a jump to the sidewalk and another into the carriage. He was a man full of vitality, and I was angry beyond reason then that he had a place to be.

The handwritten invitation to the formal dinner on Columbia Street in Brooklyn Heights arrived that afternoon. Annie, who'd grown older and wiser as I'd grown up, was the one to deliver it to me in my bedroom. "Mind you, a Catholic," she said knowingly, because she was Catholic. "Watch him," she said. Annie wasn't often wrong, but she was wrong about that detail. Juan had been raised in the Anglican church at his mother's insistence. She liked setting herself above.

"You'll need a gown," my mother said and took the dress up as her mission. Because I was a college girl, I refused to wear a dress the color of an innocent blush, and I chose a blue fabric the color of the sea at Asbury Park at sunrise. "Remember the sea?" I asked, trying for once to please her, because after all, I'd won the color battle. Of course, my mother remembered those summers when we'd gone with my father to the New Jersey shore where he was the summer relief pastor, but my mother ignored me. I pushed her. "You do remember the brightest star. Star bright..." I began with a little tune I could not hold. "We got up at sunrise to watch the Dog Star rise." I actually winked at her. I knew she remembered.

She was holding a straight pin in her mouth but took it out, stabbed it into the pincushion on her wrist, and said, "When did you ever get up at sunrise, Miss?"

"The dog days were the best days," I said. I knew she remembered because Papa was there and the three of us sat on the boardwalk at sunrise—Mother and I wrapped in silk shawls.

What I remembered best about that dinner on Columbia Street was the moment of looking at the reflection of Juan and my nineteen-year-old self in the largest, clearest window I'd ever seen. The dining room was ablaze with light, and as we looked out our reflections reversed so that, abracadabra, the two of us were looking east not west. All these years later, I've come to doubt my memories, but not that youthful image of us in that glass, already headed in the wrong direction.

And then all the dinner guests were called out to the terrace to watch as the sun set over New Jersey and made worshipful sounds that indicated they were astounded by the singular moment of a setting sun. It felt dangerous to be there with those people in all their finery with Juan's fine-boned hand resting on my nearly bare shoulder, but then the moment ended as our hostess directed us to our very specific seats for dinner.

I wasn't seated with Juan that evening as the couples were scattered about, but I could hear him. He told the woman seated next to him that his brother had recently married and moved to a home on a lake in New Jersey. "Out beyond the sunset," he said, and I thought he might in fact be poetic. The man seated on my left knew the man on my right and they briefly spoke over me until they spotted my name card and told me they knew of my father. Then I became of momentary interest. "The borough of churches," one man said, and the other added, "The borough of rubber plants." Neither comment drew the three of us into conversation. It was fine, as it allowed me to listen to Juan. I never did hear him speak of sunsets again that evening or after.

Now, after the twirling and the buttons, I had earned myself an afternoon of sleep. But as I changed back into the dressing gown, I rallied and said to Tessie that I'd like to take Alice to the park to see the swans. It was still early fall and mild from midday until late afternoon.

"Missus, back to bed," she said.

Alice was watching me, and I am sure I saw disappointment. "You only have five days to recover before the gala." Tessie was always expanding her English.

"I'll rest," I said as if I was consenting to her wishes, but in truth I felt overcome. "All that twirling," I said, because I was trying to get Alice to smile again. "After I rest, we shall read. Would you like that?" I put my head on the pillow, which was cool and fluffed. Then I was alone, and the house was stone quiet, and I remembered my annoyance at my mother when she buried herself under her covers, leaving the household to carry on in silence. It was as if she were announcing, "mind my sadness," or so I had thought. I felt ashamed of both of us.

I had been deep into writing stories about my mother when I became pregnant with Alice, and I lost my heart for it. But then, being ill these last days fueled my urge to write. "Bring me my notebook," I called to Clara one afternoon after my fever had broken. And now, such a wonderful line floated into my head that I felt joy at its arrival. "I was never fascinating to my mother," the sentence began. I relaxed now that I had that line to mull over and pulled the covers up over me. What a selfish child I'd been, but how I loved that line.

On the night of the dinner in the Commodore Grand ballroom, I began counting the round tables as soon as we were seated. Ten seats at each table and so packed together that if there was a stampede right here in New York City on Forty-Second Street, many would die. Five hundred women, I calculated—each an adornment for a man and all trapped together in this grand room.

"Now what?" I said to Juan to engage him, but he answered by simply saying, "The aviator."

As if I had forgotten.

And then I asked myself what my mother would think of such a place and how it might compare to her beloved Wanamaker's.

Juan and I were seated at a table two rows back from the stage and near the center of the room. The envoy insisted that I sit next to him as he was with no one that evening. "We shall share," he said to Juan, and even that sounded diplomatic.

"When will your father-in-law set sail for New York?" the envoy asked me, and I wanted to giggle like a girl. It was a rather amusing thing to say at a dinner celebrating an aviator. "Thirty-three hours" in the air is the first thing everyone said with reverence when Lindbergh was mentioned. "I suppose even aviators set sail," I said, aiming for the poetic, but between the question and my answer, Juan pinched my shoulder as if he were being tender and gave the envoy the exact dates of his father's travel plans. The envoy only half listened to Juan. I think he preferred women.

The sound of one thousand voices reached a pitch that reminded me of the sound of the ship that Mateo and Juan had boarded back in June. I recalled that sound washing away every thought I'd ever had. It took days for my own thoughts to return after Juan left with our son. It was the same here—I felt erased. But then the sound dipped as a man in a black robe with a shawl of many colors took center stage at the podium. We all knew to be quiet, and I thought of the power the robe gave the man who was the Pastor of the Church of the Intercession in New York City. He'd been a friend of my father's. Papa had said that church was a Gothic Revival masterpiece, and he had taken my mother to see it and they'd agreed that the tall, narrow entrance gave them a sense of entering another world. But they had not taken me. I felt my face flush. We all bowed our heads. His voice boomed, but I heard few actual words. I only heard my father.

As the pastor stepped away from the podium and took his seat, dozens upon dozens of waiters burst at one single moment into the room as if the ballroom walls were porous, allowing the waiters to seep in. They held platters above their heads on flat palms. How I wished just one of them would take a twirl and set sail. Oh my, I loved to amuse myself.

As one of the waiters arrived at my left shoulder, I saw that at each table such a man was waiting. My waiter nodded ever so slightly to Juan that he should remove his arm from my shoulder and then I understood that I was to nod or point at each item on the platter that I would like a serving of; and so, with a simple nod, I was served. Then each lady at the table was served. It was the next wave of waiters who served the men larger servings of each course with more choices. And when I whispered this observation to my husband, he patted my hand as if he adored me and said, "Now Dearest, don't you start."

The aviator was seated at the table on the stage. I watched him nod again and again to the governor, who was seated next to him. As we ate, stacks of his bright blue books were placed along the edge of the stage like a little wall a child could skip along. *"We"* in quotation marks was the odd title. I didn't bother pointing out to Juan or the envoy that Lindbergh had indeed flown solo. Being alone was the point, wasn't it, and there was certainly no "we" in any self-satisfied autobiography I'd ever read, but coffee was on my mind and our very specific waiter, who I would now recognize anywhere, was pouring.

"Colombian?" the envoy said diplomatically to the waiter and then poured two tablespoons of sugar into his coffee.

I sipped my coffee and thought about the title I'd yet to arrive at for the book about my mother, not that it mattered. Silly me, thinking writing about her might make amends. Still, I considered the other available pronouns. "Hers," I said to myself, but the young aviator began to speak, and he started with a quote.

"If I could fly on the wings of dawn," he began. Then hundreds of voices chimed in with him as if in Sunday school and the rest of the words about the sticky hands of grief were muddled. He would be a beloved man, I decided, and would be remembered for his good looks as much as for his bravery, both of which I knew were deceptive. I felt very sorry for him then, standing up there alone speaking of his instant autobiography—his own story, as he put it—when he was still baby-faced and facing perhaps a long life.

"Wings of Dawn," would have made a much better title for his book. And then, as if it flew in on wings, I realized that *Meet Me at the Eagle* would be a better title for my book.

Later, as hundreds departed the ballroom, many of us lingered, waiting for our copy of *"We."* Now that our waiter merged with the others who were clearing tables, indifferent to each of us, I realized that in all these people I knew not one other face. It was simply a sea of people with the men finely tailored and all alike, and the women each unique. As I waited for Juan to decide when to leave, I decided I'd look for specific dress colors. First, I looked for plum and found that was all too easy. Next on my list was a dress the color of a mute swan. That was when I saw the face I knew. This woman was in a black dress, but she was carrying a feathered white wrap. It looked to me like she was carrying a long-necked swan in her bare arms, and I recognized her.

She was moving toward me through the spaces between the circles. She was not following a man or leading one along behind her, for that matter. When she arrived, she gave her hand to Juan, who was then put upon to ask her name and introduce her to the envoy. Names were exchanged, and then pointing to me, she explained to the envoy, "We each have children at Green-Wood. A cemetery. It is where we met." Juan took my elbow in a tight grip. The envoy wove the woman's arm through his own as if she were a gift to him. It happened quickly, but she was skilled and retrieved her own arm while Juan still held mine firmly.

"I visit the children on Tuesdays," she said virtuously. "And I always stop by the Farrars. I'm quite taken by the stones on your parents' graves."

The envoy studied the woman with a kindness that said

he'd like to hear about the stones, and I felt my throat swell as something I could not describe welled up in me.

"Yes, they were devoted," I said. Juan listened too because the envoy was listening intently. "My brothers Jimmy and Eddie saw to the stones," I said, realizing I'd said more just then than I'd said all night.

The woman whose name I learned that night was Kate looked sincerely at the envoy and said, "The stones almost touch and Reverend Farrar's reads, 'Faith is the means.' And Mrs. Farrar's gravestone reads, 'Love is the end.'"

The envoy took her arm again and said, "Precioso. There is often poetry in graveyards." Juan had no other choice but to nod.

"Tuesday mornings," the woman said to me. Now she patted the envoy on his arm as if to comfort him, and wound her way through the room, alone.

Three days later at Faith's grave, as withered cherry tree leaves broke free in the breeze and spun to the ground, I was tempted to clear them away endlessly. I stationed Alice, who was only half sleeping—for she never seemed to be fully of this world or another—so that the sun would warm her. Shortly, two cats sauntered by dismissively, indifferent to us, looking for feathered creatures. And then Kate appeared on the hill just as she had the morning I buried Faith.

We will be friends, I thought, realizing viciously that Juan would not approve. Poetic justice, I decided.

Alice woke the moment Kate arrived, and we set her free from the carriage to wander. "Let's not let her walk toward the hill," Kate said and pointed Alice in the other direction. "They've set snares for pigeons. I've complained. About the snares, not the pigeons." She laughed at herself. "They assure me that they set the pigeons free outside the gates, but I do not believe them."

Kate kneeled on Faith's grave. It was marked only by a delicate white cross with her name and one single date. She motioned for me to join her as she unpacked a picnic basket. I had not thought to bring along much other than sweets for Alice. Kate handed me a little card with her name and number. "Mansfield 6-6746," she said. "I kept the house when we separated."

"So you are no longer married?" I said in what sounded like a question.

"What would be the point after the children?" she said, and I turned to look for Alice and held up my arms for her.

Kate went on, "Partial divorce. Not his fault. Not mine." She rolled her eyes and said, "We have one single life. But I see what you're thinking, Ruby. My husband is no Daddy Browning and I am no Peaches," and then she laughed again so loudly that Alice turned to stare at us in alarm.

"Free as a bird," Kate said, and Alice ran into my open arms. And then Kate said, "Well we all read the tabloids, don't we? I mean, the man kept a goose in their bedroom."

I thought of my mother, who would not have allowed a tabloid in her home but had died with Agatha Christie's latest book at her bedside. I looked over at my parents' graves and revealed for no reason, "My mother was the most content person I've ever known."

"Good for her," Kate said. "But tell me, would she have approved of the stones your brothers chose?"

I couldn't answer because I didn't know. I only wanted to be Kate's friend. She studied me and I finally said, "I will think about that." But I didn't. Instead, I turned my thoughts to the stone I wanted to have made for Faith's grave, something more than a white cross.

"But tell me, what is holding you back?"

When I didn't answer, she said, "From contentment, Ruby."

And then I was rushing to tell her about the book I was writing. "I have a number of titles floating around in my head,"

I said. "Titles matter. Perhaps Lindbergh got poor advice on the title for his book," I said, showing off for her.

"'Setting Sail,' might have worked better," I said. And we laughed like girls.

"Finish that book you're writing. I'd like to read it. When you know a friend's mother, you understand your friend oh so much better," she said, making me think I'd told the wrong stories about my mother.

And then Kate said to Alice, "Little one, let's have a bit of lunch."

CHAPTER 5

RUBY
1930

I was alone in the kitchen smoking and sipping hot tea to keep my head clear, when at nearly ten p.m. I heard from two floors above Nana slam her bedroom door, her meddling in my house done for the day.

Mothers-in-law, a story as common as tea, I thought.

I listened for sounds of any of my children. Mateo's bedroom was on the top floor too, and he was probably reading, his bedside light back on the minute his grandmother's door slammed, or so I hoped. He had read Lindbergh's memoir one long cold winter weekend, and so I'd taken him to the library and insisted it'd be just the two of us on that adventure. We each chose something to read by one of the big fireplaces.

My youngest daughter had long ago climbed into bed with her sister Clara. I knew this because I'd checked on them and because I often felt I knew Alice's plans before she did. Alice and Clara loved each other with a fierceness that sometimes alarmed me. My brothers Jimmy and Eddie loved each other that way. I did not bother checking in on my older three daughters, who would pretend sleep if I bothered to climb the stairs to check on them and besides, while they had big ears and an appetite for gossip, it seemed that nothing in our household was urgent to them, and surely not me.

I tapped my cigarette out and picked up my cigarette case. I heard Tessie, who now had the room off the kitchen, turn off her light. I planned to move her into Nana's room when the home was mine—because it was mine; my father had given each of his children the home of their choice when they married. A family home is what he'd promised. He believed in the virtue of the family, and I was thankful that he would not have to put up with my plans.

Tonight was the night I would make my announcement to Juan. I'd had to postpone my plans since Christmas when the children—every last one of them—came down with the German measles, one after the other well into March. Clara's neck had puffed up before I knew what I was confronting. Mateo was next to take ill, and he had the worst of it. He resisted my nursing, but Tessie insisted on sitting up with him for three nights straight to comfort him. Nana had moved back to her home and her maids for the duration. "For safety's sake," she'd said as she made her escape, but she was back now. Their home on Second Street was closed up again, as it had been on and off since the disaster on Wall Street and my father-in-law was in Colombia introducing Carlos to business associates. I knew only enough about the family business to know it was in danger.

My plans were made and were precise right down to the pressed wool, peacock blue dress I changed into before dinner even though it was only dinner with Nana and the children. I didn't want the summons to blindside Juan; I remember that.

With the wind blowing, the house quivered just enough to dampen the sound of my steps as I tiptoed across the dining room and the center hall. I'm not sure that I knocked on the door to Juan's study before I opened it. He was standing with his head in the corner closet where he kept his childhood collection of hand-painted tin soldiers and what all else, I didn't know. He didn't know I was in his lair.

My eyes skipped around the room, lit only by the last of a fire and one desk lamp. I didn't spot a single clue that said Juan was a man with a family of his own making. A map of Colombia dominated the wall behind me where there sat a seldom used sofa. The bookshelves on either side of the fireplace mostly held mementoes. Juan was not a reader. On one shelf there was a photo of Juan as a toddler with golden blond curls, but not the one of him with his nanny. I never did know where he kept that hidden.

Each time I brought one of my dark-headed newborns home, his mother would say, "Juan was a blond child," as if she'd been dazzled by her own son.

There was a single photo on his desk of him with his brother, Carlos, and his mother in some sort of wild field. It looked like Juan was holding a stalk of wheat, standing casually as if he had time to be frivolous. Or maybe the brothers had posed for that picture with their mother.

There was a time when Alice was newly weaned and my interest in life had returned enough that I'd considered sneaking into Juan's study to place the Third Rail photo on his desk. To show affection. But the arguments about having another child started about that time. I'd told him it was absurd to have a herd of children, and I'd smiled when I said that. But I saw no humor on his face. He hated being told what he could not do.

"I do not want to be pregnant again," was the way I'd turned him down repeatedly after I'd moved Alice into the tiny front bedroom with Clara.

Now I took a step forward.

Juan turned and said, "What do you want?" He had not taken time to manage his voice, and he sounded bewildered and looked shocked to find me there in the room with him.

I kept moving across the room to his prized round humidor. It was three feet across and sat like a proud coffee table. I reached down and set the thing spinning as if life—our life— was a game.

"I have things to talk to you about," I announced before he could escape his corner. I took a seat in one of the two chairs that sat across from each other, the humidor in the middle.

"For God's sake, my mother is upstairs."

We both looked up at the ceiling.

What a pair of bullies this mother and son were.

"Of course she is. Where else would she be? Surely not in Colombia with her beloved husband," I said. She was always here and growing fatter by the day, but then she didn't have a waistline in that photo of her in the wheat field either.

I could see him considering his next move by the way he pulled his brows together. He would have to step over my feet to get out of his corner. He stood, formally composed now. He reached behind him and closed the closet soundlessly. Then he pointed to his desk, which had a shine in the low lamplight, and stabbed his finger at the chair that sat in front of it. If I'd agreed to his silent command, I knew he'd have the upper hand. I did not budge. I wasn't going to sit across the desk from him as if I were his subject or a misbehaved child.

With a slight nod of my head, I began, "I've made a decision, Juan."

"This can wait," he said, and then he stepped across my outstretched legs and crossed the room to the desk. He stood behind it, confident now that he had dismissed me.

"No. Now, Juan. I've given you six children. A son. It's what you wanted." I held my hand cupped over the cigarette I was about to light. It was an effort to tap down the rage I felt bubbling.

Under his desk, I spotted Clara's stuffed swan. My father gave it to her after Faith's funeral. Pooh was the swan's name. Tessie had mended the swan's long neck several times and had hidden the darning with a blue necktie. Iciness dripped between my shoulder blades. If there was any sorrow in the room, I did not sense it. I inhaled and felt the cigarette work its magic on me. Even in the dim light, I clearly saw his deprivation.

"I'm bringing a separation agreement," I said. "I've been to the Carnegie with Kate, and Jimmy has helped me understand such things."

Juan smirked, but then he glanced up at the ceiling and his expression changed. For a moment he looked very much like our son. Just then, I saw a ghostly object fly by the big window behind his desk. Sometimes bats were out and about in Brooklyn in late winter, but this was a night bird and so I pointed and said, "Fly-by-night." I didn't know where I'd come by such meanness. I felt emptied out then, as if I were bleeding.

I waited for him to understand what I'd said. Waited for him to reply. I saw the last of the flames leap and dance in the fireplace. Finally, I stood, crossed the study, and stooped down to pick up the swan. Clara had outgrown it. Then I put my cigarette out in the ashtray he kept next to his blotter. He stared at it. Finally—it had been minutes of silence—he said, "There are breadlines. You will be left to stand in a breadline with tramps."

"Pooh is a perfect name for a swan," I said. "If you call him by name and he doesn't come, you can pretend that you were saying pooh to show him how little you wanted him."

Juan fooled with his mustache, a habit his mother had never broken. I added, "Milne wrote that—the author." I was goading him. He had disdain for writers, and so he pretended to ignore my performance.

I hated Juan then. And I had hated him in the moment he called my brother Dales a "fly-by-night" man. It was at Dales's funeral just before Christmas.

Now I watched as the shape of my husband's eyes changed. And then, past him, I saw myself in the dark window. The bird and Dales were gone as if they simply had been released.

"It's a shame, but it's come to this, Juan. Our marriage is over, and I've done my duty by you. Six children..."

I watched him smirk again. He was a man without compassion for women, another thing his mother had failed to teach him.

"This house is mine, Juan, and I am told that the court will grant me alimony."

"Reader of gossip columns, are you, like your mother?"

I was too smart to believe in ghosts, but just then my mother hovered in the room, watching over me. She'd never gotten around to telling me how being loved filled up all the emptiness after each loss. It was Kate who'd figured that part out about my mother. She'd said that being loved was the end.

Juan looked past me as if he'd forgotten me. Holding the swan to my breast, I crossed the room and pulled the door open with enough force that I knew I could slip out and still give it a good slam. Instead, I stopped and said, "How little you wanted me, how little I wanted you. That's the shame." I was shouting and added, "You will receive a summons." And then I slammed the door and Nana began to pound the floor with her cane and kept at it as I climbed the stairs and closed the door to our bedroom. Even behind the closed door, I could hear Alice crying her heart out and Clara, in her raspy voice, saying, "There, there."

Juan slept in his study that night. I knew his mother knew it too. It had never happened before.

The next morning, Nana appeared in the parlor, puffy but well corseted. The older children had left for school hours before. Alice sat next to me on the divan. She was holding Pooh, which I'd given to her when I went in to wake her that morning. I was reading a German fairy tale to her. *The Six Swans*. She was too young for the story. It might have frightened her, but the illustrations were exquisite. I liked the book for the evil mother-in-law. Kate had given me the book for that very reason. In one illustration, there was a prince whose left arm was in fact a wing with white feathers. Alice always wanted to see the picture of the boy who sprouted feathers.

"I'm at the end of my rope," Nana said. "My son is sending a car for me."

Alice could not read yet, but she pointed to the exact spot

on the page where I left off. Nana took a seat across the parlor and never spoke one more word to me or her granddaughter that morning while she waited to leave my house.

And so, weeks later, Juan and I went to Court where I was the plaintiff and Juan the defendant. It was open court, but we were alone that day, just the two of us with a judge in a dull silk gown, sitting high up on a pedestal. How easy, I thought, to be a judge. And I wondered if when he went home at night his wife made him leave the robe on the hall tree in the entryway.

I heard right off that we were to address the judge as Your Honor even though I was sure he had referred to himself as the Court and then as I stood alone at my table, I heard him say something about the plaintiff being prayed for. It was odd, and I said under my breath, "Pay attention. Your job is to pay attention."

"And so, we have here today before me the Flatbush pair," the judge said as he let his full weight fall onto his arms, which he'd laid like two black cats on his podium. I saw Juan out of the corner of my eye. I was sure he was preparing to take his seat and the judge must have seen it too because he said, "Mr. del Palacio, in my court, you stand. It's procedure we have to plow through today, like wheat farmers." And he laughed at himself and I felt sorry for all of us.

Then the judge began to read the single paper he had in front of him. Finally, he looked at me not unkindly and said, "What a pity," as if he were reading about some tragedy on the front page of the *Brooklyn Daily Eagle*. He said, "You chose to bring this action, Mrs. del Palacio? Speak your answers, dear."

"Yes, Your Honor," I said loudly because I had come here with every intention of speaking.

"How many children are there in this marriage?" he asked and took up a pen as if prepared to take it all down.

"Seven," I said. "One dead."

The judge softened. I saw that, and I said a little prayer of apology to Faith, asking her to forgive me, knowing it was unfair to use her that way.

"I see," he said and then asked for ages and names. He wrote in a large ledger. I was surprised that there was no one there to assist him. After each name, he dipped his pen. Juan fidgeted.

"I know that this is hard to swallow, Mr. del Palacio, but this is the business of the Court in America. You understand of course that you are in the United States of America. Not some South American country."

For the briefest of seconds, I wanted to feel sorry for Juan for this offense to his pride, which he and his mother wore like armor, but I could not afford it.

I could see that the judge wanted our story, the way people are when they pick up a mystery novel and quickly, as if starved, turn the pages. The man was prepared to judge no doubt, but first he'd get the story. Something to tell his wife over dinner if they were kind to one another. I looked back over my shoulder when I felt the chill come over me. It was my mother. She was at it again.

"Don't be flattered into telling your story," she whispered. I hadn't expected ghosts to show up for me.

"A separation action?" the judge began and then rambled on with a legal lecture that moved into a moral one when he asked, "And what of the children?" And then he did the oddest thing. He quoted Agatha Christie, saying, "Christie said that marriage is an extraordinary thing, and it distrusts if any outsider—even a child of the marriage—has the right to judge. But judge I must."

My mother patted me on my right shoulder. It felt like love, not pity, and then she left me.

Juan had never been taught to pay attention. Being married all these years, I knew that what he did and what he said was a reflection on me. It was the way things worked. I guess

I wanted the judge to like him, to like us both, which was stupid. Juan was looking down, in his own world, as if none of this was happening.

"Be prepared, Mr. and Mrs. del Palacio. Word will spread in the morning tabloids like seeds and tall tales will take root," the judge said. Still, Juan did not look up. "Mr. del Palacio, the Court orders you to engage an attorney for your wife. Meanwhile, I will take this matter under advisement. Until then, let the matter rest," he said, which made no sense at all to me.

Juan was out the heavy double doors while I was still gathering my things and pulling on my spring coat. Even when we were both on the street, Juan took big steps to outpace me. Finally, he stopped, squared his shoulders, turned, and said, "I have a busy day providing for my family, but I will find you your precious attorney."

In that moment, I was sure that he'd used the word precious by accident. His English was often imprecise. But looking back—the two of us standing there on Fulton Street—I think he had meant what he said. Not beloved, never beloved, but costly.

And then he left me standing on the street. People, mostly men, were coming and going and two men, walking together, made way for me, passing on either side of me as if I was never there.

I walked home that day.

It was a full week later when the attorney Juan found for me finally took my call. He said that there was no need to meet me; a telephone call would do the trick. He dove right into details about filing a motion for an order to direct the payment of alimony in the amount of two-hundred and fifty dollars a month. He reported that proudly and then in a muffled voice he added that his order would include his own counsel fee. It seemed odd to me how he was getting ahead of himself, but there was no interrupting the man.

His sentences ran together. But then finally he sniffed, swallowed, and said, "Ruby, my professional advice is that you take some time and go away. Let the dust settle, that's the ticket." He'd used my first name when I had not given it and I did not know his. "Let things cool off, that's the ticket. Take your maid with you. It is my understanding that Mr. del Palacio's mother can step in, so you need not worry about your household. I'm told you have a brother in Connecticut. There you go."

Then finally the sniff and swallow and he said, "That's the ticket." He was one to repeat.

CHAPTER 6

RUBY
1930

People of all ages filled the Grand Central Station, even mid-morning, and I thought, this is what I have been missing—people who don't know me. Kate knew which train to take into New York City and which exit from the station to take us to Madison Avenue. We walked arm-in-arm, and yet strangers seemed to carry us along in their hurry to get places.

As we exited the station, Kate took my hand and said, "Wrong direction. I've allowed for wiggle room. Not far from here there's a tearoom."

Over her fragrant whiskey, Kate played with the long rope of colored beads she often wore while she started into a one-sided conversation about herself.

"Had I been given a choice, I'd have been born to gypsies," she said.

She gave me no time to react. She twisted the beads and let them clatter on the table.

"That way, I'd have learned to pick up stakes without a second thought."

She gathered up the beads and began playing with them again.

"Over hill, over dale," Kate started humming a little song. Then she said, "Off to the next fair we gypsies would go. Of course, I'd be shared with all the mothers because I was a dazzling child. Eventually, I'd be stolen away by another family. And off I'd go."

She took another sip of her whiskey and poured what remained into my tea. The waiter was guarding the door because it was not a tearoom but rather a private club. She motioned to him, and he went downstairs to retrieve the whiskey. He delivered it in a teacup that looked just like mine.

"My father drinks here," she offered. "He and his father built ships, but once they arrived here in New York, neither one of them stepped back on a ship. 'We're sticking,' my father always said. And my mother said that one child like me was enough for her lifetime. After I was born, she dedicated herself to what she called the good life and started collecting jewelry, her own private Women's Movement of one." Kate wrapped the beads around her fist.

"'Boats rot. The sea was the only way to get here from there and here we are,' my father was known to say.

"My mother would always put her eyes on him and say, 'That man, he's afraid of the half-woman, half-bird sirens.' It went on like that between the two of them."

I was on to Kate today. Her plan was to distract me, maybe to get me talking again about my mother. I'd already gone on and on that morning about her black hair and how she wore it combed high with a coronet of braids, or her beautiful teeth—the two gold ones she was proud of or her quick steps and made-to-order hats. She was very vain about those hats. My father always complimented her on her hats.

"My mother dusted her hats with talcum powder. It was quite a job," I said. Kate rolled her eyes at me, so I said, "Your mother collected jewelry. Mine collected hats but all those feathers mold eventually." That is when Kate showed me the personal in the paper.

I never much noticed the personals that the local paper, *The Brooklyn Daily Eagle*, ran. I thought they were want-ads or notices about people joining or leaving a firm, but on May 27, 1930, the personal my husband ran reeked of contempt for me: *I WILL NOT be responsible for debts contracted by anyone other than myself. Juan del Palacio, 789 Argyle Road, Brooklyn, NY.*

That public denial of responsibility made me see red. Looking back, I think it scared me.

"I'm not responsible for Faith's death," he had hissed at me on the street in front of the Kings County courthouse that day we'd first appeared before the judge. Juan kept a pocketful of grievances the way some had a pocketful of sweets for children.

Kate explained that Juan's personal ad had run for a week, but it was the May twenty-seventh paper she brought with her when we took the train into Grand Central that day. "Show that to your lawyer," she said. "Show him how that golden boy of yours loves his own odious publicity."

"The judge warned us about spreading seeds of tall tales. He was looking right at Juan, as if telling him that it's not just women who spread gossip," I said, thinking that the judge had been sympathetic to me. But my heart did that thudding thing that had made me want to throw things when I was a child.

"Juan's trying to bully me, or maybe it was his mother who was behind this spitefulness. Yes, that's it. I can see him at his parents' house having dinner, her putting pencil to paper."

But then I didn't think I'd ever seen her write anything down and that thought distracted me so that Kate tapped me on my hand to get my attention. "Ruby, that may be true, but he knows that a separation does not have to ruin a man if he plays his cards right. So far, he's shown his cards like a poor poker player. He seems set on revenge."

I slammed my hand on the table, causing the waiter to startle.

"That's what I wanted," she said.

The law office was three blocks up from Grand Central and once there we faced three flights of stairs. The waiting area was shabby. A clerk sitting behind the knee-high fence matched the décor. She looked older than my mother had ever looked. The woman, who had been typing when we entered, told us to take our seats and then she glared at us as if we were there to commit some crime.

After a reasonable amount of time, I said, "Mr. Sisson is expecting me." I wasn't going to let some old bird bully me.

A framed copy of the Bill of Rights hung on the wall behind the woman. I'd once memorized it. I hadn't been in many offices, but in my father's office, which resided high up in the steeple of his church and required a ladder, there had been a framed picture of a griffin. And below the legendary creature, it said, "My busy day." And when that came to mind, I put on my sweet face and said to the clerk, "Busy day?"

But it was a meanness I knew, to say that, and surely the griffin was not a mean creature. The one in my father's office had feathery white wings, like a swan's really, like little Pooh's wings.

The day before, I had kept Clara out of school, and Tessie and I had taken her and Alice to Prospect Park where the hyacinths were disappearing, and the forsythia were in full bloom. My mother had always sent our cook, Annie, out to the kitchen garden to prune her climbing roses the day the forsythia bloomed. Clara found Pooh to take along for Alice. Clara babied her sister. I had let the girls run free in the Long Meadow. Only the ravine with its shaded narrow path was off-limits. "Only where I can see you," I remembered saying.

"How long will he be?" I asked, and the clerk waddled out from behind her desk like a duck and went into the office.

"How long did your case take? From start to finish?" I asked Kate as we both watched the woman return to her desk.

"I can't recall. It all runs together. It was just so many papers and then he moved out," Kate said blankly.

The woman looked at us as if we were her prisoners. "I'm going to need some air if this takes much longer," I said, and the woman shot us a nasty look and turned on her heel as if angry thoughts were her motor.

When I was finally invited into the office, I gave the attorney a minute to pontificate, and then I asked him just how long this was going to take.

"First, Ruby," he said, "we get the filing to the judge. I'd like to show the judge your goodwill. Let's call it your willingness to clear the air and keep things civil. For the children." He pursed his chapped lips into what he might have thought of as a smile and said, "That's our strategy."

But when I asked my next question and the next, he erased any hint of a smile, tilted his fleshy chin downward, and looked up at me as if I were a naughty child. And then he called out, "Mother."

For mercy's sake, the woman was his wife.

"You have children?" I asked to confirm what I already knew.

"Yes, we raised five."

His wife returned. She had one of those rolling hip walks like the ducks at the pond. Swans did not waddle; there was your difference.

The woman put a stack of papers in front of him and stood there waiting for instructions. I took the newspaper I'd been holding in my lap and slapped it on his desk. His wife did a gulping thing.

"Let's talk goodwill, why don't we?"

He read slowly. I looked his wife in the eye, daring her to read over his shoulder.

"May I keep this?" he asked, and I said simply, "No."

The woman gulped again and then left the room.

"Ruby, have you given some thought to visiting your brother in Greenwich? Why not get some country air? Take some time." He was looking down at the newspaper in front of him, and I thought he might just go on and on jabbering about things Juan had fed him.

I thought about the pale blue walls in my childhood bedroom, which looked over the back garden. For many years, one wall bore a hole where I'd thrown my shoe in temper. My mother had left it to remind me that bad temper is damaging to property and character. But then my instinct for self-preservation kicked in, because I reached across the desk and grabbed the newspaper just to get him to stop.

"Seems you already know a bit about me, Mr. Sisson, but I best fill in a few details. I own the home on Argyle Road in Flatbush. It is a detached home with eight rooms and a garage, all very modern. A gift from my father." I stopped myself and added, "And my mother." I waited for him to say something, but he was mute.

I went on, "So you see, I too have a family of some significance. My brother shares your profession, so yes, perhaps I should visit him and seek his counsel."

I stood and left him with those thoughts and gathered up Kate by waving at her to follow me and we left in a flurry.

But in truth I was thirty-six years old and in my book it was too late in life to expect my brother to save me, and it was too late to ask him for marital advice, but it seemed the right thing to do: to go stay with my brother Jimmy.

To get away.

Jimmy had a wife and a young daughter. He'd written and told me all about the home that they'd moved into after they married. Of course, that home was a gift from my father. I knew that they lived on a street with one hundred trees, but I'd never visited him before.

As we left the office, I decided that I'd take Alice with me to Greenwich. She was only in nursery school now, and that was without my consent. Nana had enrolled her in the school. She said Alice's days were shapeless. It was a Catholic school run by nuns. "We are not Catholic," I'd shouted at Louise when she came back that first afternoon with Alice in tow. Louise stared me down as if she could not be bothered to respond. "They'll make her go round and round in a circle like a little inmate," I'd cried to Tessie. The next day, Louise arrived early at the house. She had a hold of Alice by her delicate little wrist, pulling her along and out the door before I was down the stairs. I remember telling Alice not to cry and I remember Louise's carpet bag sitting proudly at the foot of the stairs. I left on the train for Greenwich alone. I knew that was Nana's work.

Jimmy's daughter Irene was in the second grade like Clara. The first time I met Irene was at my father's funeral, where all the little children sat on the little pews at the front of the Old First Church. Clara and Irene sat next to one another, holding hands. But I could tell from the moment I arrived in her home that I scared the child. I thought it was because I was given her room for my stay, or perhaps she thought I'd come to live with them for good.

"Did Clara run away from home?" Irene asked me, and her mother made one of those faces that said, "Well, of course she'd think that." Arriving childless terrified Irene and maybe my sister-in-law too.

I was afraid to put my arm around the child the night I arrived. But the next night, I took her in my arms, and I told her that I had something for her. She followed me to her bedroom, where I sat on her bed and told her that I admired her China dolls. They had been, of course, my mother's. Jimmy had many of my mother's things. I went to the dresser and took out the ruby bowtie pin from a little box I'd left sitting there. I'd meant it for Jimmy's wife.

"Oh my, oh my," Irene said. "I'll always carry it in my pocket as a charm." And then she hurried back to the parlor where her parents were waiting to be bedazzled again by their only child. She'd be their one and only.

On Thursday night, just before Irene went off to bed, she invited me to go with her and her mother to the candy store after school the next day. "We go on Fridays," she said.

That night I stayed up late with Jimmy and his wife, who was sure of his devotion to her. I was finishing my third cigarette of the evening. I was certain my sister-in-law did not approve of my smoking, but she had passed me a lovely hand-painted ashtray, which I balanced on my knees because I did not know what to do with it. I thought about the personal ad from the *Brooklyn Daily*, which I brought with me, but the time had never been right to show my brother, and now I was ashamed to show him. After thinking a few minutes about another cigarette, I said, "I only want this to be over."

Jimmy's wife stood and said she was spent. She hesitated at the doorway and said, "You stay as long as you need, Ruby." But I had not even asked about staying on, and I knew then that I could not stay long, and she knew it too.

When we heard her close their bedroom door, Jimmy began talking about our brother Eddie. He'd come home to Brooklyn for our parents' funerals, but not for Dales's. Jimmy was fighting back tears. "We won't see much of Eddie from now on. His wife has claimed him for her own," he said. "Once upon a time, we had a big fairy-tale family…"

An image of Faith in the white gown crossed my mind, as part of my fairy tale, but Jimmy was going on with his own stories.

"Our father was beloved. Eddie and I had our President Street Gang…and then it's all over. Even Annie is gone to us. You know, I tried to bring her here."

"We kept Annie from having her own family until it was too late," I said. It was true and Jimmy knew it, but it was mean of me to assign blame. "She was as round as a muffin," I said to be kind, but I felt feverish, and he must have noticed because he jumped up to pour us something. When he handed me the elegant glass, he squeezed my shoulder and said, "Tell me exactly what stage you are at with this attorney. It seems to me it is moving along," and I could see he did not know what else to say.

"Yes, my ducks are in order," I said, and he studied me solemnly, so I added, "You never did like Juan, did you?"

"Never, I never trusted him. I do not trust him now."

I was glad I kept the personal ad to myself.

And then like a confession, the excuse slipped out, and I said, "I was so lonely when I was shipped off to Bryn Mawr. Mother sent me there so she'd have an excuse to shop at Wanamaker's."

"You know that's not true, Ruby." Now I'd gone and done it. He was disappointed in me.

"You didn't miss much in Halifax," he said after he'd sipped his drink. He lowered his voice and went on, "After Eddie met his wife, the sparkle went out of things."

We talked about our father then. Our father's story was so easy to tell. "They carpeted the street in rose petals for his funeral procession," I said to make my brother smile, and it worked. What I didn't say was that it was all over for me too and I had buried a dead baby, and he had not said one thing about her. I disliked him very much just then. Looking back, I think I was disappointed. I had hoped for more.

I smoked another cigarette and thought for a second that I'd tell him about the book I was writing about our mother. But I just couldn't find a way to bring it up, and Jimmy never brought up the subject of my writing. I think maybe he felt that in writing about our family, I was stealing from him. Anyway, I left that subject untouched. Writers are always seeking flattery. Best not to go looking for that here.

My fever was gone. I felt the way I'd felt as a child when my mother had put a cool cloth on my forehead. I finished my drink, stood and handed Jimmy both the empty glass and the ashtray, and decided on the spot that I'd leave for home after the weekend.

The thing I noticed when I stepped into the mudroom of my home on Argyle Road was that my kitchen smelled of vinegar when it should have smelled of spring. I felt as if I had been trespassed upon. I wanted to shout like a child, "Mine, mine, mine."

Even my tidy mother, who liked to say, "You cannot neglect your kitchen, or you will pay a price," would not have left a room smelling like this. Colombian maids, I'd learned, were vinegar loving—except for Tessie. But I'd sent her off on a trip to see her sister in Newark while I was away at Jimmy's. She didn't expect me for at least another week. I'd only sent word to Juan that I'd be coming home. Kate asked me later why I'd notified him, notified anyone.

"You'll have to stop that," she'd said.

I held my breath as I crossed the kitchen in the vinegar fog. I thought that surely Alice would have arrived home by now from her little school and would be waiting for her beloved sister, Clara, to arrive home.

"Alice," I called. "Mama's home." The house was dim, and I didn't feel safe being there. I sensed that Nana was listening.

Juan stood in the entry hall. I only had a split second to study him before he took a step away from me. His hair looked oily, but maybe I noticed it because it was thinning, which was not like the del Palacio men. Too bad; he'd been so striking.

"Come to my study. Make it fast. The children will be home," he said.

I didn't move because I didn't understand anything about this moment and finally he said, "In my study."

I set my bag down and walked across the entry hall to his private study. He followed me in and gave the door a shove behind him.

"I've incurred no debts in my absence," I said and sat in the chair in front of his desk, arms folded tight across my chest. I waited. He moved behind his desk. He touched a thin manila folder and opened it to display a single typed page.

"That's a lease. You've probably never seen one. Your attorney drew it up." Juan used his index finger to flick the folder across the desk to me. "Put your signature there." He pointed.

"My attorney did this? At whose instruction?" I asked, but knew. "The Verona?" I said with as much sarcasm as I could muster without throwing something.

"You cannot take advice, can you, Ruby? Mr. Sisson said to go away. He did not say to go for a few days and come running back to cause havoc."

I wanted to argue with every word he'd just said. Instead, I averted my eyes from the paper and from him. The Verona Apartment building hugged the corner of Seventh Avenue and President Street and blocked the view of my father's church from our downstairs parlor. My one and only childhood friend had lived there.

"I will not sign that. I'll call my attorney," I said and stood up to leave.

"You sign or I'll have your maid and her sister on a boat to Colombia. You will never see her again. Deported for good.

"Carelessness will sink you, my dear wife," he said, as if I were his property.

"Juan, we stood in this very room and agreed on the separation. It's the best we can do, and you agreed." I wasn't begging, but I wasn't shouting either.

We both heard the children coming up the sidewalk.

"This is the best you can do? The children will never forgive you."

"Forgive me for what?"

He slapped me then, his finger hooking in my ear and pulling it. I whimpered and thought to bite him, but the moldy smell of the cigar mixed with the vinegar fumes made me gag. I closed my eyes and waited for him to hit me again. His large ring, which was some sort of family heirloom, had met my eye and it began to fill with tears. I reached behind me for the chair and dropped into it. I tasted blood, which I later decided he surely saw. The vomit I held back burned into my throat. I think it did damage.

"You bully," I said.

He crossed the room. There was such a noise in my head that I could not be sure he'd left. And I could not tell if the children were standing in a little circle outside the door. I knew it was my heartbeat that deafened me. Finally, I stood and walked to the sofa where I lay down, turned my face to the cushions, and wept the way I'd seen my mother weep when Richard died. There was no comfort on that hard sofa, and I thought that if only I had her red puff to pull up over me that I might quiet myself.

Now, months later, I woke surprised. Most mornings were like that at the Verona. I sat with my feet on the cold bare floor and moaned. What a baby I'd become. I heard Tessie outside my bedroom door. I knew that now she would go for my coffee. Seeing the clock on the dresser, I tried to calculate where each of my children would be right now, but my mind wandered. There was nothing urgent on my calendar today, and I considered pulling my feet up and burrowing under the covers. The apartment was always cold and damp. But I sat and listened instead to the steam heat as it crawled up the walls to the fourth-floor apartment. There had been no Indian summer. Snow had fallen the first week of October.

The Verona had emptied out over the summer. The lawyers, brokers, and well-off merchants left to summer at the New Jersey shore—that is, if they were still afloat—and some did not return. It was better now that many of the twelve apartments were occupied again, that there was some sign of life.

I'd had a friend who lived here when I was a girl. We'd been chums against my mother's wishes. I'd had so few friends. My mother would not let me visit Dorothy because of the mere fact that her family lived in an apartment in the Verona. "That friendship will cost you," my mother warned, and she meant reputation. I'd come to think that Dorothy must have lived on the top floor, which was the sixth floor because she'd told me that when she saw me on the street from her window, I'd looked like a mouse. It had seemed so romantic to me to live in the Verona—like living in a city—like Paris. And I'd considered disobeying my mother and going inside to visit my friend, but the entrance to the building was tucked away on President Street, and people kept an eye out for children in those days.

Precious child. I could not remember how that felt.

My dressing gown was at the foot of my bed, but all that thinking about my mother made me determined to dress properly—plans or no plans. She had not approved of me leaving my room until I was dressed for the day. And so, when I was fit to be seen, I joined Tessie in the parlor. She was in uniform—a striped shirtwaist with a white apron. Surely, I had not suggested such a getup, but when she returned from visiting with her sister, she brought those uniforms with her. Thinking back on those days, I think she'd adopted the uniform to perk me up.

When Tessie left to collect the newspaper, there was a silence in the room that was, in fact, sadness. I knew that if I went to the large windows and opened one, I could have put the street noises together with what I saw. But I wasn't up to putting things together, and instead I sat on the little love seat and wondered where in fact Dorothy and her family had gone. She'd been such a pretty girl. But my mother was right about the Verona; it was not a place for a family to make a permanent home.

Silly girls, Dorothy and I had been. We thought we would be friends forever.

I was teaching Tessie to read English by reading the paper, and she was reading me the front-page headlines when the phone rang. It made the wall it was attached to shudder. As Tessie ran for the phone, she hollered, "Maybe something will happen today."

"Missus, your attorney," Tessie called out as if she was a proper receptionist.

"Or is it the duck?" I waddled across the room to take the phone. I had told Tessie all about the attorney's squat wife.

Tessie peaked her eyebrows as if in celebration. "No, the real thing," she said. And I imagined an end to the waiting, and I told myself that now it would get easier: that the hardest part was over.

"We are going to need a fresh strategy," my attorney said when I picked up the phone. "The Court has been advised of a counterclaim." The word "strategy" rolled around in my head. And then with each answer I wheedled out of him, it got worse, until he whispered, "Adultery and abandonment."

"I cannot hear you," I shouted into the phone to give myself time to think. I heard him muttering and I said, "Claims who?"

He repeated what he had said, and I thought maybe Juan was there with him watching the performance, but it was probably only his ducky wife.

"Mr. del Palacio answered your complaint—with a counterclaim you understand—of adultery and abandonment."

"Absurd," I said.

"You did leave the home, Ruby."

I'd been standing with my head up against the wall and when I hung up, Tessie found Kate's number in my desk and called her.

"She's taken to her bed," I heard Tessie say, which was not technically true. I had gone back to my room but not to my bed. Instead, I smoked cigarettes and listened to my heart trying to beat a hole in my chest.

When Kate arrived at the apartment, she insisted on calling Mr. Sisson, but first she sent Tessie out to collect Alice at her nursery school, which was the only motherly responsibility left to me all these months.

"Take the stuffed lambs," Kate said. Kate was forever buying Clara and Alice stuffed animals and dolls dressed in colorful party clothes. Kate's babies had been boys.

Mrs. Sisson refused to pass the call through to her husband

until Kate threatened her, saying she'd get on an afternoon train to New York, and she would have.

"I'm not authorized," the woman kept saying, which I knew because Kate repeated each thing the woman said.

When Kate got Mr. Sisson on the phone, she said, "It seems to me that you sat on your hands after you pocketed the fee the Court ordered Mr. del Palacio to pay you. We both know adultery is a word men get to toss about and saying it makes it so."

He must have tried to give Kate the same lecture he'd given me, but I could see it was going nowhere and I left Kate on the phone and went back to the parlor and stood at the window and watched all the schoolchildren on Seventh Avenue going every which way. Tessie would be delivering Alice home to Argyle Road about now.

"We have an appointment with that ridiculous man tomorrow at nine," Kate said. "He said you have twenty days to reply to the counterclaim."

I kept my back to Kate for minutes on end. I heard her twisting and playing with her beads. Finally, I said, "I married a man without pity."

CHAPTER 7

RUBY
1930

We were walking across the main concourse at Grand Central Terminal—Kate and I shoulder to shoulder—moving straight ahead up a ramp now toward the Forty-Second Street exit. I had been taken to Grand Central when I was a child before they tore the old place down and started over. I couldn't construct a memory of my parents in this building, not the way I could see them in Wanamaker's. It was odd to me years later that parts of my parents' lives seemed more real to me than my own.

"I hate it when they tear perfectly good places down," I said to Kate, but it seemed to me that she was ignoring me.

Mr. Sisson was expecting us at nine, but overnight I had convinced myself that he might not even bother with us. I'd told Kate that on the train coming across the Brooklyn Bridge, but still we walked straight ahead with purpose, not making way for anyone distracted by their own life.

"I'll not be responsible for knocking anyone down," Kate said in what sounded to me like a detached voice.

And so, meaning to be lighthearted because she had set the tone, I said, "Watch out. I'm an accused adulterer now." I was ready to bluster my way across the terminal, but she still faced straight ahead.

"You are part of this," I wanted to say.

Instead, I said, "This is a waste of time. Yours and mine."

"You've paid for his time, Ruby." She did a little trip over her own feet but caught herself.

"Time and toil, time and toil," Kate said in typical Kate fashion and then added, "Not a very easy day, is it?" She'd taken to using the negative approach over the summer so that I couldn't help but agree before I knew what I was agreeing to. And all summer, she had brought her book of French fables every time we met at Green-Wood. The gilt-edged book had been meant for her children, she'd told me. Telling me things like that never seemed to make her sad.

"I thought it would be good for them to learn to speak a pretty language along the way," she explained one day, because the book told each fable in both English and French. Looking back, I remember those summer days distinctly because of the fables. "Their way was too short," she'd said one day while we sat near her babies' graves, and that day was the fable of the lion and the mouse. She read it aloud in French and she was right, it was pretty. And then she read the translation, "By time and toil we sever what strength and rage could never."

That day her forehead had looked sweaty, and I'd wanted to put my hand to it and check for heat.

"You see, the point is, Ruby, that mercy brings its rewards." And then we'd just continued on with fables.

Near the doors to Forty-Second Street, she maneuvered me to the right and said, "Silly me, wrong way." But it was all farce today. Kate never considered herself silly.

On the street it was warmer, and I stopped to remove my coat. I was wearing my peacock blue dress, which had paled over the summer from having hung too long in the sun on a line on the top floor drying room at the Verona. Tessie and I had forgotten it there, which is what happens to people who have too little to do.

"This time, I'm going into his office with you, Ruby. Nothing to gain by being good girls now. And if you do not tell him that moving to the Verona was Juan's idea, then I will make a scene."

"For Pete's sake, how will you make a scene?" I asked.

And then I calmed myself and said, "It's perfectly fine if you come in. Two against one."

"And it is high time he set things straight with that husband of yours," Kate added.

My mother had used that exact phrase with me, and like so much I had chosen to forget about my mother, I'd forgotten that. "Let's set this straight now, young lady," was how my mother phrased it. But what she'd meant was that she herself would be setting things straight.

Sarcasm took charge of me; I put a mean smile on my face and I said, "So, no mercy for Mr. Sisson."

She let that pass and said, "Just tell him that he's got twenty days to earn his pay and get this simple matter settled. And it is not, I repeat, not like you just walked out on your family to take up with some lonely old man. Ridiculous."

"I will," I said, but without enough enthusiasm for Kate, because I'd been thinking about how much Juan hated this woman.

"You have to try," Kate said and began coughing, which was another thing that had started over the summer.

"Too many spring blooms at Green-Wood. Haven't you noticed? Their vapors are thick in the air," she'd said the first time she'd canceled her plans to meet me at the cemetery. Later, she stopped making excuses although one day late in the summer she'd called and said, "I've done my best by my children." And I imagined her, like my mother, snuggled under deep layers of covers—content. But also, I knew she had acquired a white fox terrier, Puck, and I suspected she preferred to spend her day with Puck—both of them cozy under deep layers of covers.

We stopped walking and both leaned up against a building while Kate regained her composure. My heart felt crowded when I saw how pale she'd turned. She took my arm, and as we headed up Madison, she began to recite by heart, "Over hill, over dale, through brush and brier, over park, over pale, through flood, through fire, I do wander everywhere..." And when she got to the "farewell, thou lob of spirits," she was whispering. Then she added, "I'll be gone." And we were at Mr. Sisson's building by then. I felt what I now know to be sorrow hit me, but I batted it away.

"I'm ruined," was all I could think after reading the *Brooklyn Daily Eagle* article that Mr. Sisson put in front of us the moment Kate and I took our seats in his office. "This morning's paper," he said with a sly tone.

"You could not stop this? Honestly, didn't you see the snare her husband set?" Kate asked and then fooled with the nape of her dress; I saw that she was not wearing her rope of beads— not any jewelry—not even the emerald ring.

> *Marital Craft*
> *Goes on the Rocks*
> *after 15 Years*
>
> *Fifteen years of happiness. Six*
> *children romping about them.*
> *And then somebody developed*
> *a case of "nerves" and the woman*
> *yearned to lead her own life*
> *and become a writer and the man's*
> *attitude changed.*
>
> *Such is the story of the del Palacio*
> *family as told in court by Juan,*
> *the husband, and Ruby, the wife.*
> *They lived on Argyle Road for years*
> *And their joy of living made them*
> *the envy of their neighbors. And their*
> *children were described as "most*
> *beautiful."*

*She went away to her brother's
residence in Connecticut. She told
the court that her husband was cruel and
yet he said he was loving-kindness
personified. The court awarded
Mrs. del Palacio with alimony and
counsel fee. The husband then pleaded
with the court to set aside the order
and countersued his wife of 15 years
with adultery and abandonment.*

"Who wrote this thing?" I asked, and Kate flicked it back across the desk to the attorney. She started coughing and turned red-faced, and being so pale, it seemed she had caught on fire. Once she got control, she said, "Those are lies and Mrs. del Palacio will not step foot into another court to defend herself against lies. For two cents, I'd throw you headfirst out the window. You fix this." Kate glared at the man. She sounded and looked like my mother looked whenever she sniffed out any misdoings. She would begin by standing up majestically, then turn red-faced and say, "I'm distracted with you children. I will take my umbrella and go sit under a banana tree on the Gowanus Canal if you keep this up."

But my mother wasn't here. My friend was not well, and I was at sea.

"My dear," the man began and then stopped speaking as he stood and walked over to the door where his wife, who had seen us in, still stood. "You are confused," he said to Kate, which anyone who had any sense would know not to say to my friend. He patted his wife on her fat face and opened the door for her to leave. "Let's think this through," he said, then folded his hands in front of his tummy while he stood with his back to the door.

"I don't get confused," Kate said and clapped her hands like a mad woman. Maybe it was to get his attention because then she said, "Go get me some water."

"Is she ill?" he asked. He did not budge.

"Just go," I said. He let his eyes slide over his desk with uncertainty, and then he left the room. I reached across the rat's nest on his desk, grabbed the newspaper article, and tore it up into little bits of nothing.

"Hold your course without remorse," Kate said as she pointed her chin at me.

When he returned with the glass of water, he was as flushed as Kate. He gingerly set the glass on the table in front of her and, as he took his seat behind his desk, said, "Let's settle down so that I can clarify things." He shuffled through papers, sweeping the torn bits into his hands and then dropping them back on the desk. After he found the paper he was looking for, he said, "Understand, Ruby, you are being sued for divorce."

Kate drank her water and then stared at me until I said, "As my attorney, are you defending me in these charges or are you taking instruction from my husband?"

The man looked at the door as if his wife would reappear and answer for him.

Seizing the moment, Kate moved to the edge of her chair and, in a rousing voice I did not recognize, said, "You told Mrs. del Palacio to leave her home. You wrote a lease for her to sign. Is that not correct? Whose pocket are you in?"

He stabbed the paper in front of him and finally said, "There is the alimony."

I could see that Kate wanted to say more, but the coughing fit had turned her voice into a whisper.

So, I said, "I will not lower myself to fight these allegations in some gossip column."

We paraded into the lobby of the RCA building later that morning as if we'd been invited for a private tour and took a service elevator that had been draped with packing blankets.

"A garden here on Fifth Avenue?" I'd questioned when Kate overruled a return to the teahouse. "A garden is the ticket," I'd said to lighten the moment because she had scared me something awful in Mr. Sisson's office.

There was not a single bird on the eleventh-floor rooftop garden at the RCA building that October day in 1930 where we wound up after our failed meeting with the weasel of an attorney. But there was fresh air and Kate was breathing better. Papa would have marveled at such a sight as this garden if he had been able to get over the disappointment I was. In this place, the memory of him became clear. I heard him saying how we were here to make the world into a garden. I looked over at the paths and saw not one weed. Give it time, I thought. My father would not have approved of the cynic I'd become.

"It's lovely, Kate," I offered my friend, who had seated herself on a stone bench. She rolled her eyes lazily at me as if she could read my mind. Today was a day we didn't believe each other, I decided.

"Take a walk around the garden, why don't you?" she said.

"To think I could have carried on and on, day after day, with my most beautiful children, enjoying being the envy of my neighbors," I said to Kate.

I was pushing it again with the sarcasm, but this time she returned my sarcastic smile and then said, "Take a walk and come back with a plan, Ruby."

"But truly, Kate, who writes such things about people they do not know?"

"Does it matter, Ruby? I'm set on resting my own mind now. An English Garden is supposed to make us pause and think." She was speaking to me as if I was a child.

I softened my face into a smile, because she looked so French sitting there in her black.

"It doesn't look very English to me," I said and surveyed the rooftop. "I think the French had something to do with it. Look at the goose-foot pattern of paths. Parisian."

I think what Kate said to me then in French was spiteful, but I did not know French.

I walked each of the distinct paths—half a dozen times. When I decided I could behave again, I stood in front of her, and she reached into her bag where she usually kept her fables and took out an envelope stuffed with one-hundred-dollar bills that she handed me.

"Now is the time to find yourself a serious attorney."

"Where did you get this?"

"Gypsies always have a stash for when they need to get serious. Consider it fairy favors."

I had a small pocketbook with me, and I put the money away.

"If my mother were still alive for this circus, I think she would blame me," I said. Kate did not respond or even look at me, really. What I didn't tell her was that my mother's disapproval was making it impossible to write about her. Disapproval will do that to a writer. But none of that mattered now.

"Juan got one thing right. My children will never forgive me, not after this article in the paper."

"They'll never see it. It will go straight to the bottom of some gilded birdcage," Kate said. She made the sound of a bird. It was frightening. Then she lit a cigarette even though she was still speaking in little puffs of breath. She offered me one. And so, we sat and smoked like Jazz Age renegades.

"You sold some jewelry, didn't you?"

"My mother's jewelry. Not mine—never was mine. Boats rot, Ruby. I understand that now."

And now Kate laughed, which had been a long time coming.

But then she wiped at her forehead. In the slanted fall sunlight, her black dress was simmering. There was no shade in this garden, and I thought then that was why there were no birds.

"Now listen to me," Kate said. "No, your children will not forgive you for any of this mess, not until they know what happened, but maybe not even then. Who knows about forgiveness? So, why don't we forgive our mothers right now? With this damn sickness, I think I understand my mother—well, just a bit. She was French, you know. She had one fox terrier after another. When one died, she replaced it with another—all snow white. They mattered more to her than I ever did. But I forgive her that."

Kate held her delicate hands open as if setting a bird free, looked around, and said, "Of course, this garden is only beginning. I hope to see it finished." She sighed and went on. "Forgive your mother, Ruby, for not warning you what lay ahead. Maybe then you can finish that book you're writing about meeting at the eagle."

Right then, in that moment, I was flooded with gratitude for her friendship and for the way she knew me. Now, as an old woman with few friends, I can still hear her whispered voice.

Kate stood and reached behind her to smooth out her dress.

"So, what now? You decide," she said.

"I need to find someone clever to help me," I said.

Kate went to the edge of the rooftop and leaned over the wall, which was much too short for my comfort. The back of her dress was a forest of wrinkles.

"Well, we're both tired, and I'm so damned hot in all this blinding sunshine. Let's get back home to Brooklyn. Puck will be missing me."

Of course, back in the spring we'd begun to fear that it was cancer creeping up on Kate. She told me it was cancer that took her mother and I'd spent the summer trying to ignore that.

But then when I met her at Green-Wood on day eighteen of my twenty-day penance, she said it was to celebrate her angry gallbladder, said her doctor had told her a gallbladder could get pretty angry and could bear a grudge.

"I was wrong to expect the worst," she said when we met

at the Gothic gate. Then she suggested that we walk to the graves, which was not like her and still not wise, and we both knew that.

"A carriage ride will give us more time for our picnic," I said. And she agreed. We put our picnic blanket on Richard's grave this time, close to where my parents and Dales rested. It was a fine fall day to be there in view of all those Farrars. And with all the unkindness I was famous for, I wondered if Dales had managed to die first so that he could get that spot next to Mother. Well, she would have wanted it that way.

"My mother didn't care for dogs, but she loved Dales," I said, but Kate looked right past me.

"Ruby, we can be forgiven for having favorites. Good thing my mother only had one child."

I looked at her closely. There was something peculiar about her face that I couldn't put my finger on. But it was relief, I decided, and besides, I saw the emerald ring back on her long, thin finger.

And when she caught me staring, she said, "The point is, I'm not dying yet." She lay out flat on her back on the hard ground and closed her eyes.

"The pain is gone?"

"Well, no, not completely. But the spasms have stopped. The interesting thing is that I can actually see the darn thing—the shape of the pain—and while I am busy being fascinated by that vision, I forget the pain."

Keeping her eyes shut, she drew the outline of a shape on her stomach.

Tessie had made us a picnic lunch, and I began to unpack things. It looked as if Kate had fallen asleep, but I was not sure and so I said, "Actually, when I was still small, we had a greyhound. He wasn't all that smart, but he liked to lie at my mother's feet at night when we sat in the parlor, and I had to play piano for her. I didn't have the heart for the piano. But one day, the dog knocked me down on the stairs, and next thing I knew, he was given away. But my mother loved Dales." In that moment, I knew I was feeling sorry for myself, and Kate wasn't having it and she wasn't asleep.

She nodded when I finished with my story and then said, "We won't have many of these days once you move back home with your children. You will be a busy mother in a busy household. I'll bring Puck over to Argyle Road to meet the older children. Let's see if your son likes Puck. Perhaps a greyhound is the ticket."

She opened her eyes wide, and that was when I realized what had seemed so odd about her. Her pupils were enormous. It was alarming and beautiful.

"What? Cheer up, Ruby. We are both looking at a new life." She sat up and motioned for me to pass her the extra picnic blanket. She wrapped it around her shoulders, and I saw how slight she'd become.

"What?" she said again when she spotted my alarm. "I'll get my strength back."

"If either of those attorneys Jimmy found me had said one single helpful thing, I might have kept trying. You know that, Kate. They were both so stupidly polite and consistent in their negativity. I really tried and I spent your money for nothing," I said.

"Wait it out," I said, mimicking the first attorney I met with. "You blame Juan. He blames you. Eventually, it will end." And then I quoted the second attorney, a tiny man, who had said, as if he were speaking from a pulpit, "It takes two sides to fight a battle, but your husband won the war before the first battle. It's New York, Little Lady."

"Fragile beings," Kate said. "Men, I mean. We are stronger than them, don't you think? They have no idea how much they lean on women... Take my father. He was afraid to step foot on a boat from the moment he arrived in America. And that was just the beginning of his fears. 'Everything rots,' he used to come home and say to my mother, who was usually in bed getting her beauty sleep. Well, I've told you that story, haven't I?"

She handed me a chocolate, which was her contribution to our picnic. I really thought for a moment she was going to start in with a fable, but instead she said, "I can no longer eat sweets."

"Your eyes," I said. "They look strange."

"Belladonna—a nightshade," she said. "Poof, I took this powder and now I'm better. The doctor said that if the powder stopped some of the pain then it was my gallbladder and not cancer. That's science for you."

She said, "I will save you some of this magic powder for when you go to court Monday. It makes the world very bright."

"Too late for that, Kate. And besides, isn't nightshade poison?"

"So?" she said. "Small doses, my friend."

Now I pointed at Faith's grave and said, "Faith died for want of oxygen." We both took deep breaths and then I added, "I wish you could have seen that gorgeous blonde baby. The doctor said she was a blue baby, but I couldn't see that. She was perfect."

Early Monday, a basket of ruby-red pansies arrived with a note from Kate saying she had overdone it at the picnic.

"For you," I said to Tessie. "Kate knows I dislike cut flowers and I detest baskets."

And so, it was Tessie who went to court with me that Monday. "Open Court" was the way Mr. Sisson had explained it to me as if it was a friendly place. "Perhaps your brother will come to Brooklyn to support you." But it would have been asking too much of Jimmy. I was not the center of his life, or Kate's.

I understood what bile tasted like that afternoon as I took my seat next to Mr. Sisson in the courtroom. He smelled musty. My in-laws arrived with Juan, and they made their entrance through the double doors as if at a concert hall. Juan's mother had her cane hooked over her free arm while she took Juan's arm with the other. She wore a fox stole—with the head—that I had not seen before. It would alarm Alice and Clara. She had changed her hair, and the curls on her forehead looked ridiculous. She'd gone to much trouble. She cared about appearances. My mother would never have made such an entrance. She would have stayed home, but then my mother's mission in life had been much different.

My mother had saved herself for herself.

But then another title for my book came to me, and it was so much better than the other ones. "Contentment." A one-word title was fitting for my mother.

I heard Juan's mother say, "Thank you, son," as she took her seat behind the table where Juan would sit with his attorney. But my father-in-law had been waylaid at the back of the courtroom by a tall, official-looking man who had his ear. The press, I suspected, was there to satisfy the public craving for details about someone else's ordeals. Juan's father was a man who loved to see his name in the paper, craved the envy of strangers. I should have realized then that he had to have been the person behind the 'Marital Craft' article.

So diligent in their love for their son.

I have a recollection of Juan's father saying something to Tessie before he finally took his seat in the courtroom. Of course, he was the one to thank for pulling the strings to bring Tessie and her sister to the United States in the first place, and he could always send them back. I turned around and saw her bobbing her head as he spoke to her. But with everything that came after that, it was hard to recall what Tessie told me he had said to her. It was only what appeared in court reports—preserved in my cedar chest—that tells me what took place that one single day.

We stood for the judge. It was as if we'd all arrived here for him—as if we needed him to march in and set things straight.

My father had always insisted on being at his pulpit as his congregation arrived. No grand processionals for him. And here was the judge parading in, and I caught myself smirking. That I remember because the judge saw it, and I've regretted it ever since.

"Do not be too quick to judge, Lady Vere de Vere," my mother had sometimes said to me, and each time in my mind I'd accuse her of calling the kettle black.

When we were all seated again, the judge began to speak. He had papers in front of him, but he was not reading from them. As he spoke, he'd touch his chest to make a point, and then he'd lean forward again on his forearms. I don't know why he didn't just say, "I am an earnest man."

"Mrs. del Palacio has failed to reply to her husband's countersuit," was his first pronouncement. "Twenty days have elapsed." He may have said "expired." Next to me, Mr. Sisson had his head down.

"The defendant having appeared and presented his verified answers and counterclaim in the County of Kings..." The judge held his head up high in a majestic pose and then continued, "the plaintiff not having appeared..."

I nudged my attorney and waited for him to look me in the eye. The judge went on about "satisfactory proof" without mentioning any details.

"Prove it," I wanted to say. It was something I'd heard my oldest daughter say many times to her brother. But by then, Mr. Sisson had his hand on my arm and held it there. I think he was afraid I was going to bolt.

And then, the judge did what judges do. He *ordered* and *decreed* like kings have always done. I've looked up those two words many times and try not to use them—not ever.

"I decree the final judgment in favor of the defendant, Juan del Palacio, and against the plaintiff, Ruby del Palacio, thus dissolving the marriage because of adultery and abandonment. The unhappy knot is broken," the judge said without a whiff of mercy. I had misjudged him.

I thought I'd been prepared for an open court pronouncement of divorce, but the judge went on and further *ordered, adjudged, and decreed.* It seemed as if the room came alive with spirits. Spirits who gasped for breath. I turned to my right and Nana was in my line of sight. With the proud tilt of her head, I was sure that she had known all along what would come next. The judge was saying that Juan would have full custody of the children and would remain in the family home on Argyle Road. He said simply that Juan would pay me for the house on Argyle Road. I looked at Mr. Sisson but said nothing.

The judge was going on about a three-month waiting period and my mind rushed forward to January, which is an unforgiving month in Brooklyn. I saw that Nana had known this before the judge pronounced it because she nodded as if in agreement with herself. Juan's father, who was holding a cigar, was studying his hands. I was not certain about him—was never sure if he was in on this part of the plot against me.

The buzzing I heard was not just in my head and the judge must have been aware of it too because he raised his gavel to signal silence and said, "Mr. del Palacio has agreed to pay Mrs. del Palacio five thousand dollars for the premises on Argyle Road. Sixteen hundred upon execution of the divorce." He was speaking so faintly that I leaned forward and heard him say, "Balance monthly."

Then he cleaned his throat and began calling out the full name of each of my six children with their birth dates, for the record, of course. Mr. Sisson was patting my hand and whispering in my ear that I would have visitation rights and that the alimony would continue, and summers would be mine with the children.

He'd known too.

How had I not expected the worst?

But Tessie was crying so loudly that the judge stopped

what he was reading and said, "Let's give that woman a minute to compose herself. Respect the Court, Miss, or I will ask you to leave."

Then he held his gavel up like a nasty child who was poised to throw a rock and spoke in a tone that implied the judging was over. I don't think I heard a word of what he said next—speaking to Juan this time—but I've reread it so many times that I can quote it: "In the event that it becomes necessary for the defendant to leave the United States for any foreign country in the interest of conducting business in which he is engaged, he may take any or all of said children with him, but shall return said child or children to the United States within a period of one year from their departure when the said visitations shall resume."

And that was the end of it that day. The judge stood to leave, and the bailiff instructed us to stand, but I did not stand. Instead, I watched Juan and his mother, who each pretended not to see me looking at them. So, I kept after it until Tessie sat down in the chair that my attorney had left vacant and began to comfort me. I never saw Tessie cry again.

The mortuary where Kate's wake and funeral were held was on Fulton Street. Her husband had made all the arrangements. "A luncheon will follow the service at Gage and Tollner," he wrote in a handsome hand on a note that arrived the day after Kate's death. The Farrars had held many functions at that restaurant following births, weddings, and deaths. I remembered how, as a child and later as a young woman, I'd stared at myself and my family in the enormous framed mirrors that Gage and Tollner was known for. I'd be alone there in those mirrors now.

Whenever we had an event at Gage and Tollner, my father would quote a friend who worshipped the place. "Gage is a state of mind. You go to Gage and Tollner for the experience, the way you go to heaven for the climate and to hell for the company." I went for my friend on the coldest day of the year that was finally almost over. And I'd gone to the wake too. Puck had been allowed to sit by the black casket.

I had never met anyone in Kate's life before, but in addition to her husband, her father was there at the funeral home. When I finally was composed enough to introduce myself to the two men, her father said simply, "Well, here we are."

And then her husband said, "Kate and I were separated a number of years ago." He stopped speaking and seemed to be counting. Then he went on, saying, "But now that she's gone, I feel as if I've become a widower."

Kate's father did not take offense. He said kindly, "Well, I am a widower and have been for many years. When a child loses their parents, they are orphaned, but when a parent loses a child, I am not sure what it makes you."

"A mourner," I could have said. I heard my father's voice. But I was no one to give comfort.

I wondered what Kate would have made of these two sad men.

Kate's husband looked at the bereft terrier and said, "I don't much care for dogs, but I agreed to keep the dog, Mrs. del Palacio, unless you want him. Kate said I must ask you first because your son might want him."

CHAPTER 8

RUBY
1931

Juan was never in love with me. It's not that I don't remember. No matter; I was the mother of his children, and they love me. I had to believe that—especially today because I was headed to Argyle Road for my first visitation, and I was so very nervous about seeing my own children. The judge stipulated that the visits were to take place at their home.

My home too, I'd corrected the man. Kate would have been proud.

The judge had made me wait three full months, and that was long enough for Alice to forget me and for Clara to think I was never coming back home. Mateo was old enough to see cruelty at work, even if only directed at his mother.

Kate and I had talked about homes that last day I visited her. Her house was an exquisite home in Brooklyn Heights with three patios and a courtyard fitted out for Puck and all his mischief. She told me that day that she had decided the only true home we ever have is the one we have as children. "Yes, but you wanted to be a gypsy," I'd teased, trying to get her going because she was wickedly sick by then and bedridden, and I wanted her to be fanciful. Puck was at the foot of her bed and stared at her with utter devotion as she spoke. I suppose it was cancer that took her, but what did anyone know for sure about anything?

I could remember her taking a gulp of air and saying, "Gypsies bury their dead babies along the way and move on.

So, I was wrong about some of my wishes. I only wanted to wander a bit, and I never got around to that. No matter. Too late now."

I let all the gypsy business go. What Kate and I did, in my opinion, was honor each other that day.

I stopped in front of my neighbor's house on Argyle Road. It felt like someone was watching me, and so I rested my bag on the curb. I was regretting the weight of the bag. Kate's book of fables that I'd brought for Mateo was the major culprit.

A few days before Christmas, Kate's husband brought Puck over to visit me at the Verona. "We're all lonely, aren't we?" he said to the dog, who looked at him but not with the same devotion he'd shown Kate. He passed around the sweets that none of us wanted. And then he gave me a heavy box of things Kate wanted me to have including the fables, but when a knock came at the door about the dog in the building—they were not allowed—he left without argument. Over the years, I've wondered about them; how long Puck lived with his broken heart in that lonely courtyard.

My neighbor came out of her house, a sweater thrown across her shoulders, which were broad like a farm girl's. She asked me to come inside for a moment.

"I'm expected at my house," I said, wondering if she'd been the one to speak to a reporter at the *Brooklyn Daily Eagle.* She'd brought over gifts when I brought Alice home, but I could not recall her name. If over the years I'd thought about her, it was to think of her misery; her husband was a recluse living in their sunroom with the velvet curtains drawn. "A character out of Grimms' fairy tales. Bright light could kill him," my oldest daughter, who had taken up dramatic reading at school, said.

I hefted the bag back up on my shoulder and stepped up on her porch. She looked back over her shoulder at the driveway we shared. "Missus, your husband is refusing your mail. He marks it, 'Return to Sender Address Unknown.' I'd call that a lie. Let me tell you, Christmas cards arrived for you and letters too. Our postman pinched them. He didn't want Mr. del Palacio getting away with that. They are inside."

I couldn't picture the postman.

"I have an address," I said, sounding like a charity case.

My back door opened and banged closed as if a sudden gust of wind was at work, but there was no wind that day.

"Please come on inside," my neighbor said, and I spotted her name on the mailbox.

"Mrs. Gleason, I am expected at three-thirty. I could stop by when I leave."

I had a spy now.

I crossed over the driveway. The pebbles always hurt my feet, but I was not noticing that today, and I didn't notice that our garage door was standing open with Juan's car inside. What took possession of my thoughts was how ugly the bare forsythias were in winter, no better than weeds. As I pushed open the back door, I saw that the kitchen was empty. But then Louise pulled herself up from behind a tall box. She meant to startle me—I realized that later. A sneer was plastered on her leathery face and her hairnet dropped down and only her eyebrows saved her from being masked. Hate bubbled up in my throat.

"Mr. del Palacio waiting the dining room," she said.

I wasn't late, but I wasn't going to acknowledge her role in my household or correct her English.

When I saw Juan standing in the center hall, he seemed rather superficial. All I could think was that like the forsythia he'd been prettier with a head full of hair. Winter did not become him. He'd be bald soon. I smelled Louise behind me. I had a spy and an enemy. I softened my thoughts like my mother told me to do before speaking and said, "Where are the children?" I was speaking to him, but it was Louise who answered. I didn't really hear what she said. Still, I dropped my bag to the floor, turned on her, and said, "This is not your home."

I looked up and saw Alice's little feet hanging through the banister. She dangled them like a mobile in a breeze and I saw that her shoes were not polished. She was silent as she began kicking the wall, as if her intent was to put a hole in it.

"Please leave us," Juan said to Louise.

Such a fraud. He'd never said please to one of the maids before.

I stepped toward Juan so that I could look up to see Alice. "You little monkey," I said to her, but she kept kicking her feet as she met my eye. I saw resentment. But all I wanted to do just then was grab my baby girl and flee as if she was mine alone, as if it was fine to take a child for your own.

I thought of Margie. After the divorce was finalized, I'd gotten a packet from her. The kindness of that woman was a gift. She'd sent the packet from Colombia care of my father's church. That was Margie. She had desperately wanted to be a mother. I always knew that. She'd sent two letters in the packet, one from her.

"I hold you in no judgment," was her first line. I'd decided that when I was settled again, I'd write a short story and use that sentence. I was still full of self-assessed pride.

"They've found me a baby," was her second line. "A second cousin of Carlos's who lives in the countryside was tricked into giving me her baby boy. Ruby, I have dreamt that they told her that her baby died at birth, and now I am sure of it. There is a hint of Carlos in the child who is named Alberto. Carlos made a mobile of wooden monkeys to dance over the crib. I don't love this child, not even one little bit. It's Nana's doing. How could she do this to a mother and to me?"

That too was Margie, poor soul. I wanted to write her and assure her that the baby would love her and that her love for him would come along, but she had begged me not to respond and not to try to contact her. She had provided no address. "It's best that we do not communicate," she'd written before signing, "Margie, Your sister, in love." The other letter was a gift that I could not bring myself to accept at the time.

Now, I thought of Faith as I stood there in the hallway. The baby I'd lost.

Juan was looking up at Alice. "Stop it," he said. "Go to your room."

As the house went silent again, I had an abandoned feeling. I listened for Juan's mother because I believed in that moment that he had come home from his office on Beaver Street in Manhattan on a weekday to protect her from me. But I was wrong about that.

Juan blew out a mouthful of smoke and checked his watch.

"I brought a gift for each of the children," I said. I picked up the bag and handed it to him as if it was an offering. I stood there empty-handed while he went upstairs. I heard him go up all the way to the third floor, expecting to hear him consulting with the matriarch. "Mother, may I?" I said to myself and wished for Kate.

He moved to the second floor and after a minute or two slammed the door to the room my three older daughters shared, and then he appeared on the second-floor landing. He held the velvet bag, the one with the strand of pale pink pearls for Alice. They'd been mine, but the blue velvet bag was one of many things Kate's husband had brought me. It was my mother who gave the pearls to me—one for each of my eighteen years before I met and married Juan.

Juan twirled the bag around his index finger until it gained some speed and he let go. It flew with such a force that the strand slipped out and broke, and the pearls bounced, rolled, and scattered. It took many seconds for them to settle.

"Who do you think you are fooling? Jewels from your mouthy friend do not make you a fit mother."

And for some ridiculous reason—that I will never understand—I began defending myself. "The pearls were mine. Precious to me, and I wanted Alice to have them." But my mistake was kneeling to gather them up.

"Leave them," he said, and pointed at me with his smoldering cigar. I'd once told him in a fit of anger that he was sure to burn the house down with his fat cigars.

He came the rest of the way down the red-carpeted stairs. Back then, how I'd loved red.

I was still on my knees. It was a hideous moment.

I was not going to see my own children. He'd come home to keep them from me. I stepped into the kitchen. Louise was sitting on the bed in the maid's room—the door standing open. I thought for a moment that I'd go after her and clobber her.

Instead I said, "My father taught me that Catholics were dipped in mercy at their confirmation. Not you—you have been dipped in vinegar." I walked out the back door, holding it open as I recited, "Be merciful, even as your Father is merciful." My father had taught me that and had told me it was our special code for those times when we were very angry. I think he might have been pleased that I remembered.

"Might I have a glass of water?" I asked my neighbor as I stepped inside her home.

Concern rippled across her face. She said, "My husband is hoping to meet you. Come sit with him."

The sight of the man, seated in a plush green chair, covered with a red and white candy-striped afghan, weakened me in a way that Juan had not.

"Please sit," he said and pointed in the direction opposite of the sofa. Mrs. Gleason did her own pointing and then left the room as I sat. When my eyes adjusted to the gloom, for it was a winter afternoon and the windows were draped in velvet, I must have gasped. A large reddish dog was on all fours emitting a low growl.

"Meet Penny," the man said. "She was a gift from my wife who tells me she is the color of a new penny. Mind you, I must take her word for it. I'm totally blind now, you know."

He looked in the opposite direction, and I began to cry.

"Your two littlest daughters come by sometimes to give

Penny a treat," he said to the wall.

Mrs. Gleason returned and handed me a cup of tea, which was too hot for me to gulp. She set a tall glass of water on a table next to me. I desperately wanted a cigarette. I thanked her and Mr. Gleason turned his head to face us. It looked as if his eyes were taped shut.

"My daughters come by?"

"Yes, my dear," Mrs. Gleason said. "Your little Alice came looking for you the day before Christmas. She said she needs you to brush her hair. Shame of it all."

The man swept his frail arms over and behind his head, calling attention to the shelves of books behind him. He alarmed Penny, who got back up and stood on guard.

"Clara tells me you are a writer. And so, you are a reader—they always go together. Please take a book or two."

"I couldn't," I said.

"Well, you must. I am in rude health and was already in bad shape when my wife set out to reread my library to me aloud. Lighten our load, my dear."

Mrs. Gleason left the room and returned with my mail. After setting it down on the sofa, she went to the curtains and pulled them back a bit.

"Might you tell the mailman that I am living in the Verona? Apartment F," I said.

"Should I tell Clara too?" she asked.

I bit the end of my tongue—felt how my tears were puddled inside the collar of my coat. "The children know where I am," I said and looked up at the woman like a beggar.

"They think that you have moved far, far away."

She was a plainspoken woman, and so I tried to be the same.

"I'm to visit twice a week now. I'll be back on Saturday morning."

"I float ever in darkness," Mr. Gleason said and patted Penny, who had finally sat. But the dog raised its head to meet the man's hand and moved so that it could put its head on the man's slippered feet.

And when I couldn't think of one thing to say other than, "I'm sorry," he said, "My dear, there are two forms of darkness. One is blindness and one is night. My wife taught me that. She reads poetry."

Mrs. Gleason and I saw the car at the same moment. It was Juan backing out without regard for children or dogs. He'd waited, giving me time to vacate the neighborhood.

"Please tell me what books you have selected," the man said, and I went to the shelves and took down a book.

"*My Antonia*," I said.

"You are kind, my dear, to pick from the first shelf. All that red Nebraska grass is what I think of first. Would you please read me the epigraph?"

"Oh, it is in Latin," I said.

"Of course," he said and from memory said, "The best days are the first to flee." He sighed.

"Not true, is it, Penny?" The dog looked up at the man.

I took two books that day, but it was many months before I could read anything. I still have the Cather with Mr. Gleason's bookplate to remind me of his acceptance of blindness. I'd made one note in the margin where the old grandfather of the narrator prays that God will forgive and soften the heart of those who have been remiss.

When I arrived at the Verona that evening—in the January dark—Tessie did her best to get me to go straight to bed. All I could think of was my mother lying under her red puff— sometimes for days—after each of my brothers left home. Of course, my oldest brother never came back to Brooklyn, not once. But the days would pass and then she'd be up ordering me and Annie around. I'd always doubted that she'd taken to her bed when I married and left home. But now, years later, I see my wedding dress laid out on my childhood bed, and I am certain about this one thing; when I left home that day after my wedding, my parents had been sad together and then together, they fought the sadness off.

I didn't go to bed. Instead, I smoked and reran the slights over and over in my head, making my heart beat faster with each minute that passed. And so, I took out the other letter Margie had sent in the packet. It had been typed.

"Dearest Girl,

We hope we have acted wisely in writing you. We are only women. We are old now and much has been kept from us. But we are still your family. Margie has won our hearts. You would too, if only. We are your del Palacio Aunties. Understand that if you and Juan had returned here to Cartagena to raise your big family, we would have made your life as glorious as ours. We loved Carlos and blond-headed Juan from the day each was born. Such beautiful babies and beloved boys. Their father is one of our brothers. He is known to you as Grandpapa. He is proud of the men Carlos and Juan have grown into. In our world, family is life.

Do you play rummy? We three sisters spend our days playing cards on our bougainvillea-covered patio while we tend to our great nieces and nephews. Their voices are music to us and remind us that life is glorious.

Please understand that Nana is English and the only Protestant in our big family. It was her blue eyes that first struck our brother. "Que ojos" he wrote us from New York where he was living. Nana insisted that her second son, your husband, be raised in the Church of England. She has always kept her two boys only for herself. For that, we are sorry—for her sons and for you. When our brother brought his young family from New York to visit Cartagena, we had a nanny living with us. Her name was Alice and she had eyes the color of a robin's egg, but when Nana caught sight of her, she insisted my brother send the sweet girl away. Little Juan had grown fond of her because she was gentle, and he sobbed and sobbed.

We have invited Mateo to join us on the patio when he's visited, but he was not allowed. Kiss your children and tell them their del Palacio Aunties love them and pray for them and for you. It is no matter that you are not of the Catholic faith. We asked Margie to help us compose this letter, and she is our translator and typist. She will see to getting it to you.

With love,

Your Aunties"

I did go to bed then. But I could not sleep. Instead, I tried to imagine the music of my children's voices.

It was Friday noon when the phone woke me. Tessie was out shopping; unwatched, I finally slept the morning away. I didn't like answering the phone not knowing who'd be on the line. It was the secretary at my father's church. I could hear in his voice that he'd hoped to reach Tessie. He'd loved my father and so I was patient. He was always a bit too humble for my taste, but today was different. It was as if his teeth were chattering.

"Are you alone there?" he asked.

"Of course," I said.

"I have no explanation for this. A neighbor of yours on Argyle Road called here to reach you. Your family seems to have left in the night and a moving van..." He waited politely.

"Mrs. del Palacio, shall I come for you?"

And when I couldn't bring myself to say anything, he said, "I will come for you."

At the house where I had brought home each of my newborns, the lace curtains on the backdoor window were down. I could see through into the mudroom and into the kitchen where all the cabinets stood open. Then, in the glass, I saw Mrs. Gleason's reflection appear.

The church secretary stepped aside for her. She was carrying a heavy blanket.

"I saw the van when I let Penny out this morning. It was already late. There were two men on the lawn and one in the garage." She pointed at the garage, which was gaping open like the mouth of an angry lion, and I saw my mother's sewing table with a rolled red rug leaning up against it.

"I should have known there was trouble because the house was lit up all hours last night," Mrs. Gleason said.

"When did you last see my children?"

"I saw the five of them coming home from school yesterday. They were all together in a bunch and I thought it was odd the way they rushed inside."

I took ahold of the doorknob, twisted, and began to kick the door. I honestly thought to break the glass. The church secretary was muttering, and Mrs. Gleason sent him to her house to look in on her husband. "My husband is blind. Take care not to alarm him," she said sternly.

"I hate Juan," I said. "But I would never have taken the children away from him. I did not take them, that was not my intent. But he has robbed me and left me..."

Mrs. Gleason placed the blanket on the little bench that was meant for children to sit while they removed skates or boots. The duck hooks made it difficult for us to lean back. The sweater Margie knit for Alice hung on her hook.

"I cannot bear this," I said and took the sweater and held it to my face. It smelled of my child.

Mrs. Gleason put her arm around my shoulder. I think it was to keep me from falling forward. Then she told her story.

"I marched inside your front door with Penny and when I

found Louise, I threatened her with the police. But by the time I got back to my porch, I saw her pull the front door closed behind her. Saw her lock the door, cross the lawn like a sly fox, and climb into that van with those men."

Now I let Mrs. Gleason pull me into her arms and I sobbed. The world had grown so bright that I had to hold my eyes closed and a freeze took hold of my feet. I stood to regain feeling in my feet and turned to stare at the garage.

"My mother's sewing table has been left there for the elements," I said, as if that mattered now. My neighbor nodded and said she could see to that.

I began to shake and sat to get myself under control. Finally, I said, "The judge said Juan has a year if he has to take the children with him on business to Colombia. He cannot keep them forever. A year is all."

"Fine," she said. "Fine, but now let's go inside."

But I couldn't do it, couldn't go back inside the Gleason home—the pair of them—their fondness for each other would have been poison, and so I sat on the bench with my neighbor and sobbed until Tessie came for me.

PART II

CHAPTER 9

ALICE
1931

The cloud was coming toward them like a wet blanket, like it planned to sink the ship, and Alice said, "I don't like this. I cannot see."

"It's only fog. It'll lift once we get out to the ocean," Mateo said. He'd been told to stay at the railing with Alice and Clara while their father went to collect the older girls and his mother.

"Button your coat," Juan said to Alice before he left.

Alice and Clara were wearing matching black velvet coats with white rabbit fur collars and round velvet buttons, and now Clara had her mittens off and was working the buttons on Alice's coat. Clara's hair had gone all frizzy in the mist and she fluffed it, cocked her head in a winning way, and said, "Clara Bow," because her Uncle Dales had told her she'd been named for Clara Bow, the "It Girl." When she was three years old, he had given her an old, autographed photo of Clara Bow and told her to keep it a secret.

"I think we've been kidnapped," Clara said as she put her mittens back on, then gripped Alice's hand.

Their brother wiped at his eyes and said, "You cannot be kidnapped by your own father." Alice had not heard Nana come up behind her but felt her grab ahold of her hair at the nape of her neck and yank. "Do not touch the railing," she shouted and then for no reason that Alice could think of Nana slapped their brother. Clara said later that it was because he'd had his mouth on the railing, biting it to keep from crying.

Alice saw that her three older sisters had taken time to grab headscarves. She thought they looked like beautiful gypsies. But Nana scrunched up her big nose at them and said, "Milkmaids all in a row."

"When we get underway, we will be going under the Brooklyn Bridge," their father said as he gathered his family into a huddle and then added in a husky whisper, "You need to see it and remember it and remember this: We are the Griffin family for now." He'd explained about the new name to them at dawn when they met Nana at the pier. It had made no sense to Alice. And she'd asked her brother, Mateo, if griffins had feathers because he was smart that way.

"Sure, they have wings, so I guess that means feathers. But it's just a made-up name," he'd explained. She knew about lions with eagle faces that could fly and thought maybe they were dragons. Standing there now at the railing, she thought that a griffin might fly out of the fog and land on the ship. She wanted to ask Mateo what they sounded like so she could listen for them, but her father began pointing out sights and buildings in New York City and kept saying that up there directly ahead was the Brooklyn Bridge. Then he told her to stop crying, told her she was not a baby anymore. But she didn't care about bridges. She remembered when her mother and Tessie took her on a streetcar across the bridge. She'd been scared the whole way over and then they had to come back.

"I cross in my car over that every day on my way to work and back home again," he said proudly, and Alice saw he was sad. She had wanted to take a ride in his car, but not if he was going to drive on a bridge. She remembered telling him that.

"We cannot see a thing, Father. I want to go home," Alice said and once again Nana got a fistful of her hair and pulled so hard that Alice was sure she had a bald patch.

"Show your father respect," Nana shouted in English.

Just then, a man in a starched white uniform approached. Her father moved quickly between Alice and her brother, and he rested his arms around each of their shoulders. The man held a basket of American flags as if it were a basket of cut flowers. He handed one to each of them, but when he offered one to Nana, saying, "Madam Griffin," she refused to take it. And then he held his hand out to her father, and when they shook hands, Alice stepped back and took Clara's hand.

"Mr. Griffin," he said. "Welcome aboard the *Algonquin.* Will you be with us all the way to Corpus Christi?"

Their father only nodded, and the man turned to the children; pointing at Mateo, he said, "Tell me your names so that we can begin to become acquainted." And when he got to Alice, he bent down and said, "First sea voyage, young lady?" Alice knew better than to carry on with this man. Nana had told her and Clara when they were shown to their cabin to not let anyone know their business.

"You will remember this voyage your entire life, Alice, how you sailed on a big ship on your own adventure," he said. The man, who was the captain, stood and took ahold of the railing and began a well-practiced lecture. "Let me tell you, this twin steam turbine ocean liner was built in 1926. Not to worry, but she was involved in a collision in 1929, in thick fog. But then that year was a year for disasters, was it not?" He looked at her father when he said this, and looking back at Alice, he said, "This fog today, Little Ladies, is nothing. We will be passing under the Brooklyn Bridge here in a bit. Longest suspension bridge in the world when it was opened. It was the first crossing over the East River. It opened Brooklyn to the world. Listen carefully, children, and you will hear the cables humming."

"Are you the one who steers?" Clara asked. She was always interested in knowing things.

"Why, yes," he said. "And I'd best get back up to the bridge before we get to the bridge." He smiled at his own words and then spoke directly to Clara. "Sometimes we use a word, like bridge, to mean two different things." He grinned at Nana and Alice knew she might just slap him. The man was not afraid of Nana. He said, "I have a better view from the bridge. You watch closely because then we will pass the mighty woman with a torch." He looked straight ahead and said, "Mother of Exiles." Alice thought he was talking about her mother and knew her father would not like that one bit. She gulped and gulped again and might have continued, except Clara squeezed her hand so tight she had to stop.

But the captain was just going to talk more, Alice saw.

"Upper New York Bay is one thing, but when we cross the Narrows, we will be up against some strong currents. It can get downright treacherous before we get to the Atlantic. We wouldn't want to shipwreck, would we?"

"Horrors, no, we would not want that to happen," Clara said, and Nana said, "Hush your mouth." And Alice gulped again.

When the man picked up his basket and left, they all stood in silence until the ship passed under the Brooklyn Bridge. They could hear it above them. And when it seemed to Alice that no one was ever going to say anything else ever again, she said, "I can't see the bridge and I can't see where we're going."

Before she could say it again, because Alice had learned to repeat herself, her father said in a voice that told her he was disappointed in how their morning had turned out, "Mother, take Alice and Clara to your cabin. They should sleep."

But Nana did not let them sleep. She got them both undressed and, leaving them only in their panties, she made Clara lie on the metal counter and bend her head back into the small sink while she scrubbed at her hair. And then she rinsed it out with vinegar. Alice heard Clara's hair squeak, and then it was her turn. There were no maids on board with them and Alice was certain Nana had never ever washed a little girl's hair before. Nana told Clara to sit on her bunk and brush her own hair.

Clara was dripping all over the bedcovers and Alice felt very sorry for her sister. But Alice was very glad that she and Clara had decided to bury her mother's red silk puff at the bottom of the huge trunk they were sharing. It would have been ruined with the vinegar water if they had laid it out on the bedcovers. Alice kept her eyes and mouth clamped closed and behaved. Nana dug her pointed nails into her scalp and said mean things about their mother in Spanish and Alice heard her say, "Filth."

Alice was so very tired that she let herself drift off right there, lying on the cold counter. She thought she heard her mother telling her that she would be there to meet them when they got off the ship. But then Nana pulled so hard, bending her neck back, that Alice said, "Now you've gone and broke my neck, Nana. I want Pooh. I want Pooh. Miss Kate will find me."

Nana poured vinegar on her hair and didn't bother to watch what she was doing. "Tessie puts a cloth on my face before she does that," Alice said and kicked her legs and said, "I cannot breathe." Nana waited for her to settle down and then said, "Miss Kate is dead."

Alice didn't know how the captain could see where he was going; she lay there on her back and felt herself getting into what Tessie called a tizzy. The ship began to bump then and made loud sounds, and she was as sick as a dog, which is what Nana called it because she did not like dogs one bit. Alice spurted vomit out of her mouth like a dragon spitting fire. She saw Nana raise her hand to slap her. Nana could move fast when it came to slapping children and so Alice braced herself, but Nana didn't slap her. Instead, Nana flipped her over and pounded on her back.

Alice knew she'd made a horrible mess in the sink. But she was glad that she did not know how to clean the way Tessie cleaned, and besides, she was way too small. There was no one else to clean other than Nana, and so Alice hopped down off the counter without being told. She sat on the bed with Clara, who was shivering. She pulled her legs up to her face and hugged them, and then buried her face in the space between her knees.

Nana was muttering and then all of them heard the tap on

the door. Alice peeked out through her knees. Nana reached for her cane, which was hooked on the back of the door, and Alice thought that maybe she was leaving them. But she didn't move and the person outside the door knocked again. Nana said, "Get under the covers and stay quiet." Nana hooked the cane on her arm and opened the door to a woman in a crisp uniform.

"Mrs. Griffin," she said as she poked her head into the cabin. Alice made a pouty face at the woman and pushed back her dripping hair from her face. The woman took a pretty tray off her cart and handed it to Nana and said, "Ginger tea for you, Madam, and ginger twists and ginger snaps for the children. Ginger helps with seasickness." They were freshly baked, and Alice did not think she could wait another second to have one. But she stayed put. The woman sniffed the air, looked over at the dirty sink, and shared a glance with Alice.

"The captain told me to tell the Little Ladies that we passed safely through the Narrows. Of course, it was rough today, but we are safely in the lower New York Bay and on our way." The woman had a nice smile.

Clara took Alice's hand and squeezed. The woman backed out of the cabin and pulled the door closed behind her. They could hear her knocking on the door across the narrow hallway. Alice very much wanted a cookie, and she wanted Pooh, who was in their trunk, and she wanted Clara to brush her hair and sadness came crashing over her. She whispered to her sister that she was seasick because she decided that that was what seasickness felt like. It came to her that her mother would be very sad if Miss Kate died. She looked at Nana, who was sipping her tea in some sort of daze. Alice decided she didn't believe Nana that Miss Kate was dead and gone.

She stepped off the bed and grabbed two cookies and said to her grandmother, "I hate you with my whole heart." She screamed it so that the woman talking to their neighbor across the hall could hear. She handed a cookie to Clara and then she cried her eyes out, quiet crying so that Nana couldn't hear. That is what her mother called that kind of crying, but her mother always heard her, Alice was sure of that.

CHAPTER 10

ALICE
1932

"La madre que te pario!" Alice's father cussed loud enough to make Clara jump down off the bench and join her sister under the piano. They buried their heads in their arms and waited. Their father had forbidden them to speak a word of Spanish. "It will not do to be taken for Mexicans," he said the day they arrived in Albuquerque. "Not here, not anywhere."

In her bedroom on the second floor, Nana pounded her cane as if she wanted something to stop. Alice knew she didn't need anything—not really.

"Alice, go see to your Nana," her father said from the dining room where he was working on bills.

"She wants you, Father," Alice said, as if disappointed in his stupidity.

Alice heard the yellow bird, who loved the yuccas in the backyard, singing in the near dark and she joined in. The bird and its mate had built a hanging nest. Her brother said these birds were orioles and had chosen their yard because of the pond. Then Alice heard Nana shout in her low-pitched cawing voice, "Juan, do you not care that your mother is alone in a dark room?"

Even with the shouting and the pounding, Clara got up and situated herself back on the white piano bench and wound the metronome, careful not to touch a piano key, not to get a fingerprint anywhere. She kept reading the book she'd propped on the music stand, and when the pendulum slowed, she moved the bar just so, and it kept its regular beat. Alice understood Clara and didn't mind being alone on the floor under the piano, where she was pretending that she was a cat lying on her back. Once her father got upstairs, Alice couldn't hear him talking to Nana, and she wanted to know what was going on, so she crawled out to the bottom of the stairs like the cat she wished she were. Clara followed her sister and the two of them listened to their father and Nana argue. This time it was about the new white piano.

"A white piano is beyond my imagination," Nana said.

Alice opened her eyes as wide as possible and said, "She has imagination?"

"What woman, Juan, wants a white piano? A common woman. And I will not allow a dog or cat in this house. I am your mother," she said.

Clara said softly, "She must be a milkmaid." The girls didn't like their father's new woman any better than Nana did, and so she and Clara looked at each other and made first their angry faces and then their sad faces. They'd learned in the last year to amuse each other. "Stay happy," Clara would say to Alice when they put themselves to bed at night. But it wasn't easy because Alice didn't want to be happy. Once she had said to Clara that she wished she were dead and buried in the park with the white swans. She'd said it to shock Clara out of one of the books she was reading. Clara had in fact closed her book as she said, "You don't mean that."

When they heard their father say, "I need a cigar, and you need your rest, Mother," the sisters gave each other their surprise faces before they scrambled to the dining room and climbed up onto the table. Alice purposely knocked a few pieces of paper onto the floor but was careful not to scratch the surface with the buckles on her sandals.

Alice pushed her hair, which had grown back after the ringworm, out of her eyes. She'd long ago outgrown the lacy white dress Nana had set out for her to wear that day. She put her fingers inside the tight cap sleeves and made a tortured face.

"I need Mother to brush my hair or braid it. Barbara's mother puts French braids in her hair." Alice said all this in a tiny little whisper to Clara because they'd been warned not to speak of their mother. Clara looked cross-eyed at her sister.

"Okay, then tell me a story," Alice said. All of Clara's stories involved a cat or a dog. Clara looked up at the ceiling as if seeing her story and began. The story had a dog that sounded a lot like Penny. Alice liked stories about Penny and the blind man.

Their father came down the stairs quietly and crossed the hall to his study. Alice could smell that he had lit a cigar. "P.U.," she said in the same whispered voice. But then he called to them to come tell him goodnight.

They arrived holding hands. Alice said, "Father, this dress is choking me alive."

Upstairs, Alice and Clara put their matching baby dolls into their long muslin gowns and into their matching bassinets, but at nine o'clock the girls were wide awake—watching the street. Their father had grudgingly agreed that his four older children could go to the picture show that night. Their brother had driven the LaSalle. Alice and Clara thought he had a girl.

Alice returned to the bassinets over and over, saying, "oh goodness" and "hush now."

"Alice, the babies are fine," Clara said each time.

"Charlie Lindberg was kidnapped, so I like to keep an eye on them," Alice said and started crying.

Clara went over to her sister, then hugged her and said, "Charlie was taken by a stranger who climbed up a rickety ladder to the nursery. That's how they solved it. The ladder gave him away. But that was far, far away in New Jersey and father would never allow a ladder to be set against our house," Clara said.

"We are far, far away where Mother cannot see us," Alice

said and gulped air so she could stop crying. When she had gotten control of her crying, she said, "The baby died. No one was watching the baby."

Now, in the darkness, the headlights of a car turning the corner off University Avenue flooded their front yard and Alice saw their neighbor, Barbara, pull her pink gingham curtains open and peek out and wave. "Barbara is a big nosey posey," Alice said, but she didn't wave back at her neighbor because she didn't really like her.

Clara went to the door and called, "Father, they're home."

But their father was already in the front hall. The girls watched their porch light flash three times as it flooded the front lawn. Alice heard her father sigh as if he now had everything he ever wanted and of course, he had his new woman.

Alice heard him pacing in the front hall. She knew he wouldn't come into their room to tuck them in—wouldn't read them a bedtime story. Besides, Clara seemed to be fast asleep already. Alice went back to the window. She wished she were strong enough to open it a crack. She looked out across the street and saw Barbara's mother standing at the window, her outline fuzzy behind the curtains. And now, Alice waved, but the woman must have had her back to the window because Alice was sure she would have waved back if only she'd seen her. And then, Barbara's light went out.

Alice checked on the baby dolls and then climbed into bed, took Pooh out from under her pillow where she kept him, and ran her fingers over the scarring at the nape of her neck. "Goodnight, precious," she said to Pooh. And then to no one she said, "Goodnight, Mother."

CHAPTER 11

ALICE
1944

Alice snagged her nylon as she stepped up onto the bus. She stopped to free it before walking down the narrow aisle to choose the first open row on the half-filled bus and accepted a sheet of Rules for Rush from the girl with the artificial vote-of-confidence smile. That girl was the cause of the snag and was still following her too closely.

"Make a new friend, sit with a stranger," the girl said to her back.

Alice tasted the mishmash of perfumes, and the assault on her tongue was so foul she wanted to spit, but the sorority social season with the Chi O's White Formal, the ADPi's Blue Diamond Ball, or the Pi Phi's Starlight Symphony Ball could make life easier. Her boyfriend, Matthew Oliver, loved a party. Some girls already had a baby pink ballgown hanging proudly on the back of their bedroom door, some waiting for their boyfriends to come back home from fighting a war.

She settled her clutch on her lap and felt for the snag. It had run, leaving a perfect flaw. The sound of paper rustling told her to get busy reading the rules.

The driver cranked the door closed and lurched the bus into gear, and Alice saw they were going to circle back around the campus to the dorms where some of the out-of-town rushees were living temporarily. More strangers, Alice thought.

When they pulled up to the dorm, the coeds on the bus erupted into gaiety, as if one girl had caught fire and set off sparks in the next and the next. Alice didn't understand them. Choosing to get on this damn bus felt like giving in.

The year before, Matthew had pledged Sigma Alpha Epsilon Fraternity even though he didn't need any more friends. He had dozens. Just the other night, he'd focused his baby blue eyes on her, circled her narrow shoulders with his arm, and said, "You'll love sorority life. It's like having a second family. You'll see." It was as if this settled the matter for her, but it was silly. The last thing Matthew needed was another family.

Alice studied the Greek motto on the top of the page, *Freedom or Death*. So dramatic. She read the list of rules and folded the paper and slipped it into her purse. The particular order of the rules was baffling to her. *Mind Your Posture* came after *Follow Your Heart*. *Be Punctual* came last. She would have been better staying home, alone, listening to Betty Hutton sing "I Wish I Didn't Love Him So." Something about that song just grabbed her. She'd be listening, and the music would fade away, and she'd be left wondering why she loved Matthew, as if there were no alternative.

The last girl who climbed on the bus sat down next to her and immediately began tracing a pink, polished, tear-shaped fingernail down through the list of rules, nodding as she moved to the next line. Once the bus moved through the noisy gears, the two pledges in the first row began asking questions of the rules girl.

"There are some questions we are not at liberty to answer," Miss Rules said and made a cross-eyed face for laughs.

As girls, Alice and her sister Clara had practiced their individual looks. Alice did a tilt of her head naturally, like her mother, she thought. That posture always made Matthew uneasy. She tilted her head now and looked out the window, same place as always—so much brown.

When the bus finally pulled up at the front of the Alpha Chi Omega house, Miss Rules, who said her name was Midge, shouted that this particular sorority would take as many as thirty pledges this fall. Then she called off the names of the girls who should get off there. "Group One," she shouted out, and then waiting for their breathless attention, called out, "Peggy," and waited while Peggy shrieked as if she had won homecoming queen. Midge called Millicent, Betty Jean, and Lou Ann next, and then a cheer went up when she called the twins, Bertha and Betha. As the selected girls clustered at the front of the bus, Midge tapped one of the twins, motioned that her slip was showing, and then explained that Alpha Chi hosted the formal dinner dance at the Hilton, and a collective sigh went up.

"Now remember, girls," Midge said, "from here, you'll walk to your next house and the next. Check the map on the back of the rules. And the bus will be there to pick you up at your last party house. Be waiting there."

Next to Alice, the girl who'd been so diligently studying the rules said, "I'm Pauline White, from Farmington, New Mexico." She pointed somewhere off in the distance.

Alice said, "I practically live on campus. I'm Alice del Palacio."

Pauline said, "My parents want me to live in a sorority house where it's safer, and the girls look out for each other. So, here I am."

Alice watched the girls who were being herded to the front door of the Alpha Chi house. Barbara, her neighbor from across the street, was sitting in her boyfriend's car, probably necking. Then Barbara jumped out and did a little bounce. She was the kind of girl that did that. Barbara was a legacy. Everyone knew exactly where she'd pledge because her mother had been in that sorority before she upped and married young. But Alice liked Barbara's mother and so couldn't fault her. She still looked young to Alice, so much younger than her stepmother, who had white hair and a heavy step.

Alice and Matthew had double-dated with Barbara and her boyfriend the Saturday before, when they went to the County Fair. Alice and Matthew had fought behind the livestock barn about you name it: how she could do nothing about her Colombian father's "better than you" tone of voice; the way he'd pointed his lit cigar at Matthew that night when they left her house.

They quarreled a lot. That night she kept mostly quiet, and she liked the way Matthew looked stumped. He took a gulp of the pissy air, and giving Alice his once-over look that never made her heart flutter, started in again with his criticisms, mostly about her family. But then as fate would have it, he reached out and yanked her out of the path of the marching, broad-headed sheep. She didn't see the flock coming, stirring up dirt, never mind the stench of their shampooed coats. Two young all-American boys in plaid long-sleeved shirts herded them past, and Matthew, making his intentions clear, bent her over into a kiss she hadn't refused. Then one of the boys said, "Oh, sorry," and when the last sheep was past the other boy said, "Who wants to kiss in all this piss?"

That night her father sat up waiting for them in the living room, his cigar held up to chest level so that Matthew could clearly see his smug expression. He was a man who played the role of father with utter confidence that his decisions would not be challenged. "Go wash off that carnival dirt," he'd said in Spanish, only to show Matthew his indifference. Her father used indifference like a knife.

"Group Five," Midge shouted at their last stop, and Pauline and Alice stood up and began following the other girls off the bus.

Pauline turned around, grabbed Alice by the shoulder, and whispered in her ear—a hint of mint in her breath—"We just have to be ourselves."

Alice wondered if that was why all these girls seemed so much alike.

Alice held her clutch in her left hand, dangling it down around where the run began. Standing there waiting, she closed her eyes and saw the pile of clothes she'd left in her closet, the things she hadn't chosen. Her parents had left on a trip, planned to be gone for a week, an end of summer trip to Santa Fe and Taos, where it was cooler. No one was going to see that mess of clothes, but she'd have to dig through it all to find something to wear on day two. She would have to iron. Clara had always ironed for her; had said she liked the way it made cloth smell. But Clara had left for nursing school that summer, said she'd be back, but Alice did not believe her, why would she? Alice thought she'd move away too if she could, like all her sisters and brother had. Gone, leaving her alone with no one who much cared.

The stupidity of it all made her shift her purse to her right hand, and then she shoved it under her arm. The double doors to the sorority house burst open and a group of girls came out, bouncing like the fanciful terrier Matthew's family babied.

Alice recognized one of the girls holding the door open for the rushees. She was an Albuquerque High grad in Matthew's class; her family name was on the Jones Motor Car dealership. Alice regretted even knowing that. The girl acted like she had never seen Alice before. Alice tilted her head at the girl, who leaned forward as if expecting a question. But Alice rarely bothered to ask questions. She made her way to the table to take her name badge. It was Rule 5: *Wear your Badge at all Times and get a Star for your Badge at each house.*

Glitter dropped from her badge as she pinned it to her sweater.

"Alice Palacio?" the girl at the badge table said, her brows peaking into little tents with the question, as if she had never ever spoken a Spanish name before. Alice wasn't interested in a bid from this sorority, and so she didn't bother to correct them on her name. She crossed the room to the sofa, and un-invited, she took a seat.

The snag was not her fault. She'd been pushed as she stepped up onto the bus. She crossed her legs—right over left—hiding the run. Her legs were her strong point, and she knew Matthew went for pretty legs. His old sweetheart, who had left town for San Francisco, had pretty legs; everyone said so. They'd had a sweetheart agreement. The summer of '42, he'd gone out with his parents to see her and her family in San Francisco, but that girl wasn't coming back. She was working in a department store that Matthew had made the mistake of bragging to Alice about. "City of Paris on Union Square," he'd said reverently. "They have this beauty salon where they'll paint a girl's legs with this film, and it makes them look suntanned." Alice remembered she'd turned her back on him, but he went on, "Never need stockings that way." She took a vow never to step foot into the place.

Alice studied the little groups of girls, all chatting. Swell this, swell that. It didn't feel like a party.

And then, in the sliver of the doorway, which led to the kitchen, she spotted the Mexican housemother who was watching her, as if warning her. Alice let her mind drift, which it often did, just let it go until it hit on a rut. This time it stumbled over Matthew's SAE pin, that tiny gold prize buried at the bottom of her purse, given to her at the Doc Long picnic grounds after that long necking session out in the tall pines. He'd meant it to lay claim to her, buried or not.

Alice snapped into gear, sat up very straight to show her tiny waist off to the girls, and then turned to look for the housemother, thinking maybe she had imagined the warning. This time, the woman nodded at her and turned around and left.

Alice took the rules out of her purse and studied the map on the back. Some sorority girl with fine penmanship had hand-lettered the map. The Kappa house was second on her party list. She got up from the sofa and went looking for Pauline.

As Alice rested on the sun-warped bench outside the third house on her list, her new friend found her. Pauline sat and started in with a summary of what she'd heard about the Chi-Os. "Everyone calls them that, Chi-O. They're the smart ones," she said. She pointed at what now had become a run, noticing the smear of red polish—made a face—indicating it had been a mistake.

"Some Kappa came to my rescue to stop it from running," Alice said.

"Didn't work," Pauline said, and Alice decided she liked this girl, and hoped she'd get the house she wanted.

Alice stood, and Pauline jumped to her feet, not like it was her idea to get up, but because she was a willing follower. This was new to Alice, maybe why she liked the girl so much. They headed inside to meet the smart Chi-Os.

Later, walking toward the Pi Phi house, sunlight was coming in at a slant, so Alice tented her hand over her face in order to see where she was going, but at least it promised that the day was coming to an end. The Pi Phi house was her first choice. In the musty living room, two Pi Phi sisters sat on the huge sofa looking plum out of steam.

Pauline said, "That's the president and vice president. Our chances are good here. They're a new chapter." Alice took her hand and led her over to sit on the love seat that matched the sofa. Both pieces of furniture were the color of wet dirt.

Alice's nylon hung listlessly from her leg as if it had given up. She wanted to pick at the red polish.

The sorority officers called for everyone's attention and then one of them said, "Homecoming is pretty much the first event after initiation. Each sorority house builds a homecoming float, and each float has a specific thematic motif."

The two girls nodded and everyone else nodded. And then the president said they would stop talking to let the sisters sing for the rushees. The sisters formed a circle. The whole day had been about circles and Alice held her hands to her temples to stop the spinning. Then someone blew a whistle, and they began:

"When you walk through a storm
Keep your chin up high

And don't be afraid of the dark.
At the end of the storm
Is a golden sky
And the sweet silver song of a lark."

Then they all began flapping their lean, young-women arms and pointed at the rushees, calling out names and beckoning them to join the circle. Alice joined in, all of them holding hands now, while they sang together as a chorus:

"When you walk through a storm
Keep your chin up high
And don't be afraid of the dark.
At the end of the storm..."

Everyone stopped there and waited for the soloist to fill in:

"Is a sister nearby
And the sweet silver song of a lark."

Across the circle, Alice saw Pauline mouth the word "motif" as if she admired these singing sorority sisters.

Late that afternoon, as Alice sat at the Alpha Chi House waiting for her last party to begin, she missed her clutch. She knew exactly where she had left it at the Pi Phi house, during all that singing. It was next to the wet dirt sofa.

A cute girl who'd been nice to Alice when Group Five filed in was saying, "When you pledge, you'll learn all about Alpha Chi Omega history. We make it fun, like learning your own family history."

Alice stood and looked across the room at Pauline, who was sitting on the floor, blending in, her legs curled to one side. It looked painful to sit that way. Alice tried to get her friend to look at her, but Pauline was concentrating and so

Alice gave up and headed for the door where Midge stood. She hadn't seen Midge since she got off the bus that morning, and now Midge gave Alice the disapproving look of a sixth-grade hall monitor with too much power. Alice suspected there was an unwritten rule she was breaking here.

"Sorry, Midge, but I'm going back for my purse at the Pi Phi house."

Alice was in a full stomp off across the ugly brown Bermuda grass yard before she heard Midge say, "You went off and left your purse? Well, don't be late for the bus." Alice had no intention of getting on that bus.

The Pi Phi sister opened the door for Alice and stood posed in the doorway as if the sorority house was some sort of sacred place and she was the guard. The girl gave her a vacant stare even though they'd all stood together in that circle holding hands, singing, just minutes before.

Alice walked home, and for fifteen minutes she sat on the edge of the pond in her backyard studying the murky water. Even the brick wall her father had the handyman put up and paint white couldn't hold back the dust. The pond was always nothing but mud. Alice picked at the snag—prying off the nail polish—and blamed her mother for the umpteenth time for not bothering to find her, to be around to warn her about things.

When they'd first arrived in Albuquerque, Alice had decided the pond was like her own personal wishing well. She'd wasted a lot of pennies, wishing very hard for her mother to show up at their front door. "If wishes were fishes," she said aloud now and thought about all those girls on the bus wishing for boyfriends to come home from fighting a war and still wanting to go to a formal with a girl in a pink gown.

Her feet throbbed and so she kicked off her shoes. She thought about dipping her stocking feet in the dark water and thought then about painted legs. Instead, she dug her key out of her clutch and went in the back door to let out her stepmother's dog who surely would have messed by now.

What she didn't want that night was Barbara running across the street to gloat about her bird-in-the-hand legacy, and so she left the yellow porch light off. She'd sworn to her father that she would not let Matthew in the house while they were gone. Even little baby lies could get her in hot water with her father. But later that night, she heard Matthew driving up and down her street in the 1942 Buick sedan his good-natured family called Harvey. It was stupid to name a car.

He stopped two different times at the curb. Alice watched him from the dining room where she sat on top of the table, smoking. She could see the luminous dial on his watch. He knew better than to pull into the driveway. Harvey was known for the mess he always left behind, and her father would be sure to spot the grease. Alice figured that was Matthew's choice if he wanted to spend his evening sitting out there.

Two endless days later, her preference card in her hand, Alice walked alone across campus, taking every diagonal. She never dawdled. She was headed for the Student Union when Pauline appeared out of dry air, head down, crossing the street. The girl, a pretty thing, in an outfit more suited to housework than coed life, wore her starred name badge pinned to her dress. She seemed to be nodding to herself.

"Hey there," Alice shouted, though not so loud as to scare the wits out of her.

Pauline stopped in the street and said, "I'm dropping out of rush. Everyone called me Pearl."

"I'm sorry," Alice said and then said it again so Pauline would know she meant it.

They both stayed put. Had Pauline not looked so wrecked, Alice would have laughed the way Clara laughed at her whenever she came up with something silly.

Finally, Alice stepped into the street, walked up close to Pauline, and said, "They're idiots." She pointed to the nametag and added, "It says Pauline right there."

"Then I'm the idiot for wanting to join them. My mother said so."

"Those sorority girls were trying to impress us. That's all."

But even as she said this, she knew it wasn't going to do a bit of good. She'd never been able to keep anyone from leaving once they had their mind made up, not even her own mother.

"I'll take the card for you," Alice said. They both knew the rules and Rule 9 was you had to formally quit. You couldn't just make a break for it.

Standing there in the middle of the street, the thought came to Alice that she could quit too and be an independent. She was still thinking it through when she said, "My boyfriend wants to pin me so that I'll wait three years for him while he finishes college."

Pauline's expression changed and Alice watched her face reform into annoyance, but then the girl turned and walked off. When Pauline reached the curb, she said, "Call me and tell me what happens to you. I'm at the dorm."

The next morning, which was bid day, Barbara picked Alice up in her family car. She stunk at driving, put her foot on the brake at the end of every breathless sentence. Alice didn't know how to drive. Her father wouldn't teach her and wouldn't let Matthew teach her either.

The bids were handed out quickly. There was no bid for her. Alice could see that she wasn't the only girl without a bid since several huddles here and there formed around some girl who looked to be falling to pieces, mixed in with the hand-holding groups dancing in *ring-around-the-rosie* gaiety. Alice let it sink in. She wasn't a girl who would go all needy.

"We can still go meet the boys at the drug store," Barbara said as she came back across the patio to join her, acting like she wanted to take her hand but didn't. Barbara fidgeted. "They're saving us places at the fountain. You want to, right? We promised."

Alice wanted to tell her to get lost.

Alice pushed her hair, which she'd shampooed and put in pin curls the night before, back from her face, felt for the barrette and tightened it.

"They did this just to slight me," Alice said. She wasn't herself; she didn't usually beg for pity this way.

"It's not all of them, Alice. My mother said it just takes one to blackball you. It's just your Spanish last name, is all."

"How does Alice Jones sound? That would make me good enough for their girl clubs?" Alice said and knew she had spoiled something important for Barbara. Alice looked around and then nodded at herself, thinking how pleased she was that she was wearing her seersucker sundress. It showed off her tan and her neck. She didn't fit in with the girls in sweater sets. They were sweltering.

"Sorry. You go on," she said to Barbara.

"What should I tell Matthew?"

"Up to you," Alice said.

"Tell me where he can find you."

"I'm going to see my friend at the dorm," she said even though she had not known she was going there.

She felt an explosion of hot willfulness. Her mother, that narrow-waisted woman with her hot temper, had risen up inside her.

The front desk attendant at the dorm sent someone upstairs to get Pauline.

"I'm almost packed up," Pauline said. "My parents are driving down for me. It'll take them until late to get here."

"You're quitting school because of sorority girls? You know they never say anything they mean."

"I don't need this, Alice."

The two of them walked down a hallway to what Pauline called the living room. It smelled old.

"I was blackballed," Alice said, but Pauline kept her eyes on her feet.

Finally Pauline said, "My mother told me to quit before those girls had a chance to exclude me."

Alice only had one chance to be honest, she figured, so she said, "I don't have a mother. So, I guess I never know what not to do."

"I know. You told me." Pauline picked at her nails.

Alice had no memory of telling Pauline about her missing mother. She tilted her head at the girl and said, "I did?"

"Well, you told me about your stepmother, so I figured it out."

They paused because the room was filling up with emotional girls, and then Pauline whispered, "But you have a boyfriend, Alice."

Alice's heart fluttered as if a butterfly had found its way in. Her mind slowed down, and she asked Pauline all sorts of things about her plans, all the things a good friend would ask. And then Pauline took out a pack of cigarettes and offered Alice one.

When Alice walked out into the sunlight, Matthew was standing there across the street, one leg hooked behind him, up against Harvey, balanced, but looking like he wasn't sure he had a right to be there. His Levi's were freshly pressed, and he'd rolled up the sleeves of his shirt. The shirt was milk white—his teeth too, she knew, but she didn't see them. He wasn't smiling. His eyes followed her every move. She nodded at him and crossed the street.

"I had to hope you'd come out of there eventually." He sounded like a little boy. He didn't try to touch her. He knew better.

She could smell the Juicy Fruit on his breath and knew he could smell smoke on her.

"Barbara said you were visiting your new friend."

"Pauline decided college wasn't right for her," Alice said, looking straight at him, and then she opened her hand out to him. His SAE pin sat there in the middle of her palm, sparkling like she'd put a shine on it.

"You want me to take it back?" he asked. She stood there silently and watched his face change. He seemed sad, very sad. In that moment, she decided.

"Pin me," she said. "And then take me home."

It was no sweetheart agreement, but it didn't feel like giving in either.

CHAPTER 12

RUBY
1944

I was crossing the cloister garden of winter-bare dogwood, with the magnolia tree at its center, startled as always by the aroma of chamomile and germander; threading my hand along the glossy boxwood—at the edge—looking for the damaged leaves that gave off a sweet smell when bruised. Morning glory blue crocuses—always the first to bloom—had popped up in the grass overnight. Those flowers placed me back in my childhood on a wispy spring day walking along the Gowanus Canal, my mother protecting us with her umbrella. But here and now, a gang of schoolchildren were trampling the flowers. It wouldn't matter; there were no sighted children here.

I was meeting with the headmaster. His office overlooked the crescent-shaped front drive. It was gated for the peace of mind of the parents who'd left their blind children at the school, believing that a beautiful place was a comfort to their children, like Green-Wood was for my Faith and for Kate's babies, I thought.

Dead babies comforted by tranquil beauty. I did amuse myself.

The headmaster's secretary, Rosalie, looked up from a messy stack of papers. She was always overwhelmed with papers because her boss kept such an uncluttered desk. She reached over to the radio that had been emitting mostly static and turned down the volume. "Air raid over Paris," she said. I watched her bite her lip as if she had been ready to say something more.

But I didn't encourage her to carry on.

"He's ready for you. Tick, tick, tick," she said and pointed at her tiny wristwatch.

When I first arrived at Overbrook School for the Blind, I'd let everyone welcome me as a generous spirit. Early in the war, I'd become braille qualified in Puerto Rico. I'd thought that after the war, this training could take me to Paris to the National Institute of the Blind. War had given women like me much to do, but we were not supposed to want to work so much as be willing to work. When it was over, we'd be sent home to keep house, but I had no house.

Overbrook offered me a place to live, and I was needed. At my interview, the headmaster actually clapped his hands when I walked into the room, as if he had found some rare species willing to sacrifice itself for the children. I allowed him that and any number of misunderstandings about me.

"Miss Farrar!" he said, as if I'd been missing. He took my hand as I passed his desk like a man taking a partner in dance. I thought had I not released his hand, which was warm, he might have twirled me.

"I hope that the reports for the Council were not too much trouble. We didn't intend to rush you, Miss Farrar, but you have spoiled us with your efforts."

I nodded and tried not to behave like a six-year-old child being complimented about a fancy party dress. But I was still standing there holding reports to my chest like a schoolgirl loving flattery.

"Sit, please," he said finally. I stepped around his desk, purposely moving my nosy eyes over the book he'd left face down, Anderson's *Winesburg, Ohio*. I watched him lift it and then heard the faint sigh when he closed it without marking his place. He placed the book on his desk face up, inviting my comment, I was certain.

"Better the poverty of silence than the risk of flirtation," my mother wrote on her stationery and left on my bed when

I was first seeing Juan. These days, I often bumped into my mother in this manner. I think she'd come back to sweeten my heart.

"It won't do to show anyone the complexity of what you are thinking. Withholding your thoughts makes your thoughts more interesting. No man needs the whole story." She'd written that in a letter to me when I'd started college in Nova Scotia. I kept none of her letters and pretended to forget what she wrote.

The silence I'd let hang had gone on too long, so I blurted out, "This is the summary progress report. There is, of course, a separate report for each child, including the one we lost—the one who couldn't stay." I handed the papers to him across his desk.

"Yes, the boy's defects were so much more than blindness—ghastly—half-witted," the headmaster said, closing his eyes. "Who will take a blind child who cannot speak? Robbed of all his senses."

I thought to correct him when I thought of the damaged leaves and the chatter of the parakeets at Faith's grave.

I didn't, and instead I aimed for a particular tone before beginning the speech I'd practiced in my apartment, wishing for a mirror. "Overbrook is well prepared," I said. "Young children in our care could thrive." I took a breath and added, "I fully understand it will be my job to convince the Penn State Council for the Blind of this."

The year before, the Council had approved the reconditioning of the headmaster's former residence into housing for the thirty very young students I had identified. I too was housed in the residence; in a large bedroom with a sitting room that this man must have known. The rooms had carmine red walls, and I discovered early on that the dark walls somehow reflected daylight from the windows when the drapes were pulled back.

While I spoke, I watched the man's hands. He was fidgeting, but he was listening. Juan had rarely listened to me. And he had never bothered to chat with me. I thought again of the parakeets and how the males chatter to the females as a way of gaining their attention.

"I believe, Miss Farrar, that there was another matter you wanted to discuss," he said, coming around the desk and sitting next to me. It was something my father would have done.

"Oh, yes. Something I was considering. Perhaps another day," I said. I was in a period of lurching ahead followed by stalling.

He looked up as if he'd just decided something. He slapped his hands on his thighs and stood.

"So, I'll keep the reports, yes?"

"Yes, they are yours. I made two carbons."

He covered his book with the reports. I said something about a child waiting for me, and by way of goodbye he said, "What would we do without you?"

With a long evening in my sitting room ahead of me, I pulled out a magazine with a short story I'd been saving to read. Set in an upper middle-class neighborhood of detached homes, the story was about families separated from one another by their walled yards and stubby paved driveways and at the heart of the story was a man who took a pledge to mow his yard weekly. I finished the story, thinking surely the man was lost and that I too was lost and wandering. I decided I'd go back and read Sherwood Anderson story by story.

I had other reading to do. The things Father James had assigned me to read sat waiting. He'd counseled me with compassion, and only then took my halting confession. It was my first step in the new life I had chosen. He'd told me that his given name was James, but like my brother, he'd always been Jimmy. He said that when he became a priest, his nickname was the only thing he missed, and then he'd stopped talking and wiped his eyes. My brother Jimmy and I wrote to each other now and then. I owed him a letter. I was putting off telling him about my conversion. Stalling for time, I knew. But it was better kept to myself; I was, after all, fifty.

I pushed those papers aside and decided that before I could read them, I had to stop my mind from circling. My confession kept floating into my head and bumping around. "God the Father of Mercies," I mumbled. It had been nothing more than excuses. I knew it and Father James, who was hidden behind the screen, knew it. Six children, some of them small, taken to Colombia. What could I do?

Now I only wanted the evening to be over. I looked at the gilt clock on the mantelpiece—my mother's. It needed winding and still I didn't stand. I studied its face. It was the only thing of merit I owned. Merit was a ridiculous word for anything. I needed to get some sleep; writing was beyond me.

I changed into a gown and ran my mind over the conversation I could have had with the headmaster if I had mentioned that I too had read *Winesburg, Ohio*, as a young woman. It was the odds and ends of thoughts about lonely, solitary people that were circling round in my head and now fed by that novel read so long ago.

When I answered the timid knock at my door, it was the duty nurse, not the child with her, who was trembling. The nurse held the disfigured child—with difficulty—by her thin wrist. The child was the scariest looking thing, her face a bluish color with mottling on her neck. Her sooty brown hair was pulled back.

"Pearl will eat her hair if you do not keep it pulled back," the child's mother had warned. Tonight, the tight ponytail exposed her empty, deep-set eye sockets. It was not in the records of course, but a stranger might have thought the child's eyes had been pecked out.

Snot dripped from the child's chin that either from birth or by some hopeful but unsuccessful intervention hung slack from the left side of her face. As if by a sleight of hand, the nurse passed the child's wrist and the book she had tucked under her arm to me and said, "Here."

Once, I had admitted to the head nurse that I could not imagine how surgery could have made anything better for this particular child.

"Well, she can breathe now," the nurse said, as if I were stupid.

Only Pearl's ears were perfect. They were close to her head and a gold heart hung from each earlobe that no young man would ever kiss.

"I asked her if she was homesick," the duty nurse said.

"I am not sick," the child said through her stuffy nose. "I want to read."

"Leave her," I said. "I'll bring her back and put her to bed. Set her gown out, please. You won't be in any trouble." I tried to recall the nurse's name but did not care enough to ask her.

The nurse tried to embrace the child, but she had a grip on my gown, and so I nodded at the woman to leave.

"We will sit at the table across the room," I said, and the child went down on all fours to crawl.

"No, you must stand up and walk," I said.

In January, I had spent a full day with this child's parents.

"We tried not to spoil her," the mother said while the father sat silent. I could hear his stomach churn. "Blindness is going to break our home," the mother added with the certainty of a woman who knew all life's merriments were over and done with. They had three older children to consider, the woman explained. I had seen this before, parents who held a sacred belief that the one crippled child was better off if sent away, and that the new wounds inflicted on the family from abandoning a child might be healed by the effort the family gave to getting on in the world.

"Steady now," I said when I sat the child in the antique chair meant for adults. I pushed the chair up to the table and the little girl grabbed the book the moment I set it down in front of her. I opened it and placed her fingers before I had the table lamp on, but the light, of course, was only for me.

I watched while the child traced her tiny fingers across the symbols on the page, turning a heavy page back and finding her place. I was cold—there had been no time to find my robe when the knock came at the door. I went to take it off the hook and asked the child if she was warm enough.

"Miss, I want to read to you."

And so the child read the story over and over, something about two children, a boy and a girl, and a red ball. I'd noticed from the time I started working with blind children that they adored games with balls—objects they could not catch, that they chased endlessly.

I let the girl read, and then I got up and got a hairbrush and took down her hair and brushed it until it was shiny. The child was not reading now; she was telling me a story about songbirds. She put her hands in her lap and glided the fingers of her left hand over the fingers of her right hand. She never once put her hair into her mouth.

"Do you like my story, Miss?" she asked.

"Yes, I do. You are very expressive," I said.

"I dream stories. I can't help it," she said and tossed her hair so that her face was hidden, and she looked like any small child.

"One day I will teach you to write in braille," I said softly. I had no business making such a promise, but I just went on, adding, "It's called night writing and it is special. And then you can write your stories down for other children to read." The child held her palms together as if in prayer. Something she'd been taught, I was sure.

"I write stories too," I said. I closed her book, thinking it was certainly time to take her to the dorm and put her to bed.

"Tell me your story," she said and squirmed in her seat, as if settling in for a long tale, and I thought it must have been Clara who had done that, who had loved to read, too.

"I have five older brothers..." I said.

Before I could go on, she said, "Oh bother."

I was thinking that someone must have read to her when she nudged me with one little finger. Finding my breastbone, she said, "Well, tell me."

"My brothers had quite the gang, especially the two youngest who were just older than me. One day they went to the park with their pair of bearded goats pulling their wagon. Some days they put me in their wagon, but not that day. That day, they went to collect a baby alligator and when they got home, they put it in our bathtub."

I watched her face, saw movement behind her closed eyelids before she spoke, rushing her words, "Did it splash water on the floor?" She waited for an answer, and I said "Yes," about the time she said, "One more story, please."

"One more," I said. But I couldn't think what might be cruel or might be kind, so I just headed into the vision that came into my head. "One summer, my mother and father and I took a train ride to Asbury Park, which is on the Atlantic Ocean. We stayed in a small cottage with a screened-in porch."

It was a good way to begin a story, I thought, because her eyelids were jumping about again.

"Every day, my mother let me ride the merry-go-round on pretty horses of every color," I said.

"Round and round," the child said, and I nodded, but of course she did not see that. "Exactly how old are you, Miss?"

"I'm fifty just now," I said.

"You think you've counted correctly, Miss? That is a very high number. Are your parents dead and gone?"

"Yes," I said and was stuck in my own thoughts, thinking that this child's parents had given her expressive language, when she poked me and went on with her questions.

"Did your mother cry when you went round and round?"

"Perhaps," I said, but I didn't think the child was looking for an answer now.

"At night when I go to bed, I wish for wings like dreamers do, but in the daytime, I need my fingers." She wiggled her ten small fingers, and I realized that they too were very perfect.

The wiggling made me laugh, a real out-loud laugh, and I saw then that the child could manage—with difficulty—the trace of a smile.

CHAPTER 13

RUBY
1944-1945

It had been months since my brother's wife had died in the night while he slept on. "For hours, I slept," Jimmy kept repeating on the phone when he called to tell me of her death.

So, I went to Connecticut for the services and stayed several days. I watched my brother weep for hours on end. I'd almost felt envy, but of course his grief was crushing, and so I sat by his side and held his hand. Jimmy's wife had been ill several years—long enough to make her wishes known. She had not wanted to be buried at Green-Wood, had said that the Farrar family was never her family. Through tears, Jimmy told me that this was one of the saddest things in his whole life. I've wondered since if her devotion to him was less than his to her. Who measures such things?

On that condolence visit, I told my niece, Irene, that I'd converted to Catholicism. Jimmy was too deep into grief in those first days to hear about my life going on. Best to keep it between Irene and me. And I told her that I'd hoped the confession would make me feel like an innocent child, and she'd said, "Don't tell Uncle Eddie. We all know Episcopalians are touchy about the Catholics—especially Eddie." And then she'd winked, which was something my father had done, but then maybe he'd stopped that too when he stopped whistling. So many memories were lost to me.

At the funeral, Irene wore the ruby bowtie pin I'd given her long ago. After all this time, I had honestly forgotten it. Jimmy sat stoic through the service, but one time he leaned across his daughter to say to me, "It makes me sad that Eddie did not come to perform her service."

My conversion had come with a great deal of mail and had given Rosalie, who handled all the mail for the school, a sense of proprietorship over me. One day earlier in the year, Rosalie came looking for me in my classroom. She'd hugged a packet of materials to her chest and waved me over. Pearl came with me as I crossed the room.

"Go back over to your table, Honey, touch and learn. Touch and learn," Rosalie had said to the child and patted her on her head like she was a dog. Rosalie's voice stuck in her throat, sounding as if she had suffered a terrible blow. Pearl grabbed ahold of my leg and wouldn't leave, and Rosalie said, "Ruby, you could have shared with me that you are a Catholic. After all, we are friends—or am I wrong about that? I'd have taken you to my parish." She made a drowning sound and then pushed the materials to me. I wasn't sure if she felt sorry for me or herself.

"A new Catholic," I said, and I stepped back so she could not embrace me. I'd always known to hold her at a distance, because she had a look that said, "Tell me more." She made me feel cruel. I made up my mind then to leave Overbrook before she learned about the vows I'd be taking.

It was months before a short letter from Father James arrived, telling me that he had made certain arrangements. I would need to come back to the church to meet with a Chancellor Benjamin. Father James had been the one behind that screen offering me absolution, and yet here was another person to judge me. I would go, but I would make no more excuses.

"There is a matter to be dispensed with. Signatures must be obtained from your husband," the Chancellor said as he pointed behind him to a certificate on the wall that said "Notary" in block letters. Then he shook his head like a wet dog and added, "Your Colombian husband."

"Ex-husband. Father James knows about my divorce," I said and added, "It happened years ago."

The man looked past me. Then he got up and went to his filing cabinet and began gathering papers. He put one of the papers in front of me and said, "Sign," and then I realized we were done.

Now the creamy white winter honeysuckle was back in bloom in this season of decorated fir trees, and I was still waiting for word from Father James or that horrid Chancellor Benjamin about my pending petition to take my vows. Sometimes I forgot all about the Carmelites in Paris.

But of course, the priests were into their season of lights and carols, and then Pearl told me that she adored Christmas lights and I believed her.

We put up a Christmas tree in the dormitory for the little children and strung popcorn garlands, while the children sang "Have Yourself a Merry Little Christmas." Pearl was the only one of the little children who was not going home to be with family over Christmas and so the idea flew into my head to take her to Wanamaker's for their Christmas extravaganza. I hadn't needed or wanted any help with the outing, but Rosalie had already invited me to Christmas Eve mass at her church, and so I had no choice but to include her.

Two days before Christmas, Pearl and Rosalie and I were outside the Overbrook front gates, waiting in the bitter cold for the city bus. Pearl was a different child than the one who'd arrived earlier that year. Today I brushed her hair, which had grown past her shoulders, dressed her in the red velvet dress her mother mailed to the school, and put the mother-of-pearl barrette, which had come with the dress, in her hair. Her hair was now honey colored after all the time she had spent in the Overbrook pool that summer. Confidence was Pearl's strong point, and now she was sure that she'd be able to smell her way to the Christmas tree in the department store.

When Rosalie and I took our seats on the bus with Pearl

between us, the child took Rosalie's hand, guided it to feel the hem of her dress, and said, "Velvet."

"Before we go home, we will have tea and croissants in the Crystal Tea Room," I said. Rosalie let out a giggle.

"I never imagined in my whole life that I'd get to go on a field trip," Pearl said before she began pulling out the barrette and said, "This perfectly horrid thing in my hair is too tight." Her hair was thick and with the pulling, she was hurting herself.

"Let me," I said, and after I got it out of the tangles, I handed it to Rosalie and whispered, "I hate mother-of-pearl."

The child said, "I heard you, Miss Farrar. You must never hate your mother."

It was a startling thing for a child to say, and my first thought was to defend myself. But then her words settled into a meaning, and I said, "It's a type of stone."

Pearl nodded as if I'd said something wise. And so I sat in silence. And when the bus turned onto Juniper Street, I said, "It looks like we have arrived in Paris." Each store window was decorated, and a long line had formed to go into the Grand Court.

"Goodness," was all Rosalie could manage before she giggled again. It was one of her annoying habits—meant to please others, I thought. Laughing like a girl was a silly thing for a woman past fifty to do.

I took a red knit hat out of my purse and put it on the child. I pulled her pretty hair free of the hat and feathered it so that her face was mostly hidden. Strangers could be cruelly consumed by pity, and we needed none of that this afternoon. I took the precious child's chin in my hand and kissed her forehead. I saw that her nose was wet, and I brushed it dry with my gloved hand. "Red suits you," I said.

"Well, it is Christmas, Miss Farrar," she offered.

We could hear the organ as we waited outside. Often in the last month, I had played the music from the *Nutcracker* for the little children. They'd all pranced around to the "Dance of the Sugar Plum Fairy."

As we made our way inside, Pearl sighed and said, "We are in the Land of Sweets."

Rosalie was as mesmerized as the child, and I wondered what Christmas Eve mass would be like with her.

"The stuff of sweet memories," I said to Rosalie and added, because I felt bad about being so annoyed with her, "My mother loved this room."

"Your mother?" Rosalie said, wanting more from me, and I regretted my kindness.

"Here we are at the bronze eagle," I said to the child. And then I said the very thing I'd been taught never to say to a blind child. The words spilled out, and I found myself saying, "I wish you could see how big this eagle is."

But Pearl only wrinkled her nose and pointed off across the enormous room, in the exact direction of the tree.

I felt my mother nearby in that moment...felt her lift my hair off my face...felt her put a cool hand on my forehead. Heard her say, "I'm here with you." It was real.

"We'll be at the tree," I said to Rosalie.

Once Pearl and I joined the crowd that circled the tree, I said, "There are fairies dancing. They have pale pink feather wings, and there is a little girl your size dancing around the tree. I believe she must be Clara from the *Nutcracker*."

"I love her," Pearl said. "I wish I could hug her."

I tightened my grip on her hand and said, "I had a little girl. I had a little girl named Clara."

"I'm very sure I'd love her too," Pearl said.

On New Year's Day, I did what I always did that day. Before I got out of bed and got my footing in the New Year, I would count out my children on my fingers and the age each of them would turn that year. Of course, I longed for a cigarette as part of this ritual, but I knew full well we could not afford a fire at Overbrook. Still, I craved one.

It was an easy year for my calculations: 1945. Mateo would turn thirty this year. His childhood, like mine, a distant memory. But then, childhood was such a fraud. The three older girls would turn twenty-nine, twenty-seven, and twenty-six. Clara would turn twenty-three this January. She'd been born on a raw day. And Alice would turn twenty.

I'd forgotten their voices.

But 1945 was the relief I'd been waiting for. I'd been twenty when Mateo was born and still hopeful. Juan would turn fifty-seven this year, I told myself and nodded. I'd been hoping for so long that Nana was dead that I'd lost count of her age. She'd be past eighty if she'd lived, and she was mean enough to have lived, and my own mother dead now all these years.

"Stop this," I said out loud. I put my feet on the floor and went to the window to check the day. It would be warm for January first. When you are alone year after year on the holidays, you stay busy, and you straighten your back. New Year's Day could be mean, and so this year I was changing things. I had a ticket for the train to New York City and then onto Connecticut. Jimmy's daughter, Irene, would pick me up at the train station.

"I'll be away four days. To see friends," I'd lied to Rosalie, who didn't know or need to know that I had a brother and a niece or had had a family and lost it. Poof.

I rubbed my fingers across my forehead. It was how I read my own mind these days, even the lies.

I went back to kneel at my bedside for morning prayers, hoping this time, just maybe, to be humbled. I always played with Kate's emerald as I prayed. I'd worn it since the day Kate's husband had given it to me, and over the years the stone had grown darker in color. It was a lovely thing, and I would give it to Irene on this visit and maybe tell her about Kate. I dressed quickly in the clothes I had set out the night before and headed out to catch the bus.

Irene and Jimmy were the only people in my life who knew that I'd filed a petition to become a nun. I'd told them how Father James took my hand as we sat in the front pew of his gorgeous church and how he said, "Let us begin together on the journey for you to become a nun." They knew too that I was still waiting for my petition to be approved. Waiting, this late in life, was not worth the breath it took to talk about.

Irene had almost married a boy in the days before he went off to war. So many girls were doing that back then, as if it was their duty to buck the boys up for what was coming. But then Irene's mother fell ill, and Irene left college to go home to take care of her, and the boy left for the Pacific. And then Irene waited for him to return.

Now, it seemed to me that she was afraid to leave her father. I feared for her that it would go on like that because Jimmy would never heal. This trip was not a condolence visit. This time, I would ask Irene to tell me about the boy she had almost married.

Jimmy was in the kitchen making us sandwiches while Irene and I sat in the living room surrounded by all the ghastly fairy-tale figurines Jimmy's wife had collected over the years. While I smoked, Irene told me that her beau had been in the Bataan Death March.

"The American boys had to surrender, you know," she said, and I nodded. I had not known that, but I wanted her to go on with her story.

"They were treated like cowards by the Japanese. I didn't know if he was dead or alive," she said. "He was listed as missing for a long time and then the Red Cross wrote that he was a prisoner of war all that time. And then I got his letter." She was twirling Kate's ring on her finger. It was too large for her.

"He sounded quite changed in his letter. He said he'd tell me things when we were together. And then another letter arrived from his family telling me he had died. I think he starved." Irene sat there shaking her head in disbelief as if it had just happened.

"Do you girls want lunch in the kitchen or on trays?" Jimmy asked from the kitchen.

"Trays, please," Irene said, and she hopped to her feet to go in and help her father. But first she turned to me and said, "I think he wanted to tell me he was dying, but who can write such things in a letter?"

When we were all eating in silence, Irene held up her hand and said, "Look, Daddy, what Aunt Ruby gave me."

"You have your mother's ring if you ever marry," Jimmy said. It was a cruelty I would never have expected from my brother. Irene let it pass, but three days later when she took me to the train station, she was wearing Kate's emerald ring. I could see adhesive tape on the back of the ring.

A letter from Father James was waiting for me at Overbrook when I returned from my holiday. "Done," I thought, but it was only to tell me about an appointment with the Chancellor the next week, and I knew better than to think that this time Father James would be in the meeting. I went to see the headmaster that afternoon to make arrangements to be out of my classroom. Rosalie stood up at her desk as I left his office, waiting for a full explanation. I waved her away and she said, "Ruby, you didn't lose your ring, did you?"

The Chancellor offered no welcoming hand as he nodded at the one empty chair in his office. The smell of Listerine was strong. He began without any pleasantries. "The Consul General of Colombia has arranged for to you write personally to your husband's brother, a Mr. Carlos del Palacio. The Consul will ensure that he receives the letter. He's a go-between," he said and stared at the fingers of his right hand before he began chewing on one of them.

I clamped my teeth as my stomach hit bottom—it was the horrid smell. I'd hoped for more from a priest.

He said, "Write to this man at once. The letter must be written in your own hand for authenticity. And return it to me for mailing." I wasn't to be trusted.

A cut-glass decanter sat on his desk and an inch of brown liquid was brewing in a jelly glass near his left hand. He played with the rim of the glass. It was the Listerine. My mother said that Listerine was invented as a cure for vile behavior in the First World War. She wouldn't have it in her home. The man kept looking at the glass, wanting it, but we were not done.

"Understand, it is your job to make it clear to Mr. del Palacio that the Carmelites require your husband, Mr. Juan, to state in writing that he will not ask for your return."

A weeping fit came on me like an allergy. The Chancellor took up the jelly jar and sipped while I cried. Then he sat open-mouthed, breathing out the vile fumes.

I wiped at the tears with a tissue from my purse. I'd out-grown handkerchiefs. I wadded the tissue and put the germy, disposable thing on the edge of his desk where it sat looking a bit like a white dove.

"Certainly, there are no children involved," he said. But he wasn't looking at me. He was looking at his two hands now, which he had flopped down on his desk. His nails were ragged.

But this was not a confessional, and there were no longer children to consider. I pointed at his glass and said, "What is it you have there? Might I have a sip of something before I head back out in this weather? January can be so very raw."

The man, who I decided was nothing more than a record keeper, was not about to serve a woman a drink. He scooted his chair back, and I could see that he had caught his robe somehow, because he wedged his fat index finger into the neck of his robe. His face quickly took on a choked color. I did not want to have to revive the man, and so I said, "You've caught your robe on your chair. Just stand up and I'll free it."

Even then, he waited a moment before taking my instruction. After he did as I suggested, he took a full minute to re-cover. He put his back to me while he stood at his filing cabinet coughing from the pit of his stomach.

"I can provide stationery," he said finally.

"That will not be necessary," I said. "And it is not Mr. Juan, it is Mr. Juan del Palacio. I trust you understand."

When I stepped onto the city bus, a woman in the second row, grandmotherly in her choice of laced black shoes, scooted over to the window seat. Philadelphia was known as the city of neighborhoods, and this bus would, without a doubt, make a stop in every damn one. I never liked to sit with anyone on the bus and never invited conversation when I did find my-self shoulder-to-shoulder, knee-to-knee with a stranger. The woman nodded at the open seat and then at me and began to talk.

"Children…" she said as I settled the leather pouch where I kept my petition on my lap. "They never grow up. Now this one needs a sitter, another—a boy at twenty-five—needs mon-ey. So, I have to be the one to go cross-town midday. I won't get home until after dark."

I tried to relax my mouth and neck and calm myself so I could compose the letter in my head that I would write to Carlos. My husband's family had always turned to their older son to solve things. My own children had preferred Carlos to their father; at least when it came to gaiety. I thought of him visiting us on Argyle Road. I'd put him in the room with Ma-teo, and he'd turned the household into a carnival; yard cats were invited inside for supper and a blue-tailed parrot he'd brought with him on the ship was allowed to wander from room to room. But of course, we didn't keep that parrot, as Juan wouldn't have that filthy thing in our house. I never knew where he took it after Carlos went back to Colombia, but Ma-teo told me in secret that he thought his father had simply let it go. I couldn't let Mateo believe that cruelty, even then, and so I made up a story.

"Do you have children here in Philly?" the stranger asked. I was looking at her shoes.

"I'm a Carmelite," I lied without hesitation.

"No!" She strung the word out as if it were a tiny little sentence. "I'd never guess you for that."

"Well, a novice. Perhaps it doesn't show yet."

"You have pretty hands for a nun," the woman said with a sigh.

This business of sharing confidences had never been for me. My mother had discouraged it.

"Sometimes I wish…" The woman looked out the window and didn't finish with the wish. And then she said, "Well, if it's what you want," and she patted my hand and left her hand there on top.

I did not want the woman to be wrong about me, and so I held her callused hand in mine as if we were girlhood friends with no need to say anything more to each other. I composed the letter in my head and looked down at my hand now and then, expecting to see it moving.

Overbrook School for the Blind
Malvern Avenue at 64th Street
Philadelphia, PA
January 15, 1945

Dear Carlos,

Following the suggestion of Mr. Jorge Ortiz Rodriquez, Colombian Consul General in New York, I am writing to you although it is with regret that I find it necessary to intrude upon you.

My request has already been made at some length in a letter which Consul General Rodriquez informs me has been referred to you. Therefore, I shall not go into details but merely ask you to be kind enough to obtain the signed statements from Juan which Church law re-

quires me to present in my petition for the Carmelites.
It is my hope that you and Margie will understand my
wish to become a nun. I will have a family again, this
time in Paris, which my mother taught me to dream of.
With many thanks for your offer of cooperation,
Sincerely,
Ruby Farrar

It had been two weeks since the Chancellor posted my letter to Carlos. Those days were long and moody. I'd kept track of them—counting them mostly as days of regret for the admissions I had made to Carlos—for groveling. But still, I thought Carlos would not begrudge me. Now, I crossed my apartment, touching my mother's sewing table, which I always placed next to my bed. It had worn unevenly over the years. I sat on the bed and held my head in my hands and thought that by now, so close to joining the Carmelites, I should know how to pray. I had come to think it must be like reading, some magical process. Writing was like that for me sometimes. Something would take control over my hand and the words flowed as if bypassing my conscious thoughts.

The Chancellor had ordered some underling to deliver his handwritten copies of the letters to me at the school that day. They rested on my table in a messy stack.

I shifted to lie back on the bed, thinking I might sleep. I needed more time. Down the hall, children shouted. It was just now their bedtime.

Finally, I stepped to the window and pulled back the drapes, and found my reflection. I looked like my mother but without her Paris blue eyes. Jimmy got my father's great mane of dark red hair. He had my father's soft brown eyes, too. I knew my eyes were hard and bitter.

When I fell for Juan, my father asked if he loved me. My father said his world would lose its whirl if this were not true.

Later, after I had already given birth to three children, my mother said, "You chose to be coy and alluring, Ruby, and it misled that man into thinking you were what he wanted. Now you need to learn to be content with what you've got." Even then, I had not considered that she had known all along.

I allowed myself a coy smile now, to see if it softened my eyes. But in the window glass, I couldn't tell if it worked.

Alice had gotten those blue eyes. My mother would have loved that child. I moved back to the table, turned on the lamp, and lined up the letters.

It was not Carlos, but his son Alberto who replied to my request. I'd never met him, of course, and I wondered if Margie had learned to love him. I had never even seen a photo of him. He was a bit younger than Alice. Alberto's letter was not addressed to me but to Chancellor Benjamin, which was one more small cruelty. He wrote that he would enclose with his letter a signed statement from Juan releasing me. "As requested," Alberto had written in the margin and "for purposes of formality"—his choice of words—he'd sworn before a notary that the signature was that of Mr. Juan del Palacio.

Then there was also a copy of the Chancellor's response with his effusive best wishes, "Trusting that God Will bless you," was his closing.

Both Alberto's letter and the Chancellor's had been copied onto tracing paper. They would smudge. Finally, there was a letter to me from the Chancellor on his personal stationery saying only, "Now that you have been released from your marriage, we may proceed with your petition." I had not been bound to Juan for years upon years, but I was given no further options for making this clear.

Down the hall, the children had gone silent. Some, I knew, slept with their eyes open.

My eyes ran over my worldly goods. Everything was to be given away when I was taken into the religious community. The Seth Thomas striking clock should have gone to Tessie. Each year on Faith's birthday, she sent me a card with true blue forget-me-nots on it and would tell me about her visit to Green-Wood. And then one year, nothing. She was dead at thirty of mumps, her sister wrote, and so I'd decided I would give the clock to Pearl and would teach her to wind it; my books to the headmaster, because I wanted someone to know what I had read. There never had been anything to pass on to my children, who were like a bruise I'd inflicted on myself but couldn't recall doing.

I turned off the lamp and returned to the window and looked out beyond the gardens at the runaway honeysuckle. It lined the walkways, growing there as a border.

"Free as a bird," I said to my reflection and wondered if Juan had ever in all these years felt bound to me.

Three months later, on a blue-sky day, I was settled in the cloister garden, writing. The boxwood was sweet with the damage of the blind children. I held my head in my fingers while I went searching for a bit of truth inside the stories of my life I'd been writing. Paris had dimmed. It would have been so very sad there and I'd be lonely again. I was free, after all, free to stay here. I'd been such a silly woman, I'd decided, in these last months, to allow a church to grant me relief and a man to release me.

I watched the children playing their game of Mother May I and thought that a dog with a wet nose would be good for them. I'd propose it to the headmaster.

I often talked to Kate in this garden, but it was my mother's presence I felt today. Today, I was recalling how she loved sweets.

If only I'd shown her that I needed her—if I'd let her know that I felt so very sad for her when Richard died—she certainly would have called me into her room. She would have shared the madeleines my father had brought her, and she would have made a place for me under her red satin puff. How I wished I had gone to her and told her that I loved her truly. I wish I'd told her that I missed my baby brother.

I put my hands—not so pretty, really, and aged brown—in my lap and closed my eyes so that I could rest. It occurred to me out of thin air that my mother had sent me madeleines when my baby died, and I felt forgiven.

I breathed in the sweet smell of boxwood, and then I heard my mother and Kate whispering to one another.

Kate said, "It is a good thing for Ruby to write what it was like for her. A cautionary tale. An American fable."

And then my mother said, "My daughter's stories will no doubt be fascinating. But now, with her ducks in order, she needs to get on with living."

CHAPTER 14

ALICE
1954-1955

Alice went with her son, Tony, out to the playroom, which was really a converted single-car garage. She set the tub of blocks he loved on the floor next to him and then returned to the kitchen and rested her heavy belly on the edge of the kitchen table. It was not a lady-like thing to do; Miss Rules would have been mortified. She took deep breaths and reached for the phone to call her neighbor, Teresa, who picked up immediately and jumped right into a story about her three-year-old son negotiating with her the night before, how he got all the particulars for his next day set. Teresa said he had made a plan to be up early so he could eat breakfast with his dad, and he had.

Alice lodged the phone between her ear and shoulder, and with hands free wiped the sink, folded the tea towel, and hung it neatly on the hook next to the sink, knew she'd tidy up like this half a million times in her one lifetime without creating any memory of it. Habit was like that.

"Let me tell you, Alice, nothing else would do but that Bobby take the trike out to the garage the minute his dad left for work. Of course, he didn't want to wear his coat, and after a few times around, he pulled it off."

"Boys," Alice said and patted her belly as if soothing the child—a second boy would be fine with her. Bobby was Teresa's only child, and likely to stay that way. Teresa and her husband married late.

"Big Bob painted the trike on Saturday, and then we had

to let it dry all day yesterday. It's hard to paint over pink. It turned out this milky green."

Alice's husband, Matthew, did not approve of a grown man being called Big Bob. Alone in their bedroom, Matthew would sometimes waddle naked across the room, mocking Big Bob, who did walk like a duck. Alice had to admit that. She winced at her own thoughts, which had wandered.

"I watched Bobby go round and round, learning where to coast and how to lean left, and then right, for balance as he rounded the corners. Finally, he took a break and slept on the sofa for a half-hour, but he's back out there now—revived."

Alice finished at the sink and, still listening, gazed out the west-facing window. The morning light in her kitchen was nice, but afternoons were brutal. She wound her fingers around the flesh-colored phone cord, held it tight in its spiral curl, and then let it go. It sprung loose as if alive. She considered the bare cottonwoods, trying to remember shade. Teresa had stopped talking, her story over. Alice didn't mind bits of silence, but now she took her turn.

"I'm standing here in the kitchen admiring my new wallpaper," Alice said and then added, "Well really, where else would I be?" They both laughed, and both knew it was out of some sort of obligation.

Teresa had helped Alice hang the paper the month before. It had been no trouble to pick out the paper. Alice hadn't bothered to cart home any heavy sample books. She just chose one of the patterns the shop had put on display in their model kitchen. Black-eyed bluebirds danced across her wall, and the wording in a fancy script repeated itself from panel to panel, "Dishwashing is for the birds." Alice flipped off the light switch, and the blueness of early winter darkened the room, calmed her.

"Call you right back," Teresa said without an explanation.

The women on Indiana and Illinois Streets—those who were friendly—were playing bridge at Teresa's at noon. They played monthly, and so Alice had her day all planned. She had set her hair in rollers that morning, and her dress lay on her bed. Alice's two daughters would be in school until three. Tony would nap on the double bed in Teresa's bedroom with Bobby. If Bobby slept, Tony would too. Tony would do anything Bobby did, but he couldn't pedal, not yet, and Alice knew there was no teaching a kid to pedal if he wasn't ready. There was time for that.

Alice went through the kitchen to the utility room to look in on her boy—heard the chest freezer click on. It began to hum. Her husband had insisted on buying it and stocking it once a year with a side of beef. Sometimes, Alice unplugged it for an hour or so just to hear silence.

She watched as her son carefully took apart a Lincoln Log cabin. The previous owner of their home had turned the garage into the playroom. "Wall-to-wall carpeting," the real estate agent pointed out when they first saw the house. The playroom had not been a selling point for Matthew.

"It'll make resale tough. People want a garage."

The phone rang. "I'll get it," she said so that her tender-hearted boy, who noticed her watching him, would not look up and find her gone.

The wall phone made the kitchen wall shudder when it rang, and Alice had discovered that it made the birds flutter. Those birds had been a mistake.

When she heard Teresa's voice again, she snagged a kitchen chair with her foot and pulled it close to the wall. She leaned the chair back on two legs; balanced, figured she had a good ten minutes to talk to her friend.

A pile of toast crumbs lay on the kitchen table. Alice was sure she'd wiped it up before she'd sent the girls to the hall closet for their coats that morning. Resting the chair on all fours, she stepped to the table and swept the crumbs into her hand. She didn't know who'd taught her to lead her life this way. She opened the cabinet under the sink and dusted her hands off in the brown grocery bag. She'd have to empty that before she left for bridge. She stood at the sink, not really paying attention to her friend, who was telling her something about how she'd set up the bridge tables.

"I'm using the china. You just watch. Blossom will roll her eyes when she sees it. But I bet she'll like the standing ashtrays. I bought one for each table. They have this tiny trap door for the ashes." Alice knew Teresa had recently inherited some delicate bone china; she'd helped her unpack it. The pattern was Marlow—English—but they'd both decided it looked French.

Out the kitchen window, Alice watched as two trash men stepped into her backyard. They had come from the graveled alley. That alley would be full of green tumbleweeds in the spring. Through the kitchen window, she saw the men see her standing there doing nothing, and she put her hand to the rollers in her hair. Each hefted a beat-up metal can to his shoulder and marched out. They were in the middle of a conversation, were good friends she suspected, and she felt a swell of thankfulness for Teresa.

"Teresa, I'm bringing Creamland French Onion dip this afternoon."

Alice heard the click that people make when they take a cigarette out of their mouth and suck at a breath. Teresa said, "Good." Alice heard disapproval. Teresa didn't approve of her choice. Even if it was the wrong choice, the dip was all she had. She couldn't zip Tony into his car coat and make a special trip to the Safeway based on the silence that followed that one gulp of breath before the artificially enthusiastic "good."

Then with a full breath, Teresa said, "Thank you so much for loaning us the trike," as if they were both making up. It had been that "good," that tiny failure of friendship that made Alice hot with anger—made her lips tremble.

"We'll have a bit of everything this afternoon," Teresa said, and then she said something else, but the trash truck rumbled past, down the alley away from Alice toward Teresa's home, and the words were lost. Alice started in, asking Teresa to repeat herself. She didn't want to misunderstand what with the trash truck and the freezer.

"That trash truck," was all Alice said before what sounded like a sonic boom, which was normal when you lived near an air base, sent a shock wave through the neighborhood. From the window, Alice searched the sky, but only saw in the glass the reflection of the frantic bluebirds.

Alice was one of the first neighbors to arrive on the sidewalk two doors down from Teresa's home; flames were jumping inside the open-mouthed garage. The two trash men practically carried Teresa to the street. "Barefoot," the Albuquerque paper had said. A fire truck and then an ambulance pulled up, and Alice held Tony tight to her chest as people ran across Big Bob's neat lawn. Alice kept patting Tony's head. He began to tremble and said, "I saw a green dragon."

"It's only a trike," Alice said and wished she hadn't.

The women were doing their best to confine Teresa and one of them said, "She's out of her mind." Alice saw Teresa's eyes quiver like a little bird that was sure it was going to die. Two firemen held fast to a hose and the strength of the water put an end to the flames.

Teresa screamed for them to stop and shouted, "My boy is in there! My baby boy!"

"Oh, Honey," someone said.

But then Teresa fixed her eyes on Alice alone and said, "Big Bob will hate me."

Alice froze.

Being happy was such a joke.

While the firemen scrambled up a ladder to the flat roof, shouting at one another, the neighbor women pulled a circle around Teresa.

"The roof is going to cave," a fireman yelled, and all of the men scrambled down, moved the women across the street, and watched. Blossom arrived with her youngest son, but Teresa said nothing more. They all stood there while the ambulance idled at the curb—waiting for Big Bob.

Finally, when he drove up, Alice said she needed to take Tony home, but her brain was telling her that she needed to go into her closet and scream. Teresa looked at her then, looked directly at her heavy stomach, and then, as if she were turning a memory over, said, "Well, I lost my boy."

Alice could not bear to set Tony down when she got back home, could not bear to let him nap that day. Matthew's mother, Janie, picked the girls up at school and made dinner and stayed until the baths were done, hair was brushed, and the children were asleep.

Not yet thirty, Alice had planned her family, so she'd be finished with pregnancies before she was out of her twenties.

"Now what?" she sometimes asked herself before she took out her vacuum.

But she kept house and stayed on her feet all day, which kept her hips slim. Nursing the new baby helped too. With her two oldest in school now, she had some alone time when the little ones napped—she used to like having time to daydream. But all that had changed since the accident—a child dead and gone—how could she take pleasure in dreaming now, with memories of a child haunting her?

In the evenings, between baths and bedtime, her husband wanted her to sit and watch TV with him, and she tried to do that if only to perch on the arm of the sofa for a few minutes. Sitting down made her wish for a cigarette. Her sisters and brother and father smoked, and her stepmother too. But Matthew hated it, told her that kissing her was like kissing an ashtray. He said it like he wanted to curse but wouldn't. What he wanted was to talk, especially during TV shows. Matthew had been raised in a family of conversationalists, who all knew how to talk without talking about anything much. They did it out of habit, afraid to let their minds linger, and none of them, especially Matthew, who was the baby of his family, was going to outgrow that.

The neighborhood party was an opportunity to be happy—or act that way. Alice was not sure which. It had been planned so far in advance that none of Alice's neighbors had an excuse not to participate. She would have to start right after church getting her family ready. They'd probably run late. She'd been rushing since Saturday morning, what with shampoos and pin curls, polishing all those shoes, pressing her linen skirt and jacket over and over again, and then going downtown to the train station to pick up her friend, Pauline. They'd almost been sorority sisters together. Pen Pal was Matthew's nickname for her.

Pauline had written a short letter after she'd received the christening announcement saying, "I'm not letting another year go by. I'll take the train—can get there Saturday morning in plenty of time for the christening and neighborhood welcoming party." Alice had to put her on a borrowed rollaway in Tony's room. Before she even got unpacked, Pauline helped Alice make the bed, which required sitting on opposite corners to flatten it out. It had made them both laugh. But then Pauline said, "Life is work. Don't spend too much time cleaning your house. It's a waste of time." And then she fell back on the bed like a spent teenage girl and said, "And forget anger—it is piss-poor consolation for anything, even cancer."

Sunday morning, after the christening, when Pauline strolled into the kitchen, she stopped short, studied the wallpaper, did a double take like a cocky teenager, and said, "Tell me that paper came with the house." Tony had a fistful of Alice's linen skirt, and she pulled him along as she led Pauline into the utility room where the lacy, borrowed bassinet was temporarily parked next to the freezer.

Pauline said, "Alice, you're shaking like a bad girl in church." The shaking had started in the car on the way home from church, the seven of them packed in. Alice stared at Pauline, who gave her a knowing nod and said, "That's natural. Nursing will weaken you like that."

Pauline knew what she was talking about because she was a professor of nursing. "Only an adjunct," Pauline had said that morning when Alice introduced her to her mother-in-law.

Alice grabbed hold of the bassinet for balance. Tony held his arms up to her and she smoothed his hair into place along the part. His hair needed cutting.

Pauline leaned over and retrieved the baby girl and the ribbon-bound pink blanket all in one sure-handed scoop. She passed the bundle to Alice and said, "I love the blanket. Don't tell me, Janie made it. Right?"

"Yes. But I didn't need another one."

"I liked Janie, and I like the blanket," Pauline said and winked.

"Not my mother," Alice said to herself. It was her habit when someone raved about Matthew's mother—which was always, but damn if she didn't love her with a fierceness she could not explain.

"Go nurse Clara Anne," Pauline said and took Tony's hand and marched him out to the playroom like she knew her way around. Alice followed and stood at the door. Matthew was out there in what he called Playland, still in his church clothes, straightening things. Alice watched her husband, who had kept his student-athlete build. He held the opinion that Alice didn't need friends; she had him and the kids, and his sociable family always included her. Pauline started right in with him. She wasn't the cautious type and could match him in conversation if she wanted to—and she wanted to. Matthew looked at Alice as if asking permission, making sure. He'd been looking for jealousy in Alice's eyes for years now. But she didn't have it in her. He wasn't going anywhere. She retreated to her backyard.

March was not Albuquerque's best month, but it was finally calm today and the two cottonwoods, one male, one female, were getting ready to bloom. Alice did not care. She sat on the first step of the cement stoop and stared at the dirt that had accumulated in the corner around the new cinderblock enclosure. After the first of the year, the neighbors had gotten together and hired some workers to build each of them a wall to pen in their trash cans, a tiny labyrinth of sorts, and in their case it also caged in a rotting telephone pole. Now the trash men could collect the trashcans and drag them into the alley without entering the backyards, as if a statement was being made that these men would not be needed to rescue anyone, not in their wildest dream would they be heroes again, or worse.

Her OB, who everyone in Albuquerque tried to see, blamed her blues on an infection, but he was a simple man and wrong. Alice's eyes wandered to the roofs of the houses behind them on Illinois Street. She heard the Illinois Street Gang playing over there, baseball, she suspected. She unbuttoned her jacket and unsnapped the flap on her nursing bra, put the baby to her cold breast and let her mind wander, wondering if her mother had breastfed her. Surely not. How could a mother leave a child after that?

The baby was asleep when Pauline held open the screen with her hip and let Matthew pass out. They had both changed clothes. Pauline wore a dress with a full pink skirt that had black panthers parading playfully here and there. Alice noticed the sequins that snaked along the yoke of her dress—they glittered. Matthew had exchanged his suit for Levi's and a golf shirt, which did not go with the jeans and did not suit him, but his mother had given him the shirt for Christmas. Matthew had a tray of sandwiches and Pauline had three beers, held by their necks. She said, "Kids are eating in front of the TV. I granted permission for one day only, tomorrow back to your rules. Let's eat."

"The party is at four," Alice said. She was famished, but had not thought to feed her family or her friend.

"I'm just looking out for you; beer is good for nursing mothers, and we'll have time to sober up," Pauline said. Then she cocked her head at the picnic table where Matthew was setting the places and said, "If I lived here, I'd eat out back all the time. Love those trees."

"Even bare?" Alice asked.

"Especially bare. The better to see the birds."

Alice could not remember the last time she'd spotted a bird in her yard. Monarchs, yes. They were out of hibernation and looking for mates. They'd lay their eggs on milkweed and then it would start all over again.

"I give up," Alice said and moved to the sunny side of the picnic table and settled the milk-breath baby in her lap. She helped herself to a sandwich; picked out her beer and let the two of them talk.

Pauline stayed back with her when Matthew walked across the street with the girls and Tony to the block party. Pauline said that she would watch the baby while Alice got dressed. "Spiffed up," Pauline put it.

"Tell me about the woman who lost her little boy," Pauline said and sounded more like a nurse than a friend.

Alice couldn't form a picture of her husband telling Pauline the story. Pauline had sat between Janie and her sister, Clara, at the christening. She suspected Janie had told the story of the turpentine-soaked rags and how they'd spontaneously combusted. "No one was to blame," was how everyone ended the story.

Now there was nothing to do but answer questions while Pauline sprawled across her bed, crushing the red silk. Alice's stepmother had told her to take it. "Get it out of my house before the moths get at it. Your mother adored red, not me."

Alice wondered how she would know such things.

Alice wanted to tell Pauline not to squash the quilt, wanted to tell her about her mother disappearing; how as a child she'd fantasized about her mother coming back to teach her to read, to walk her home from school. She didn't want to say another damn word about the explosion.

Pauline must have sensed something off because she said, "You really like this puffy thing? It's nothing like you." And Alice didn't know if her friend had come here to see her or simply to make her think twice about everything.

"So, these neighbors left town or just the neighborhood? Temporarily?" Pauline asked and then nodded at herself when Alice nodded.

Alice stepped into her walk-in closet, which was something to be proud of, but not before she saw Pauline move to the rocking chair. Neither of them had bothered to walk across the room to look into the bassinet, which they'd kept dragging from room to room that day.

"Bob and Teresa are living here in town. Bob's work is at the Air Force base. The house is sitting empty. It smells, Pauline. When the wind blows, and in this place it blows day in and day out in March, there is this stench. No one has started any repair work. It just sits there with the garage door blown off."

Pauline nodded slowly and said, "Nobody can fault any of you for celebrating today. Let me tell you, you can't be sad for other people. It never works. I mean, you can be sad *for* them, but you can't do it *for* them. It never helps."

So, Matthew out there in their playroom had ratted her out about the sadness, told her own friend about leaving the baby and Tony with the two girls, who were little girls, while she locked herself in her closet in the dark. Mutinous anger rippled through her. But she didn't want to be angry and didn't have the time for it. Pauline would just disappear again, back to her two young children and her sick husband. He had cancer—something in his spine—and was bedbound. Pauline wanted him to enjoy the short life he had left, and so they'd had a second child after his diagnosis. Pauline hadn't minded sharing that story. Why would she? Nothing about it saddened her. She'd written all that in her letters.

Alice was taking longer in the closet than she needed. She disliked Sundays more than any other day of the week—it often brought her up short—and today she could taste a sour apprehension that there would be trouble. Sometimes, Teresa drove down Indiana Street, back around Illinois and down Kentucky; the neighbor women had all seen her, even on Sundays.

A neighbor from a block over greeted Alice and Pauline at Blossom's back door. She was twisting a purple balloon, and the stupid thing was shrieking. The woman and her husband made a team. He blew up the balloons while their two beagles sat at his feet. Today, they'd dandied the dogs up in matching red checkered bandanas. Sometimes, the pair of dogs did tricks. That would be later. Matthew usually wanted to leave the neighborhood parties before the beagles performed.

"Let me at that baby," the neighbor said as she tossed the unfinished balloon sculpture at her husband. She made that "Give me the baby" gesture that all women knew, even the childless ones.

Alice lost track of Pauline in the first few minutes in Blossom's kitchen as she stood there admiring the sheet cake that one of the women had baked and decorated as the Hundred Acre Wood. They'd chosen a Pooh Bear theme for Clara Anne's welcome party and there was a stuffed bear for each child. Alice hoped they would have the good sense to keep the fourteen bears safely hidden until the end of the party.

Alice left the baby with the woman and headed outside. The party stretched across two backyards. She decided not to bother hunting anyone down. Kirk headed for her, a cigarette dangling from the rosebud center of his mouth. His face was always slightly sweaty and made her want to reach up and check him for a fever. He pulled the cigarette out of his mouth and, checking his back, passed it to her. She took a long drag and he said, "Better?" It was his backyard—he was married to Blossom—and their four all-boy boys were lined up on the six-foot-high cinderblock wall, waiting for their turn on the rope swing. It hung from an amazingly tall cottonwood. The Oliver kids would not be swinging on that rope, Matthew would see to that. Kirk draped an arm around her shoulder like the solid friend he was.

That night around eight, Alice left Matthew and the children in Blossom's den and took a seat at the kitchen table with the women. She didn't bother to catch up with the chatter. She passed the baby to Blossom, who wasn't much for babies, but said that since it was a girl, it couldn't hurt. When Teresa walked through the back door, her face was bloodless, her eyes defiant. She wore a spring coat that looked like it might slip off for lack of shoulders. She held her right arm under the coat, clutching something. When the neighbor women talked about it later, they agreed it had mostly been scary what with her arm hidden there.

Teresa's eyes skipped around the kitchen and found Alice. She pointed her chin at her and came closer. Alice felt her milk let down. It was warm and it dripped into her lap and ran down one of her legs. Alice knew it would stain the red, polished cotton dress that Janie made for her, and she felt badly about that.

Without a break in her voice, Teresa said, "You could have invited me. It's my neighborhood too." Alice saw unfiltered blame.

Pauline got to her feet and put her arm clear around Teresa. It looked like they were set to do a line dance. Pauline said something about them not meaning to exclude her, and then Teresa said, "You're Alice's old friend. Don't patronize me." But she was not resisting the tight grip Pauline had on her. Then with the tip of her chin, she pointed at Alice and said, "It was like this. I wanted so little. I only wanted one child."

It was just a tiny, glossy pink package Teresa clutched under her coat.

After she left, the women sat in silence until Alice opened the gift. She passed the delicate diamond stud earrings around. Pauline approved of pierced ears on baby girls, and since she was a nurse and planning to stay for a few days, she said she would see to the piercing before she left town. Alice was too busy trying to calm herself to bother with little piercings that Matthew would never allow.

"Bedtime is my favorite time of day," Alice said by way of explanation as she got up from the table to take her children home. Matthew, who rarely had more than a couple beers, was a shade drunk, and said he'd follow her home in a bit. Pauline was involved in a conversation but stopped long enough to say, "Come back over, Alice; we'll keep Clara Anne."

"Put the porch light on," Matthew said as she left.

A memory of her own mother putting her to bed flitted through her mind as if it had wings. They were all living under one roof, with her older sisters and her brother, Mateo, in a handsome Victorian with a striking clock and a blind neighbor. Her mother had been happy. She wouldn't have wanted to be separated from her children. Mothers knew such things about mothers.

Alice's house was quiet except for the settling noises it always made at night. She laid her son on his small Birdseye maple youth bed. He rolled over onto his tummy; played out. She went to help the girls into their nightgowns. They didn't fuss when she turned out the light. She went back through the shared bathroom to get Tony undressed and into bed. His Pooh Bear lay face down on the rollaway, but Tony was gone. Alice's first thought was that he had escaped back to the party, but the front door handle was too high for him.

Her beating heart hurt her ribs as she searched the house and finally went through the utility room to look out back. She found him curled up in the new bricked-in enclosure, wearing snow boots. He was not really hiding, and it was not a new thing. It started one night in January when he spotted the sparkly green glass insulator atop the creosoted telephone pole that was parked proudly in their backyard as if it were a handsome iron lamppost. He'd called the thing his fairy.

Sometimes late at night when Alice was trying to sleep, she could hear a soft sound like a hum coming from the pole.

"Mother, Tony's out in the milkweed," her oldest daughter, Robin, had screamed when she found him there one afternoon. "It's poison."

Now, for maybe two minutes Alice stayed there, leaning up against the still-warm wall. It held the heat of the day. She felt like a good mother in those minutes.

In the dry New Mexico air, the green light beam had nothing to deflect it, and it rested on her son.

"Star bright," she said aloud.

"Bobby made the fairy promise not to take me," Tony said.

"I wouldn't let anyone take you, Sweetheart, not even a fairy," she said.

Without warning, she was so very sad for her mother. Such debilitating sadness that she didn't trust herself to lift her son up from the dirt. But then he stood and held his arms out to grab hold of her and said, "Mom, fairies are not afraid of dragons."

Matthew studied the snow boots on his son's feet and said to her, "You better get back over there to that kitchen debate before your neighbor ladies get Pauline all loopy." Alice knew that even though Matthew had sisters, he never would understand women. He crossed in front of her and pulled off the boots. Tony was playing possum for his dad.

"What did all those Teddy Bears cost?" Matthew asked and then when she tilted her head at him, he put that look on his face—the one he used when pretending he was only teasing.

"It all came out of the neighborhood pool," she explained, but was guessing.

They were working around each other. Matthew stood back and let her pull the covers up over the little boy before he said, "What is it, Al?" She hated being called that tough name. Her father would have backed him into a corner and explained Colombian manners had he heard it, but then the two men never saw each other now.

"Al?"

She closed her eyes and said, "I think Teresa has forgiven me—the earrings, you know."

"None of it was your fault. There is nothing to forgive, Sweetheart."

But he was wrong and as she let go of something that felt like blame, it felt like a clean breeze washing over her.

"Now go back. I'll watch you get across the street."

The women made a place for Alice at the smoky vigil around the kitchen table. Pauline sat across from her, balancing the baby in her lap and smoking a bummed cigarette. She cupped her hand and waved the smoke away, but Alice didn't much care about smoke. They were catching Pauline up on how Bob and Teresa had taken their boy's body back to their hometown in New Jersey, and how the service—there had been no viewing, no silk-lined coffin—had been for family only.

"No gravesite in Albuquerque," Blossom said and sighed. That was sad, they agreed. Blossom added that Teresa and Big Bob would never move back into their house on Indiana Street. "Story is that their marriage is going bad," she said.

Pauline put out her cigarette in the ashtray that kept moving around the table like a rumor and said, "You tell me what marriage wouldn't go bad after that."

They all agreed, the nodding passing now around the table, that Teresa had a wounded look. "She's lost so much weight," someone said. "Too much," someone said.

"Anger," Pauline said. "It'll eat you alive."

PART III

CHAPTER 15

ALICE
1955

Alice's older sisters had told her that their father had not kept one single thing that belonged to their mother. But Alice had kept her mother's red satin quilt and remembered refusing to leave home that night in Brooklyn without it. It had been on her mother's bed. Alice had screamed like a brat when her father told their ugly maid to take it from her. Alice always gave herself credit for biting that woman and had hoped she'd given her ringworm, because by the time they'd arrived in Albuquerque Alice's head was a mass of sores and her grandmother, Nana, had cut her hair off to her scalp.

"It's that red scrap of fluff you dragged around out in the yard that made you sick. You let that filthy dog chew it. See what you did?" Nana had said as she took after Alice with the scissors. Clara had run upstairs and hidden the quilt. It stayed hidden until Nana forgot that problem and started worrying about the woman she called the "garden-variety American" and the white piano Alice's father had bought for her.

In those early years in Albuquerque, Alice was sure her mother would come back for the quilt and would take her away and her sister Clara, too. Alice was sure of that and having this sureness was as close to having faith as she ever came. She remembered pulling the quilt out from its hiding place when Nana was away and calming herself to sleep by rubbing her thumb over its stitching and wishing very hard.

Old wishes.

And now her son, who already knew loss, truly believed that the light on the moldy telephone pole in their backyard on Indiana Street was a fairy come to look after him. It was a comfort to him. Late at night, Alice sometimes caught herself leaning into her kitchen window, watching for the fairy to light up. When Clara Anne was old enough, Alice would have Tony tell her all about the fairy.

Sitting in her parents' living room, Alice looked past her stepmother, Fran, out the big picture window at the sour pond and the green tumbleweeds that always took root in their backyard in spring. There wasn't a single real tree. All along the bottom of the window, Alice could see the nose smears their old long-nosed collie left. The dog had a foul smell and bald patches where it lost lumps of hair to the lacy-winged mayflies year after year.

"You'll see what she was," Fran hissed at her with the threatening tone Alice knew so well. Alice could see spit flying from the woman's mouth.

"Her name is Ruby," Alice said, but Fran didn't move. As a challenge, Alice held the baby up so that her stepmother could see her clearly and said, "I had planned to ask my father today if he thinks Clara Anne looks like I did—as a baby. He would know." Alice checked the baby's forehead for a temperature. A habit now. She bent over and placed the baby on the sofa and built pillows up around her. The sofa was a sectional, which was all the rage now, but it always split apart when Fran or her father sat there. Fran was a broad-shouldered woman, much bigger and taller than Alice. Alice turned back around, faced the woman, and lied when she said, "I'll need to nurse the baby soon if you don't get on with it."

It was a war between the two of them. Nothing new.

"Tony, let's go sit at the piano and play while Fran goes for the papers my father told her to go get." Tony was still teary-eyed. He had burst into tears when Alice and her father had shouted at one another. She'd been standing there holding the baby and had to gather up Tony in her spare arm. Just then, her father had taken the opportunity to turn his back on her.

"Give her what she wants," her father had shouted at his wife and, being a man who was free to leave the room when he wanted, he grabbed the collie by its collar and dragged it along into his study. Alice watched him kick the door closed. She knew he had immediately relit the cigar he'd been playing with from the minute she'd arrived.

"He's going to burn the whole damn house down one day," Fran said, as if she and Alice were allies. It was odd the way Fran sometimes did that, but dangerous to take her bait. That was when Tony had covered his face with his little hands and sobbed.

"He's afraid of fires," Alice said.

Clara Anne had slept through it all and was asleep now on the sofa. Since the baby's emergency surgery three weeks earlier, she'd grown content, could go hours without being fed, and hadn't once vomited blue-white milk across a room. But she was emaciated. Her little chest had been carved open, and she bore an angry scar from the top of her breastbone to her tummy button.

"I'm not leaving without the divorce papers," Alice said.

"Your father's divorce never was your business..."

Alice saw the woman swallow her next words and knew that those words would have been, "you brat." Fran had said it so often when Alice was growing up here in this house that it wouldn't have mattered, but it would have started Tony up again, and both women knew that Juan, on the other side of his study door, was listening to every word.

Alice lifted Tony up onto the piano bench. The piano sat in front of the west-facing picture window and over the years had turned an oatmeal color. Alice sat, composed herself, and played a minor chord and began, mostly speaking the words: "I love Paris in the springtime." Alice had heard the rumor from her oldest sister, probably started by Fran years ago, that her mother had become a nun and gone to a monastery in Paris. Fran took off in a stomp, and the parrot that lived in her father's study began hollering. Alice made a silly face at her son and he mimicked her.

"Mama, where is Polly's nest?" Tony asked. Alice's parents were slow-witted with names. The collie was named Lassie.

Alice said, "I don't know," and realized she'd never considered that before. Her grandfather had brought the parrot to her parents, from Colombia, at least ten years earlier. Alice's brother had wanted to name it Contraband, but he didn't live in Albuquerque and the name hadn't stuck.

"Parrots don't have nests, I guess," Alice said and the two of them studied the backyard. It was a wreckage of weeds.

Tony said, "Polly has a cage."

Alice could hear Fran upstairs. She thought for a moment about how Fran had to feel being ordered around by her father. But if only Fran had been sorry just once for her or her brother and her sisters maybe, Alice would feel some compassion. The moment passed.

"Not Fran's fault," Clara had tried to convince Alice over the years. Maybe not, Alice had admitted, but she didn't need her sister's permission to get the divorce papers. And so, she hadn't told Clara what she had planned. And she hadn't told Matthew either.

"I love you. Isn't that enough?" was what Matthew liked to say when she brought up her mother and how she intended to find her. But one night after Bobby died, she'd said, "No, it is not enough that you love me." He'd slammed his fists into the arms of her one fine piece of furniture and left the house. He was gone until late that night and their oldest daughter, Robin, had started a crying fit that woke her sister and brother. Alice didn't like thinking about that night, and so she put her hands back on the keys and played a little lighthearted song.

It was five minutes before Fran returned. Alice put Tony's hands on the keys and said, "You play something now." Fran hated children playing her piano.

Alice moved over to the sofa and unwound the red blanket from Clara Anne. Alice had requested red when she brought Clara Anne home from the three-day hospital stay. "An eternity," she'd told Janie, who'd looked after her other children while Alice sat in the hospital nursery staring at her tiny baby.

"Only male infants get pyloric stenosis," the pediatrician had declared after Clara Anne had vomited across his exam room, hitting the walls and his shoes. "Better than new," he said the morning after the surgery, his tone of voice different. And so, Janie had gotten right to work on the blanket. "Gladiola red," she said, but then she was a gardener.

Fran slammed a leather packet on the coffee table and lit a cigarette. Once she had taken a drag, she said, "Your mother was a bad apple. These papers prove it. Never in all these years a word from her. The modern woman taking off without a care." But then Fran read romance paperbacks.

Alice heard the blood pounding in her ears and heard Matthew's words, his kindness late that night when he finally came home after he'd disappeared. He found her on the back patio, smoking. "Careful, Alice. I'm on your side, but you don't know what you'll find if you go looking. That's my only concern."

Alice took the papers and stashed them in the diaper bag. She checked the baby and then wrapped her loosely in the blanket and nodded to Tony to come help her with the bag.

"My father is a coward," Alice said. "He kept his children from knowing their mother, and you helped him." Alice paused to see if Fran had anything else to say and then said, "You can call him out of his hiding place. You wouldn't want him to burn down your precious house." She was speaking way too loudly and woke the baby, but Clara Anne didn't cry. Alice let herself out, and as the door closed behind her, she said, "Go fly a kite."

She didn't know how she came up with such things, but it

made Tony smile.

"Proud of you, Little Man," she said to him because she knew it was what children wanted, to be cherished.

Two weeks later, Alice was still rearranging the few memories she had of her mother into a new story she was telling herself. The divorce papers included a short list of things, mere things, Alice thought, that her mother was allowed to take from the marriage. Alice kept reading the list over and over, trying to convince herself that she remembered the bookcase in the sun parlor and the antique chair given to her mother by her mother. And she was certain she remembered the brass-banded cedar chest. Her mother had also been given the personal possessions of Tessie Casanova. Alice remembered Tessie picking her up from nursery school and walking home with her.

Clara had so little free time. She lived clear across town and worked nights as a nurse at the Crippled Children's hospital. Her three boys usually ate dinner with their father on trays in front of the TV. When Alice called and told her what she'd done, how she'd confronted their father, Clara had said only, "Oh, Honey."

Clara never did hold a grudge. It was as if she forgot any slight Fran threw at them and every cruelty of their father. She just carried on, staying cheerful and busy. Alice loved her dearly.

That night, after she'd told Clara, she told Matthew. She gave him the six typewritten pages to read. The baby was down, and the children were asleep, and he had the TV on, but he flipped through the pages. "Your mother was the plaintiff?" he said without looking up. "How'd that happen?" Alice watched as he withheld any further judgment as he read. He was not much of a reader. He often told her he'd read everything he ever wanted to read in high school. He always looked pained when he read, and he looked that way now. But she hadn't given him the memo that had been tucked in the back of the leather pouch that she'd come to think of as the *Let the Matter Rest* memo. And she hadn't told Clara either. She needed to think about it.

Alice had always loved those hours after everyone was in bed at night when, if she held her own breath, she could hear them each breathing. It was her time to put on the TV. It used to be her time to smoke too, but she'd given that up or told herself she was trying. But these nights, she just sat in the silence and mourned her mother and cursed her silently for what she might have intended. Some of her worst suspicions about her father had been proven true in the papers. Still, Alice could not settle her mind on his blame and yet the memo made it all so much worse. Plus, she'd never seen a legal document before and she didn't know anyone who was divorced. A neighbor who lived a block over, who she'd met once at a bridge game, told everyone she wanted a divorce. It had put a shadow over the game. Said she'd head straight to Reno if she had the money. She must have seen the look on Alice's face because she'd said, "Don't fret, Honey, it happens."

In the next weeks, Alice lavished attention on her children, babied her two oldest daughters, while they were still young enough to believe that she adored them and admired things they did. She started French braiding Robin's hair each night and played cards with them in the afternoons after school and she took them all to the library where she studied maps of New York City and Brooklyn. She checked out *A Tree Grows in Brooklyn*. It made her remember things, and she was unable to finish reading it. She tried hard to remember her mother reading to her, brushing her hair. She tried not to quarrel with Matthew so that he would finally agree to take her to the laundry convention he went to every other year in New York City with his folks. Excelsior Laundry was the Oliver family business.

"When Clara Anne is two, I'm going," she said to him one

night when she was getting into bed. He said, "That's awfully young to leave a baby, Al." And then he simply turned the lights off. She felt fury turning her into something dangerous. She waited until he was asleep and went into the living room and smoked until her anger exhausted her. The next day, she lost her balance on the back steps and twisted her ankle, making it swell up, and she used it as an excuse to take time off from housekeeping and told Matthew to bring home dinner from the Chinese restaurant on Central Avenue.

Early one morning when Alice knew Clara would be home from working her night shift, Alice called and told her about the note in the leather pouch and said, "I want you to see this memo for yourself. I don't want to read it to you over the phone. You have to see the handwriting and the stationery."

"Okay, Honey," Clara said. "Come over tomorrow. It's my day off." And so, in the chaos of Clara's home, baby Clara Anne slept in the playpen that Clara had left standing in her family room all the years since she'd brought her first baby home. Tony played with Clara's three-year-old son, who had a teepee filled with a collection of cars and trucks.

Alice laid out the divorce papers on Clara's kitchen table. She'd already told Clara what they said and had read parts to her; had read her the list of things their mother had been allowed to keep. But now, Alice pointed to the paragraph that began: "*Further ordered, adjudged, and decreed that the defendant, Juan del Palacio, shall have the sole custody and control of the six infant children.*" Clara shook her head like she was trying to clear it. They'd already agreed when talking on the phone that infant meant children. They both read on silently, only pronouncing the names of each of their older sisters and their one brother. They read about their mother's visitation rights. "*Twice weekly visits to be within the State of New York.*" The document spelled this out and even noted the times and days of the week.

The two of them took a breath and looked at their children playing together and the baby sleeping. Clara was pregnant with her fourth child, and she patted her stomach and lit a cigarette. She had offered Alice one earlier and Alice had wanted one, but it was on her list of things to stop.

Alice punched her index finger at a line below the paragraph they had just read and read aloud, *"In the event that it becomes necessary for the defendant to leave the United States of America for any foreign country in the interest of conducting business of import and export, he may take any and all of said children with him, but shall return said child or children to the United States of America within a period of one year from their departure."*

Clara shook her head as if she had a tremor. Alice stood and went to check Clara Anne. But she really didn't look at the child and wouldn't have noticed if Clara Anne was missing because when she stepped back to the kitchen table and took out the memo, she had to go back to the playpen and check Clara Anne's forehead.

"Come check her, would you?" Alice said.

Clara held the child's wrist briefly, pulled her top up to look at the scar, and said, "She's peaches and cream. A perfectly healthy baby."

The undated memo was typed and double-spaced, and the paragraphs were numbered. In the margin, someone had written two notes in a fluid script. Alice and Clara knew it was their Uncle Carlos's hand. All through their childhood, he'd sent the six of them letters and books he personally inscribed, writing each of their names with a flourish.

```
1. The final decree provides that the ex-
   wife is entitled to visit the children
   twice a week in the State of New York.
   The exception to the ruling is in the
```

event that the husband is obliged in the pursuit of his business to leave the United States in which event he may take the children with him but must return them within a period of one year.

2. The husband is not now residing outside the United States so that for the period for which he has been residing within the United States in some other state than New York, he is technically in contempt of court.

3. It is unusual for the punishment for a contempt of court to amount to anything other than a small fine. This contempt of court would in no way affect the custody or control of the children

4. This contempt of court in my opinion is not punishable in any state other than the State of New York.

   The net result is that although in technical contempt of court, in my opinion, nothing can be done about it by the ex-wife. She cannot in any way disturb the custody or control of the children. Her only remedy is if the husband comes back to New York, to apply to the court to have him punished for contempt of court. If he doesn't come back to New York, there is nothing she can do.

   If I were in the same position as the husband, I would be inclined to sit tight and do nothing with the possible exception of writing to the lawyer who handled my divorce proceeding and explaining to him that financial conditions being what they are it was impossible for me to make a living and support my children in New York. By reason of this fact, I was obliged to go to another state to earn my livelihood and support my children. That I have not the means to return to New York and furthermore, it is unlikely that I would be able to make a livelihood if I did have the means to come back to New York.

Juan, I would not write such a letter as Herbert suggests.

I would ask the lawyer who handled my divorce whether or not under these circumstances it would be possible for him to apply to the court for a modification of the original decree giving my ex-wife the right to visit the children twice a week and have some other arrangement substituted.

Juan, I would not do this. Let the matter rest.

"Okay, here's what I think. Some lawyer named Herbert wrote this," Clara said as she flipped back to the first page. "He's telling our father to sit tight and do nothing." Clara put her hand on Alice's. Then she turned to the last page and read aloud the handwritten note.

"I would not do this. Let the matter rest."

"Contempt," Alice said. "How can we forgive our father for doing this?"

And then Clara, who was equal parts scatterbrained and quick-witted, said, "Mother must have believed we were taken to Colombia. But it looks to me like he left her there in Brooklyn waiting for us to return after a year."

"And we didn't, did we? And we didn't go to Colombia," Alice said.

"Mother did visit us once," Clara said.

"I remember," Alice said. "There was so much shouting. It was winter." The memory was frozen in Alice's mind and always had been, but she'd never been able to tell Clara what she remembered most—the pearls.

So instead, because Alice saw that Clara was near tears when they both should be livid, Alice said, "You had a kitten and we had Tessie who loved us children, especially you."

Clara cleared her throat and said, "And our father always took care of us children. Maybe he had his reasons that we don't know about."

"Don't make excuses for him. Contempt is a crime. He took us away, and our mother was left with nothing."

Alice started clearing up the pages. "She's probably dead," she said, and Tony left the toys he'd been playing with and came running over to put his head in her lap.

"It's fine, Little One," Alice said.

Clara got busy making them all snacks, and Alice nursed the baby. And then while the boys played in the backyard—careful of the many rosebushes that Clara loved and babied—the sisters talked about Clara's pregnancy and how it would be her last. Clara put her feet up on one of the chairs and told Alice how her feet killed her after her night shifts at the hospital. And then Alice put the papers in the diaper bag and promised her sister it would not be so long before they saw one another again.

CHAPTER 16

ALICE
1961

Alice was on her own in New York City—standing in line at the Metro Theater two blocks from their hotel, studying the map her husband had marked up for her—when she spotted the New York City Public Library nearby on Fifth Avenue and Forty-Second Street. Alice turned—faced the street—putting behind her the posters of Audrey Hepburn in her long black dress, black gloves past her elbows, and her hair teased and frosted and swept up in a style impossible for Alice to try for herself. Her own hair had been thin ever since she'd had ringworm. She touched the scars it had left on her neck and ignited what she knew was a far-fetched resentment at a mother who let this happen.

She didn't want to step out of line after waiting all this time in the cold. But she did take a big step to her left, briefly, to look up the block. She squinted to read the cross street she was on. She'd only just recently learned the term cross street.

Forty-Ninth.

Matthew had walked her here after lunch and stood in line with her until he had convinced himself, or so it seemed, that she could take care of herself and would make it into the theater safely and back to the Waldorf Astoria on Park.

"On Park," he'd shouted to her from the corner after he'd put an extra ten-dollar bill in her hand and smiled broadly as if he wanted her to be beholden or grateful. She tilted her head at him and tried to look grateful, but it was at such a distance that she knew it didn't matter.

Alice decided that she could walk the seven blocks to the library. It would be easy. Blocks here in New York City were short. Brooklyn was out of the question though, a bridge and trains and all the rest. She'd given up on that.

She studied the map some more, but kept losing Broadway the way it snaked around. The hardest part would be trying to figure out which way to turn once she got to Fifth Avenue. It was not like Albuquerque. You'd have to be a fool to get turned around in that town with the barrier of the deep blue Sandia Mountains in the east and all that blinding sunlight coming from the west.

"The avenues are the wide ones," Matthew had repeated over lunch that day. He loved this city, had been coming here since 1953—with his parents—for the bi-annual American Institute of Laundries convention. He and his dad were both officers in the organization now.

Four trips without her. He had a bag full of reasons. Four years earlier, when he had refused to let her make the trip with him, she had started speaking to him in detached tones. She'd thrown a vase at him. It was made of thick leaded glass, too sturdy to shatter. "Sometimes, I want more than you," she'd shouted and then let him leave town without truly making up with him. She'd kept the apology letter he'd written on stationery from the Barbizon-Plaza Hotel. He'd sent it via Special Delivery.

He'd written, "I do hope there is a little love in your heart for me, and that you will forgive me for all of my selfish ways."

It was now nearly two o'clock and already winter dark—the third day in a row without a hint of the sun. To her way of thinking, it was a relief from Albuquerque's winter sunshine. Torrents of dirty rainwater had run down Park all morning. The blue-black afternoon shadows were calming as she stood in line for the romantic comedy.

Alice turned back to the posters. In the glass doors, she

caught the reflections of New Yorkers, mostly men camou-flaged by their two-button grey wool suits, as they passed by, never taking notice of her. It was pleasant watching them going about their business with hats on their heads and places they needed to be. Suddenly, the day lightened, the sun found a way to angle up Forty-Ninth as it headed west. But the blue sky was less real to her than the blue shadows had been, and she wondered if she was in the mood for a comedy—if she ever was—if she had developed a taste for sadness when she was a child.

"Lady, you going in to see this movie or not?" a man behind her she hadn't noticed in all those minutes said. She turned to face him. Without waiting for her reply, he raised both his unkempt eyebrows and then gave her a head bob. He wasn't looking for an answer, and she decided she didn't owe him one.

She could smell the man's damp raincoat. She wanted to wave her hand at him and tell him to shoofly, but she didn't have the nerve. She let herself wonder if her mother would have been the type of woman to shoo a complete stranger. And she asked herself, like she'd done a thousand times, what it might have been like to be her mother.

She turned and, in her own time, caught up with the two women in line in front of her. Then the line moved into a lobby and she could smell the matted, stained carpet and she real-ized this theater was long past its glory days, even though the bellman at their hotel said it was once known as the cathedral of the motion picture. An usher pointed his light at her feet and marched down the aisle, and before she was even seat-ed, the newsreel began. She didn't much care about current events. Her mind was made up that she would leave here in thirty minutes—news or no news. She tried to read her watch, but it was too dark and didn't illuminate like Matthew's.

The newsreel assaulted the audience with what felt like alternating flashes of light and dark. The expansive beach in

Cuba, and then a barbed wire and concrete wall separating what from what she did not know. Then even as Khrushchev, wearing a suit that did not fit him, promised, "We'll show the imperialists what we can do," she was thinking it wasn't a bad thing to want to know who her mother had been. Finding out did not mean anything more than knowing. She squirmed in her seat like her daughter Clara Anne had a habit of doing.

Why did she feel like she was planning a crime?

She watched the movie to the beat of her heart thudding. On screen, a yellow taxi pulled up to the curb and Audrey emerged—an independent woman. She was alone in the early morning wearing her evening clothes—a slim black dress, a pearl choker—looking into the windows of Tiffany's, a coy smile on her face. It was hard to figure that smile on a woman who was alone. Alice knew she wouldn't need to stay to the end of the movie to know Holly Golightly's story. Besides, she knew the music and the ridiculous words to the theme song, "Moon River." Her two older daughters had the sheet music and were learning to play it. Those lyrics didn't sound a whit like they belonged in a comedy.

Alice's second oldest daughter, Rhonda, thought the song "Moon River" was very romantic. Rhonda liked romance. Shortly after school started that year, Alice found a chunky gold necklace in Rhonda's pajama drawer when she was putting away the laundry, bundles wrapped in dark blue paper that Matthew brought home twice a week. Rhonda first told a telltale white lie about the jewelry, and when Alice gave her a look of disbelief, she sobbed her way through the story, her lips quivering. Jimmy Eaton had given her the necklace.

"His mom is okay with him giving it to me," Rhonda insisted.

"I don't blame you for wanting to keep it. But when a boy gives you something you don't have to hide, it will feel better," Alice said.

And Rhonda, her little sweet lips still quivering, said, "But

Mom, you have to agree it is so romantic. I know I'll remember it my whole life." Alice saw the pearls scattering. It was the sound of each of them hitting the floor that haunted her, and she always wondered if they'd been left there to find a spot to rest.

Alice couldn't get comfortable sitting there in the dark theater, plotting her afternoon, with time ticking. She stopped squirming and fell into the film, thinking she'd ask Matthew to take her to Tiffany's. "I'm crazy about Tiffany's," she'd tell him. And now Audrey was pulling on a little dress, tying a sash around her tiny waist. And then a big hat like Easter Sunday. Matthew wouldn't care much about a hat, and so she'd tell him how pathetic they'd made Mickey Rooney out to be with ugly teeth—no longer cute little Andy Hardy fudging the truth and mooning over Judy Garland.

Audrey was in trouble, lost or hiding from someone, and so pretty and so sad, and yet here she sat in this dark theater. She thought about her four children sitting together in the dark, haunted KiMo Theater. The night before, she and Matthew had called home and surprised the heck out of the sitter, or at least Alice hoped so.

"Mom, the babysitter took us to the wrong movie, *Babes in Toyland*," Tony had said in a rush of words. He explained about trees that came alive and how Clara Anne cried when a boy was locked in a birdcage. "First, the bad guy tried to sell the boy to gypsies." Tony sounded as if his heart was broken. It was a lot to sort out when you and your husband were sharing a telephone booth in the Waldorf Astoria lobby—in another world.

And then, Robin reported when she finally—as the oldest— took the phone back to summarize, "Can you believe she took us to the KiMo Theater—and get this, her boyfriend went with us. He lives out in the desert someplace in a trailer. We had to go pick him up."

"Robin, don't let her hear you tattling."

"Don't worry. She's outside smoking. She does that while we eat dinner alone. It's not even dark yet. Then she comes inside and stands guard while we do the dishes, like she's too good to do dishes. She calls me 'Mother Goose' and Tony, 'Little Boy Blue.' She's mean is what she is."

Alice heard Clara Anne sniffing. The children had never been left before. She said hurriedly because Matthew was motioning to end the call, "Robin, I am very sorry, but can you help Clara Anne so that she doesn't cry? Please."

Matthew took the phone and said, "Your mother is having a ball. You should see her in her cocktail sweater. She misses you kids." He hung up and brushed his hands together. An optimist was what Matthew was. He just wanted it all to be good.

Alice had in fact made the sequined cocktail top herself, a silver sequin on every other stitch of azure wool.

Knit, purl, knit, purl.

It had made her dizzy as she mostly listened to Jack Paar late at night—her husband and children sound asleep. She'd made her skirt too, of midnight black taffeta and had left the hem raw, carefully pulling threads. Her skirt had tickled her calves when she was already dizzy with the sound of her children's voices ringing in her head, the smell of her own French toilet water, and the hum of tall people dressed for evening crossing the lobby in every possible diagonal.

"Damn that woman," Matthew said. "I heard you tell her to take them to see *Hatari!* at the Hiland. Those buffalo skull lamps at the KiMo would scare any kid out of their wits."

But then Matthew's parents had arrived in the lobby—very smart looking—her father-in-law smelling of hair cream and her mother-in-law of rose water. Matthew perked up and stood taller. His mother was wearing a violet brocade suit she had sewn. The lapels flared stiffly, and she looked like a tulip. Her pearls had dipped down dangerously into her cleavage, and Alice watched as Janie clutched them at her neck and reeled them in.

Alice complimented her on her dress. She had seen the

fabric when Janie bought it and had watched her as she sat at her black sewing machine. Alice's mother too had sat at a black sewing machine, sewing for her and her sisters. She and Clara had thought the machine looked like a baby elephant. It was one of the few things Alice remembered from their home in Brooklyn and it too had gone missing.

"Talked to the kids," Matthew announced to his parents. "Got some stories about the sitter; well, she is no substitute for Alice."

"Of course she isn't," Matthew's mother said. She then turned to Alice and said, "Look at us all dressed up in New York City." Janie didn't hug her—kept her distance and left Alice to walk with her own husband. They weren't girls, after all. Janie took her husband's arm. It was a kindness Alice knew to expect from Janie Oliver.

And then as they stepped into the ballroom, Alice took in a big gulp of air and collected this one single moment in her life. Pauline had told her to do that very thing. "Collect one single moment and freeze it. Then when you think of this trip, think of that moment. I'm telling you, make a memory of it."

And now, standing outside the Metro Theater, all it took for Alice to catch a taxi was stepping to the curb and raising her arm. She had not known it would be so easy to do this all on her own. But it was disorienting to zip away in the opposite direction from where she thought she needed to go, splashing rainwater up onto the sidewalks.

"Forty-Second Street Library. Fifth Avenue entrance?" the cabbie asked.

Alice told herself that Matthew wouldn't come looking for her, door-to-door committee meetings and all that. He wouldn't be waiting outside the Metro Theater when the matinee ended. Well, she was in the taxi now. Done was done. If that happened—if he showed up and leaned against the wall waiting—she'd tell him she left early...bored with Audrey. She'd tell him she'd taken a walk.

"Where you from?" the cabbie asked, as if he was interested in every little bit of personal history that stepped into his cab.

"Corpus Christi, Texas," she lied. Reluctant to give the truth. It was the way she distinguished herself from the Oliver family.

But then, remembering her manners, thinking too late it might be something only a tourist did, she asked where he was from.

"Big Ivan from St. Petersburg, Russia. Founded by Peter the Great, the Bronze Horseman," he said. Then he began to recite a poem in what she knew was his version of a Texan accent. He waved a hand in the mirror and said, "We Russians all have big bear hands. Do you have bears in Texas?"

Lying always got her in trouble.

But today, she was sure of her own persistence because she said before she knew she was going to say it, "I was born in Brooklyn."

"Brooklyn, the American Motherland," he said as if in celebration. "That explains those blue eyes. I sure didn't think Texans had blue-eyed girls." He turned around to grin and took a corner on two wheels, and she felt as if she were in a cartoon with Goofy at the wheel. Ivan had big ears, too.

Softly, in Audrey Hepburn's French accent, Alice heard herself say, "I'm not in a terrible rush."

As if in response to her concern, he slowly glided to a stop at the curb and held out both his open paws at the proud marble lions lounging on each side of the many steps leading to the library.

"When you go in, you pass by Patience there on the left and by Fortitude on the right." And then he offered her his hand from across the seat and said, "In friendship." Here was another moment to capture, she thought, and heard Pauline saying, "Click."

She took his hand and then handed him the ten. He gave most of it back.

"Please," she said to him, offering a dollar. He waved that away.

When she stopped several steps beneath Patience, she looked back, but another woman was stepping into his cab.

The scent of the huge winter wreaths that each of the lions wore made her wobbly. A memory came to her, and it wasn't about Albuquerque or her home on Indiana Street. It was Brooklyn...a wreath on their front door. She took two more steps and grabbed the base of the platform where Patience stood.

In the giant lobby, she retraced her steps twice before she found the card catalog room the information lady had directed her to. "Can't miss it," the woman said.

Alice sat patiently in the Main Reading Room, waiting for her number to be called. The room went on forever and the blue ceiling with the billowing white clouds kept her distracted, like the tourist she was. The woman who called her up to the front counter took a book out of a tube, handed it to Alice, and said, "*Little Talks to Little People*, sounds interesting."

"It's by my grandfather," Alice said. And when it was clear that the woman was willing to listen, Alice explained that he was her mother's father, a minister, and then Alice asked where she'd need to go to look up things in a newspaper. "About my mother," she added.

"I see. Farrar is your grandfather. Women are harder to research. It's still possible. You need one room over for newspapers. That way. But you can't take the book. We don't lend."

The woman seemed sorry.

"Why don't you take a seat and read some first?" And then, to coax her away, the woman said, "Just to get a flavor. It's referenced as a book of vignettes."

Alice did not step away, and the librarian was not really coaxing her. She was wrong about that. The woman reached for the book and flipped to the back and took a card out of the yellowed envelope. "Look here," she said. "This shows when it's been requested over the years." She pointed to a stamp—in blood red—on the card tucked into a little pocket. It said, "Missing."

The librarian stabbed her finger at that word and said in an unforgiving voice, "A patron most likely walked out with it in 1932. See there. And then, lo and behold, it reappears in 1934, in March. Not requested again until 1950. Back then we lent out. See there. After you take a look, just drop it in the return slot and you go look for your newspapers. Wait, hell with the rules. Bring it back to me and I'll keep it at my desk in case you want another look."

Little Talks to Little People was a nice title, Alice thought. She took a seat at one of the long tables and placed her grandfather's book under the lamp. She made a few notes on one of the cards in the stack left there for patrons. She smiled at herself—a patron. But she could not spare more time, not with what she wanted to look up down the hall.

She had to wait behind several men before she could return the book to her librarian. "I will try to come back," is all Alice took time to say.

In the next room, a man behind the long, high counter said without looking at her, "I need dates, name, subject," and then when he took a moment to look up, he said, "Let's start with one of each. Is this an obituary?"

She couldn't answer. She heard Matthew speaking to her—"Careful what you wish for." But he hadn't lost his mother or his memory of her.

"A wedding?" he asked.

"Yes, a wedding, 1914, Ruby Farrar and Juan del Palacio."

He nodded and without so much as turning his head to look behind him, took a book off a shelf.

Looking up again as he flipped pages, he said, "This is New York City you're after? The Grey Lady? So, this wedding was here in New York City?"

Alice felt her nerve leave her.

"Where was this wedding, Sweetheart?"

"Brooklyn, I think."

"Well then, you need the *Eagle*. Hey, Sallie," he called over his shoulder as he reshelved the large book. "I'm sending you a lady looking for a wedding.

"Persistence," he said. "Sallie will find your wedding. Those are the easy searches. We New Yorkers love society and not just high society. Of course, we don't shelve the tabloids here—whole other story on those pages."

"But listen, it doesn't have to be just weddings," Sallie said as she climbed up onto a tall stool behind the counter. She put two heavy ledgers on the counter and said to Alice, "I always start with two decades. Rare for people to be sure about dates."

The man winked at her and hit a bell, calling up the next patron.

Alice spelled the names for her, and then while she waited, she watched people taking their newspapers and finding a place at large desks to flip through them. She felt like she was in an old movie. The librarians were not bothering to be quiet, but the patrons were silent. The only sound they made was turning pages.

Alice was so busy figuring out next steps that she did not see Sallie slip off her stool. She'd disappeared. Then Alice noticed the wooden plate Sallie had placed on top of the two books on the counter. It said, "Sallie will return." And so, Alice waited. But Sallie did not return to the counter. Instead, she came up behind Alice and said, "Let's take that desk there by the window."

Sallie was the one to turn the pages. With the paper open wide, she said, "Upper right, front facing. Nice. Pretty woman." She looked up at Alice.

The photo was faded but her mother didn't look feral. You didn't hear such things said about your mother, things Fran had said over the years, and just wipe them out of your head.

Sallie read through the article and then whistled as if interested and said, "Quite a legacy, Miss Farrar had." Alice finally looked away from the photo.

Sallie read aloud:

"Dr. and Mrs. James Farrar's daughter Miss Ruby Farrar was a bride last night. She was married from her father's home on President Street to Juan del Palacio, a very representative Colombian (South American) family doing business at #16 Beaver Street in Manhattan. His family rests high in the mercantile world of New York.

The season's array of pretty brides includes beyond a question Miss Ruby Farrar who made the most attractive of pictures at her home, 857 President Street, last night at the residence of her father and mother. Dr. Farrar being the famous minister of the First Reformed Church on Seventh Avenue.

Dr. Farrar married his daughter, being assisted by one of his sons, Edward Farrar, who is now an Episcopal divinity student.

There were white roses in the library and pink Killarney roses over the rest of the house. The bride's mother wore a gown of orchid net draped in silver. Miss Farrar wore white satin with a bodice of lace. Her veil was of tulle, in a comb effect. She carried a bouquet of lilies and a French blue lace handkerchief, a gift from her mother."

"Oh my, you will want to copy this out, won't you? I'll help. Some days no one comes for the *Eagle*."

"Yes," was all it took for Sallie to go retrieve a stack of larger paper and two well-sharpened pencils. Alice could feel herself grow dizzy—her mother carried lilies—it was the lilies. Alice had always hated the thick sweetness of lilies. She shook her head and made a memory of that address—857 President Street—and froze the thought of a gown of orchid net draped in silver. Alice didn't know how someone could be draped in silver.

But instead of taking one of the pencils, Alice opened her purse and took out the map. She asked Sallie to show her where Beaver Street was. Her father, now that he was in his seventies, was forever talking about his glory days with his father and brother Carlos on Beaver Street. "16 Beaver Street," he sometimes shouted at her before he started into one of his stories in Spanish, but she had not been allowed to learn Spanish, and so he had no real audience for his stories.

"Right here," Sallie said. "May I?" and when Alice nodded, she put a big star on the map with a #16 next to it. "Right off Broadway."

People came and went. Alice read to Sallie, who copied the article out, and then they exchanged jobs and Sallie read as Alice checked for accuracy. The librarian had a lovely hand.

"Did you keep that blue lace?" Sallie asked. Alice shook her head, meaning she hadn't, and Sallie patted her on her shoulder and said, "I didn't find any obituaries for your mother or your father in New York City or Brooklyn papers. I know, you didn't ask me."

Alice walked out, carrying the pages in a manila folder. She stopped briefly at Fortitude. Or was it Persistence? She could not remember, the lilies and all.

Streetlights were coming on. She checked her watch. It was not yet five. She turned right on Forty-Second Street and then left on Park. When she saw Forty-Third ahead, she knew she was headed uptown, and knew she would have to skirt around Grand Central Station. She and Janie had visited Grand Central the day before with a tour for the wives. They were not infatuated with the place, and it was cold. "Dated," Janie said.

But Alice wasn't cold now, not with her face burning hot. The streets were wet though and her shoes were taking the brunt of the short walk.

It didn't matter. Shoes could be brushed clean, dried out.

But she wanted to get back to the room before her husband so she could put the pages away. Not everything had to be discussed. She was not ready to share. Six more blocks was all.

That night, Alice and Matthew grabbed a late dinner with his parents at a small Italian place the hotel recommended. "Short walk," Matthew had said.

Janie had spent the afternoon with old friends she called the "Laundry Queens." Janie was a social creature, but she looked done in.

"Big shoppers," Janie explained before she began listing the gifts she'd gotten, one for each of her grandchildren.

"Seventeen," Alice's father-in-law said by way of emphasis.

Alice didn't mind the distraction. Her husband had been looking at her as if he had a sixth sense ever since he'd let himself into their dim hotel room. "Good, you found your way," he'd said, as if he had been truly afraid she would not come back.

She had changed into another dress, something not quite fancy enough for her kid dress shoes, but her others were drying out after she'd done her best to scrub off the water stains.

She hadn't noticed the blisters until she stood up after dinner. They'd walked over to Madison was all, but she would be limping by the time they were back to the hotel.

"Would you take me to Tiffany's in a taxi?" Alice asked Matthew, knowing this was the exact time to get her way, what with his parents there to hear.

"Alice, they have to be closed."

"Oh, I know. I don't need to go inside. Just the windows will do."

"Janie and I will be turning in," her father-in-law said. He was a dear man. His grown daughters called him "Dear Daddy." Alice could not bring herself to call him that, as he wasn't her father.

Matthew whistled for a cab. His father stopped in his tracks and glowed as if he might applaud and announce for passers-by, "That's my boy." But then Matthew was the apple of his father's eye. Janie took her husband's hand while they waited to see Matthew and Alice climb into the cab.

The cabbie said that of course he knew Tiffany's, that it was the heart of New York.

"I thought that was Grand Central Station," Matthew said, because he loved to make people laugh.

"That'd be the brain," the cabbie said and then everyone laughed.

"Have you got your map, Al?"

She handed it to him, but it was too dark in the cab, and so he closed it and put it in his coat pocket. When they pulled up on Fifty-Seventh, the driver said, "Shall I wait?"

"Well, I was trying to see on the map what kind of walk we have ahead of us," Matthew said.

Alice felt her stomach drop. She wouldn't make it back to the hotel.

The driver opened his hand and Matthew surrendered the map over to him. Alice saw Matthew point at the hotel. He had marked it.

"I better wait," the cabbie said.

Alice posed for her husband in front of Tiffany's, and he said he wished he had a flash for his camera. Then he said, "What is that starred on the bottom of the map?"

She felt faint-headed.

"My father's and grandfather's office. It was on Beaver Street. Number 16. Way downtown, I know. Far." She thought she was talking like Holly, but he wouldn't know. He wouldn't see the film she knew.

"Hey, Buddy," Matthew said as he leaned into the window of the cab. "What would it cost me to go down to Beaver Street, near Wall Street, and back to the hotel?"

"I don't need to," Alice said. "It's a silly thing to do. And I've seen Tiffany's."

But her husband said, "Let's go. Someday my grandchild may go looking around downtown Albuquerque for Excelsior

Laundry. I'd like that."

"I got blisters today," she said as he climbed in next to her.

She thought she might have smiled at him because he said, "Oh, Alice," and reached for her foot.

CHAPTER 17

ALICE
1962

For ten minutes, Alice sat in the church and tried to remember her wedding ceremony here in this very place. How she'd hated her dress—forced on her by her stepmother—the color of fog. The church had been torn down and rebuilt since then and renamed a cathedral. Not that she knew or cared what that meant. Once, standing in line at a fabric store where she and Janie shopped, Alice heard a woman ahead of her say, "We are members at St. John's Cathedral," as if that gave her some dignified status. Alice had wanted to ask her if members got some sort of badge.

Alice didn't know why she got so riled up sometimes.

She had to admit that St. John's was stunning, but it disoriented her terribly. Light filtered blue by all the stained glass hovered like a vapor, refusing to land on the thick carpet. This church, where she was married, was nothing like the church she and her husband attended now, along with his parents. Sunlight poured through the clear windows of that Presbyterian church where each of her children had been baptized. The Oliver family preferred simple and sunny. Alice wondered if she'd grown accustomed to their outlook, because the darkness was haunting her here and it was as if she was hearing prayers spoken during some long-ago worship service.

Old prayers. Old services. Old wishes.

Alice thought maybe it was the rancid smell of Sunday's roses sitting in a foot-tall vase at the altar that was disorienting her thoughts. They made her think not of her own wedding, but her mother's. The *Brooklyn Eagle* newspaper article had said there were Killarney roses scattered all over the home where her parents had been married. Alice had asked Janie about that type of rose and she'd said they were known for being able to grow in shade.

"Are you Alice Oliver?" A woman's voice came from somewhere in the dark, behind the altar. Alice had not heard anyone come in. Whoever it was had been lurking. Alice wasn't going to answer to someone she couldn't see.

"I told you on the phone that your meeting with Rector Sims would be in Cathedral House, not in the cathedral."

There it was, that false dignity again.

The woman made her appearance, not that Alice much noticed or cared what she looked like. Short was all she could have told anyone.

"I thought churches were always open," Alice said and wanted to add, "for prayer," but she didn't wish to be the one to put on airs, not here, not with all those prayers left behind. And then Alice said too softly for the woman to hear, "I cannot believe you'd shoo someone out of a church."

The woman wasn't bothering to listen, and as she walked away said, "Cathedral, not church. The Rector will see you in his office." Then she flipped her hand over her head and pointed to the door where Alice had entered. Alice stood and whispered her own little prayer of thanks. She had not known how to address the man she'd be seeing, and now she knew.

Rector was it.

Alice stepped out onto the courtyard. The grass was bluegrass, long-bladed, reminding her without warning of a childhood birthday party. They had been playing games on a shady lawn under tall shade trees, and all the little girls twirled their full skirts. Her sister Clara had gotten grass stains on her white sundress. It couldn't have been here in Albuquerque, not with that shade, not with that long-bladed bluegrass, but it had happened. Dreams never came from nothing.

Albuquerque was known for its Bermuda grass. It made Alice's skin crawl the way it grew out of cracks in the pavement. But the grass here at the cathedral was different. Someone had taken care to water it. It surrounded a circle of painted pavement with a pattern Alice knew to be a labyrinth.

She checked her tiny gold watch and saw the minute hand quiver. Still ten minutes early.

She walked across the concrete slab to the center of the design. It was not how it was supposed to be done. A person was supposed to wander their way into the center. She knew that but thought of hopscotch and decided maybe there was more to that childhood pastime than she'd ever realized. Clara Anne adored hopscotch.

Once Alice had brought her two oldest daughters here to this courtyard. She'd been pregnant then with Tony, and her obstetrician's office was nearby. The two girls had sat in her doctor's waiting room while she was seen. Afterwards, she'd taken them to lunch at Woolworth's and Matthew had met them there; the four of them seated in a row at the lunch counter. Matthew always let the girls spin on the stools. After lunch, she'd wandered around downtown with them, even if it was no longer the place it had once been. Even then, the movie palaces were losing out to the Hiland Theater with its big car park out back. Then she had remembered the labyrinth and took the girls there. They began at the outer opening, each trying to find her own way in with no help from her and when they'd found the center, they began spinning in the fall sunshine. Finally, they'd gone over to sit on the short wall, on either side of the stone cherub. Alice wished she had a picture of her little daughters sitting next to that round-faced, winged angel. But it wasn't an angel—had no wings—Alice saw that now. It was an Indian child sitting cross-legged.

But then she saw that the Indian child was holding a large bowl, a birdbath, and a tiny brown bird was dipping its wings in the quarter inch of water. Maybe her daughters had seen that bird. In all these years, she had not thought of that afternoon.

Alice threaded her way back to the opening of the design, which was just paint stained into cement.

"A pattern with a purpose," a man said in a dry, elderly voice. She knew he was the rector because he wore a collar. He'd officiated at her wedding, not that she remembered him. But now he had a doddering way of walking as if he knew he was prone to falling. Alice watched him make his way to the grass.

The rector took Alice into the office building, past a fancy oak desk where the woman she'd seen earlier was sitting. It looked as if she'd just polished the desk. Alice watched how the ceiling light threw a pattern on the polished surface.

"Just so you know, I leave for lunch at 11:30," the woman announced.

"I'll mind the phones," he said and nodded to Alice that she should go ahead into the office.

A few stray toys lay on a dark red carpet in one corner of his office. Stepping in behind her, he went to the toys as if to collect them and then didn't. "Mothers often need to bring their little children along," he said.

Awkwardly, he directed her to take a seat and then took her hand in a handshake as if they had just met and then crossed himself and mumbled a question that sounded scripted.

She told him that no, she wasn't here about her marriage, but that she was here to talk about finding her mother. He waited calmly, as if he'd been trained not to be thrown by the first thing a married woman revealed.

Alice had told her husband about her appointment at the church, but only that morning. She'd waited past Christmas, past summer, and then waited until all her children were back in school. Covering the lunch hour when her two youngest children would walk home from elementary school required advance planning. Her neighbor, Blossom, had agreed to have Tony and Clara Anne come to her house for lunch. Blossom was Catholic and her boys were parochial schoolboys. Those kids didn't come home for lunch and so Blossom was free as a bird all day long. Alice knew she liked watching daytime TV and having a smoke out back between programs.

None of her neighbors had time these days for morning coffee at each other's kitchen table or afternoon card games; they'd all gotten so busy mothering, everyone said, but Alice thought that was an excuse for women who'd grown to like being alone or maybe they no longer wanted to talk about marriages that had melted away into their second decade.

Blossom hadn't asked why Alice needed to be away at lunchtime and Alice hadn't offered; they'd never been that type of friends.

The rector wrung his hands as if he was polishing an apple, and when she stayed quiet, he said, "Of course, I remember your family. Your father and mother were some of my first parishioners." He hesitated and then said, "I understand when people move to the heights. St. Marks up there on the mesa is a handsome parish." He gave her an honest smile and said, "Plentiful parking." And then he rubbed his hands together one last time and said, "Alice, would you like a cup of coffee?"

"I would," she said, because she'd been rushing that morning and had time only for one cup that had been cold by the time she finished it, and because it would be the secretary who would have to go to the trouble.

He pressed a button on his phone and then, holding it while it turned the rather long fingernail of his index finger red, he said, "Gladys, two coffees please. Bring cream and sugar." And then he let go of the button.

Alice was holding her purse in her lap and took a moment to open it and pull out a large manila envelope. She put it on his desk, pancaked her hands on top of it, and then began. "Of course, you have only met my stepmother, not my mother. My parents were divorced when I was five years old."

He shuddered as if cold and reached for a handsome pen that rested next to his desk protector. A pad with the Episcopal seal sat there waiting for him, and he tapped it with the wrong end of the pen.

"That was 1930. There were six children. I'm the youngest in the family. Only my sister Clara and I live here in Albuquerque."

"I see," he said and wrote on his pad.

"My father moved us here to Albuquerque when I was little." She started to explain that he had business interests here, which was their family story, but she left it unsaid.

"Where was it you were born?" he asked, and when she said Brooklyn, his face turned sad as if she were a refugee. She knew the look. She and Matthew sometimes took the children to potluck dinners in the basement of the Presbyterian Church where they watched slide shows about refugees. They always brought nonperishable can goods to those dinners along with a casserole. But she could see on the rector's face that he was catching up; he had taken her father for a widower who had found a new wife. He swiveled in his chair and turned to a framed document behind his desk. He pointed to the fourth line down and read, "Episcopalians recognize that there is grace after divorce and do not deny the sacrament to those who have been divorced."

Alice was trying to figure her way past grace when Gladys made a crashing sound into the closed office door. It was the rector's signal to get to his feet. He stepped gingerly over the telephone cord and went for the door. Gladys carried a polished silver tray. The rector made no offer to take the tray from her and so she set the tray down on his desk and said, "I'm leaving for my lunch hour. The phones are yours."

"I believe you already warned me, Gladys."

The woman had pulled on a snagged cable-knit sweater. It sagged at the elbows. She glared at Alice, making her glad she was wearing her new sleeveless shift. Jackie Kennedy had set the style for sleeveless, even for women like Alice who were well into their thirties.

"I'll muddle through," he said as the door slammed behind the woman. Then he and Alice were silent as they stirred sugar and cream into their coffees. The china cups were too delicate for coffee. The cups also bore church seals. As a child, she'd been taught the significance of the nine blue crosslets. She could not explain them now.

Then in a voice that no longer sounded elderly, he said, "How can I help you find your mother?"

"My father left my mother behind in Brooklyn when we moved here. From that day on, he only allowed us to live in *his* past. We were warned never to speak of her. But I've learned that he never even let her know where he had taken us. She was left behind. You see, we traveled by ship from Brooklyn to Corpus Christi under an assumed family name, like criminals."

Alice sipped her coffee, put it down, and picked up the envelope. She removed a single paper and passed it across the desk.

"My mother's maiden name was Farrar. Ruby Farrar, the daughter of a famous pastor in Brooklyn, New York. In 1914, my grandfather and my uncle, Edward Farrar, who was an Episcopal divinity student, officiated at my parents' wedding." She pointed at the words on the page. "They married at my mother's parents' home in Brooklyn. I copied that out of the *Brooklyn Eagle*."

She nodded when he said, "May I?" She finished her coffee, which had never been hot, while he read. He put a crippled index finger on the page and traced it across each line as he read and then said, "Reverend Edward Farrar sounds to be ten years, give or take, my senior. Divinity student, you say? This is who you wish me to find—right? I take it you are thinking he can tell you where your mother is."

She nodded again, impressed by his skill at sniffing out her motive for being here.

"Perhaps you have other information about your mother?"

Alice set her thoughts in order and said, "I know I look like her because there was a picture of her in the paper I read when I was in the New York City Library last year. I know she might be dead. If not, she is at least sixty-five. I've heard rumors that she had the notion of becoming a writer or that she became a nun and moved to Paris."

He was writing it all down.

Then he said, "So, you never saw your mother again?" He shuddered. "You didn't hear from her?"

Alice knew that if she said anything at all, it would have to be an explanation, and she did not have one. So, she waited, and he said, "Can you tell me what *you* remember about her... small children often have the raw material of memory. Sight, smell, touch—those things." He looked over at the toys.

No one had ever asked her this, not Matthew, not her sister Clara, and not her mother-in-law.

But then the phone interrupted, and it took three rings for the rector to compose himself enough to push the button and pick up the receiver. A woman's voice thundered through the line.

"I have your tuna sandwich sitting here, growing stale on our kitchen table."

The rector had his eye on his notes, and so the woman, who was certainly his wife, said, "Waiting." And when she got no response from him, she said, "Leaving it in the refrigerator unless you want me to give it to the cat."

He said, "Thank you, dear. The refrigerator will do. I must have stepped into the wrong pew today." Then he replaced the receiver gently, as if laying a baby down to sleep. Alice decided to answer the question he had not asked.

She said, "When my last daughter, Clara Anne, was born, I made a vow to myself to find my mother because I decided, well, I just knew in my heart that my mother could not have given up her children. Especially not little ones like me and Clara. It would have been like having a child die to lose us the way she did." Alice looked around the room, back over each shoulder before saying, "You must understand that I'd grown up hating her for not looking for me. And then I thought of the Golden Rule and decided I had to find her. And it has taken me so long."

Alice wanted to reach back and touch the scars on her scalp. It helped to do that when she got lost in a loop of thought. And here she was, wondering if he left his office every day to go home for a sandwich with his wife. She might have gone on that way in her thoughts had he not said, "Actually, Alice, you've happened on the Silver Rule. But the important thing is that with either of those rules, they mean nothing unless you understand, the way you do, that it is *your* move."

What she liked about this man was that he was not trying to console her. She reached her hand back and rubbed her finger across the largest of the scars.

"I remember that my mother had a sewing machine. She sewed clothes for us, and she smoked. She smelled like cigarettes. She had lots of books, and she read to me when she put me to bed. After she left us, I could not fall asleep at night."

"A nun in Paris? Catholic, you think?"

Alice noticed the sparkle in his eye and said, "I never believed it. Just a rumor passed around by my stepmother to make my mother look bad."

"I can make some calls," he said. He held up one finger at a time and said, "You'd like to know if she's well, where she is, if she has died, and you'd like to speak to her. Is that right?"

"I'd like to know what happened unless she's dead. Then I'd like to know where her grave is. I am so very tired of hating her and blaming her." Alice thought she'd go on, but she could see he understood and there was nothing left to say.

"I don't think you've shared this with your father. Am I right?"

"He can't know," she said and then decided to say it all. "I want her to know what happened to me and my brother and sisters. Especially to Clara and me. We were so young."

Alice wasn't really hungry when she left St. John's. Food had never been her thing, but she thought that the lunch counter at Woolworth's would be nice for old times' sake, and she needed the walk—had the time because the elementary school did not let out until 3:30. She came out of Cathedral House and headed north and turned on Central. She passed by an old dress shop and saw two salesclerks, arms crossed, standing around on tired feet, looking like caged animals. The Sunshine Theater was still open for business. She and Matthew had had their first date there. She passed by the Burns Brothers Pharmacy—closed down years ago and now a pawnshop with bars on the windows.

Alice ordered a grilled cheese sandwich and watched the cook melt a chunk of butter before he got busy. She had the counter to herself; it was late for the lunch trade.

She'd left her car parked two streets up from the church, and she headed straight there after lunch. She drove up Roma, skirting around the two blocks where the laundry that her husband and father-in-law managed sat. She imagined she smelled freshly pressed linens. On Tuesdays and Fridays, her husband gathered up the stuffed laundry bags that hung in their utility room and brought home freshly laundered things on Mondays and Thursdays. It was her job to put things away. They didn't own a washer or dryer.

And then she was turning right when she did not need to be going that way at all. She'd drive up Central past the University; thought maybe she'd make a loop around Spruce Park where Matthew took her to park once, but when she got there, the traffic was heavy, and she passed by the turn and kept heading east. At Nob Hill, she turned onto Campus Boulevard and drove by Matthew's childhood home. Her mother-in-law had babied a garden of lilacs and hollyhocks there, so old-fashioned now. The lilac bushes were still there, just green bushes now in fall, but the house was ramshackle.

Turning back now, she took a left on Central and then finally turned onto San Pedro and then Constitution Avenue. She was in her neighborhood now and began to see children walking home from Mark Twain Elementary; it was a proud brick building, which pleased her. She wearied of the stucco. She spotted her own two children who looked to be deep in conversation. Clara Anne would be the one talking. They didn't see her pass; they didn't know to be looking for their mother.

She turned onto Indiana Street; thought she'd wait in the car for them, take them for ice cream floats at the drive-in. Her older girls had after-school activities and would not be home until later, and so there was time yet before she started dinner. But the children never saw her sitting there in the car in the driveway. They walked right past her to the front door.

"Mom. Let us in," Clara Anne called out in a hungry wail. This child of hers was always hungry.

Alice stepped out of the car, and Tony shouted, "There she is."

Alice tossed the house keys to him and he reached up and caught them.

It was nearly time for Matthew to pull up in the driveway when the phone in the kitchen rang and shook the wall. Tony continued playing out back with Clara Anne, but Robin and Rhonda had tucked themselves away in the bedroom they shared. Robin had a stereo record player, and Alice heard the same song over and over. Robin sprinted from the bedroom for the phone, and took the time to put on a face that said to Alice, "Why would this be for you?"

But it was for her, and she took it, not knowing who to expect this late in the afternoon when families were soon to sit down for dinner.

"Alice, this is Rector Sims. May I give you a short report?"

"Okay," she said and nodded at her daughter to move along, back to her teenage music. It took a second, more severe look to get her moving.

"It required no detective work on my part to get to this point. I found an Edward Farrar in the master church directory, retired and living in Florida. Then a few calls later, I reached the wife of Reverend Edward Farrar." Rector Sims cleaned his throat and said, "She called her husband to the phone, but I was certain we had been disconnected. Finally, he answered politely but cautiously. I think maybe he was expecting a death. We spoke only a short time. I caught him unawares. Several times, he asked me to repeat who I was and where I was calling from. As is often the case, I think he heard Mexico and his mind went to south of the border."

Alice took a pad from the junk drawer and stood at the sink watching her son who went back and forth between the monkey bars and his little fort in the back corner of the yard where Alice knew Clara Anne would be hiding. The boy from next door had hopped the fence to play with them. Her husband would have brought in ponies if that kept any of their children playing out in the backyard year after year.

Rector Sims said, "But once he got his wits about him and understood who I was and what I was about, he said that he wasn't authorized to reveal any information about his sister. I let him sort it out rather than insisting. He talked in a few circles but wouldn't tell me if she was alive or where she was. I think we can understand that a brother would be cautious. And I believe that if your mother was dead, he would have said so. Done and done. He certainly wasn't protecting you, Alice, by being secretive. He was protecting her. He said he would contact another brother who would know better what to do. He said it would likely take some time to call me back. There we have it—for now."

Alice had nothing to write on the pad.

"Did you tell him who was looking for her? I mean, which child."

"Ah yes, I explained that her youngest daughter had been

in to see me."

"But he didn't ask about us?"

The rector took a long breath and Alice heard his wife's voice in the background. He had called from home. Alice thought of that tuna sandwich. Then he said, "I caught him off guard, Alice. I'm betting it was as if someone had come back from the grave. He was exceedingly surprised, or so he said. Let's give him and his brother time. You've made your move. It's their move now."

"Yes," she said. "I suppose it is, but I don't think we will ever hear from him again."

The rector said, "The other brother's name is Jimmy. Edward said Jimmy was the one best able to handle this."

"He'll call you back?" Alice asked and wondered if anger would eat her alive if he didn't call back.

"Oh yes, of course. I asked him and he promised. Alice, it was as if this was simply a matter between two rectors who are trained to look out for others. And you must believe that this is only our first step."

Alice wrote on her pad, "Jimmy Farrar—Uncle Jimmy," and then wrote "Rector Sims" and below the names she put the date.

Later that evening, she went to the small desk that sat in their entry hall. She kept her parents' divorce papers in the desk drawer along with the *Let the Matter Rest* memo. She clipped the page from her notepad to the manila envelope. She put everything back into the drawer, locked it, and went to her dresser to hide the key under her stockings.

The fragrance of spring grass came to Alice that night in her fitful sleep. She thought that bit of memory might have lasted a second or two at the most. The fragrance had come in on a breeze—woken her—and yet the room was still, and then she remembered her mother on the lawn in the green gown. It was as if Alice was seeing that day rather than remembering it. "Uncle Jimmy," she said to herself and then in a whisper she said, "Uncle Eddie," trying to push herself back into sleep.

Matthew didn't move a muscle.

Anxiety kept her awake for another hour at least. Why would anyone need protection from her own daughter? But still she got up in the soft morning light when she could be alone before her day started. Standing at her kitchen sink, waiting for the coffee to perk, she looked out the window and steadied herself. Some part of her still expected to feel another blast from Teresa's garage, but what she felt instead was a sort of relief wash over her. There wasn't going to be another blast, and anger wasn't going to eat her alive. It was over. She had done her best.

CHAPTER 18

ALICE
1963

Rector Sims was sitting on the little wall in the garden at St. John's near the statue of the Indian child, where he said he would wait for her. It was early spring and not yet full dark at six-thirty. He said, "We have time, Alice, to make a round of the garden." He walked her slowly around, pointing out the night-blooming primrose. "It's a treat to be here past dark. When you leave tonight it is sure to be in bloom. Some gardeners consider it a weed, but I baby it for the scent."

He then walked her to his office and pointed her to his worn chair that sat behind his desk and showed her how to make the call. He'd put a cup of hot tea next to the phone and said, "I thought it might be too late for coffee. I'll be in the sanctuary listening to choir practice. Come by before you leave, would you?"

Alice said that she would write him a check for the long distance. She had saved out a check from the ones Matthew gave her for groceries, but he said that'd be silly, that this was church business, this business of rebuilding a family.

Alice took the card with her mother's phone number out of her purse and put it on the desk protector. She then wound the phone cord into a tight circle, held it tight, and thought that just maybe her mother had not wanted to be found. Alice thought that had she been a Catholic and had Rector Sims been a priest in a confessional, maybe she could have told him that she was worried that her mother had never been lost but rather had been hiding all along. But face to face, Alice could not tell him such things. She didn't want him to be sad for her.

She dialed and when Ruby said hello, Alice said, "I hope I'm not calling too late."

The silence hung and so Alice had no other choice but to repeat, "I'm sorry; I know it's late where you are."

She regretted her sudden apology and sat up straighter in the rector's cushioned chair and fought the panic that told her this had been a mistake—all of it. Matthew had told her as much, repeating his worn-out warning, "You don't know what you will find, Alice." It was his way of telling her that she was making a mistake. As a man accustomed to being the apple of everyone's eye except hers, Matthew had always been a bit cautious of telling her what not to do. But he had his ways.

She'd had to argue with him to let her drive downtown at night. "I'm going and that's that and I'm going alone." She'd stopped short of calling him Mr. Oliver, which is what her mother-in-law called her husband when she got her back up and Alice's back was up. She pointed her pretty, long finger at her husband and then pointed him toward their kitchen because while they could not see them, they both knew their four children were waiting at the kitchen table and Clara Anne no doubt would be taking in every word. Clara Anne fretted whenever they argued. "The children are waiting on dinner for you," Alice said. "It's Robin's turn to wash and Tony's turn to dry."

Her mother answered before Alice had her wits about her. "This is a good time," Ruby said.

Alice wondered if they were destined to go on like this, being polite and saying nothing much. But then as they each said in unison, "Thank you," Alice's panic ebbed, and she had no idea why she'd said "thank you." And then they both laughed nervously, which was a type of honesty, Alice figured.

"All the children are in bed now and mostly asleep here at Overbrook," Ruby said.

Alice thought maybe she was smoking because of the pause, but her voice had been soft, not rubbed raw like a smoker's.

"My brother Jimmy told me that you were the one to find me. I am grateful to you, Alice."

Ruby stopped short then, as if she'd been interrupted or had changed her mind about saying something more, or at least it felt that way to Alice. There was no ease in any of this, it was all hesitancy. "Be merciful," Alice told herself not for the first time that day.

Alice knew exactly where they were starting. It was a joke to think it was a fresh start, like making a new friend. But it was the gratefulness part that threw her. She's scared of me, Alice thought. My own mother scared of me because of what might happen to her. But it was apparent to Alice then that if anything important was going to be said, she'd have to start. And so, she blurted out, "I never understood. I was a child, and I didn't understand, and I waited and waited to be told what happened. I needed to know how you came to leave us. Clara thought we had been kidnapped." Alice fooled with the scar at the nape of her neck.

Ruby cleared her throat, her voice thin now, and she said, "I loved you. I loved each of my children." Ruby paused again, and it gave Alice time to admit to herself what she might tell Rector Sims when she found him in the sanctuary; that she could remember loving her mother fiercely when she was small, but grew to hate herself for loving such a selfish person as her mother.

Ruby was speaking again, "Jimmy tells me that each of you children have children of your own…"

"I'm thirty-eight years old. We are no longer children. But when I was a child, we left on a ship, and we were in a heavy fog that just hung over us and I was frightened and seasick because it was rough seas. And then I had ringworm and Nana shaved my head." She wanted to say then that she hated Nana too, but it felt like a confession she did not feel safe making.

Her thoughts were a jumble. She saw herself slamming the heavy black phone down to be done with it.

"Alice, I was terrified that you children would never forgive me. And now that you have your own children, it is too much to ask. I know. Finding me won't change the past. I am terrified all over again."

Alice wondered if she was crying.

"I think, Alice, that it would be best to get to know each other first by talking like this on the phone now and then and maybe writing to each other."

Alice said quickly, "Okay." And for the first time in memory, she felt oddly cared for, like a child should be made to feel. And she repeated, "Okay."

"I'm getting a phone for my parlor," Ruby said. And now Alice had a passing vague impression that she sounded like Clara. It was the cheerfulness in the middle of all the sadness.

"Okay," Alice said again.

"But before we go," Ruby said, "tell me please the names of each of your children and their ages and just a bit about each one of them."

Alice listed them out, saying that her youngest, of course, was named Clara Anne after her own sister. But it was hard to choose one single thing to say about each of her children.

And in the bit of silence that followed, Alice wondered if her mother would then ask about her sisters and brother—ask to be told one little thing about each of them. But when she didn't ask and didn't mention them, Alice felt judgment seeping in and squinted her eyes to look at the statement about grace behind the rector's desk. And so, she said, "I'm told you teach braille to blind children and live there with them."

"Yes. Overbrook is a beautiful old place with gardens and enormous old pin oaks. There is a shady lawn where the children can run and play, and I sit out there often and read and watch the children. Some children live here for years and some for only a short time to learn how to manage their blindness.

Some are abandoned here." Ruby waited a few seconds and then said, "I've lived here many years and I love teaching braille. It is a gift for the blind to be able to read."

Alice thought about Rector Sims waiting for her in the sanctuary and thought maybe he tended his night garden to avoid his wife. It was a hateful thing to float into her head just then, and she thought maybe it was the scent of jasmine making her loopy.

"Do you remember the beautiful shade trees in our front yard?" Ruby asked.

Alice did not. Why would a five-year-old remember trees?

When she had hung up, Alice sat there with her hands at rest in her lap. In the days before the call, Rector Sims had met with her twice for what he'd called gentle counseling. He had told her, "Just know, Alice, that it is human to float between affection and condemnation." Looking back at the phone, she thought that maybe she should have left it there and let it all go.

She was so tired of floating. But still she sat there letting time go by, until she decided she'd write her mother right away and would send her the picture Matthew took of her at Tiffany's. And she'd begin the letter, "Dear Mother."

CHAPTER 19

ALICE
1989

It was Clara Anne who found Teresa. "It's what I do," she'd said when she called her mom with all the information on their long-lost Indiana Street neighbor. And then Alice wrote Teresa a note explaining that Clara Anne, who was a reference librarian, had recently moved to New Jersey with her family and that she, Alice, was coming out in the spring to help Clara Anne with spring break. Alice had fought with herself over the wording and had used a piece of lined notebook paper to write out several drafts. She had hesitated to mention Clara Anne's three little boys.

"It just so happens I live one town over from Clara Anne," Teresa wrote back in a note on pearl blue stationery embossed with her name. It was the same last name as it had been all those years ago even though Teresa and Bob had been divorced forever, or so it seemed to Alice.

Midmorning on Friday, Teresa picked Alice up at Clara Anne's house. She called ahead to say she would toot her horn.

"Pretty house," Teresa said when Alice climbed into the car. Alice saw in a glance that Teresa was still pretty, and it pleased her. "I'll enjoy meeting Clara Anne in person soon. We talked on the phone quite a while, you know. I hope she will be happy here in Jersey. I am. But it's where I'm from."

"She's working at it," Alice said.

"Yes, there's that. I bet she already knows her neighbors and having three little boys will help her get to know people."

Teresa turned to Alice with a wide smile that Alice remembered, and then Teresa reached over and grabbed Alice's arm above the elbow, squeezed it, and said, "It's okay, Alice. We were good friends. Remember? And now we're going to have a good time at the Colony Diner. Let me tell you, Jersey does diners best."

Teresa led the way into the diner, which was narrow like a train car with counter service on one side. She headed up two steps to a sunlit room off to the side. Teresa seemed to know some people and did a little wave and head nod to a group of four women packed shoulder to shoulder into a booth.

"We can get comfortable back here. I like Erma's section. She'll keep filling our coffee cups until we ask for a check. Oh, unless you smoke—that section is in the back," Teresa said and made the gesture for someone taking a puff. So very sophisticated, Alice thought, and realized after all these years, decades in fact, that Teresa looked like Audrey Hepburn, had her fine chin.

"Not anymore," Alice said, and Teresa said, "Me either," and Alice knew they both meant more than they'd said.

Erma set identical plates of eggs with hash browns and thick crisp bacon in front of each of them and winked when she said, "Enjoy."

Then Teresa said without any lead-in, "Here's the thing..." She put her hands palm down on each side of her plate and she looked to Alice as if she might levitate.

"That day when I found the Teddy Bear you left on my front porch, I felt as if I'd been showered with mercy for what I had lost. Simple as that. I knew it was you, and I knew it was Clara Anne's bear. Am I right? I still have that little Pooh bear." She paused, but she didn't touch her food or her coffee.

"When we moved back here to New Jersey, I thought I'd put the bear on Bobby's grave, but I couldn't part with it and Big Bob didn't know how I'd sometimes drive by our empty house. So, I hid that little stuffed bear from him. Showing emotion was not his thing." Teresa paused again and made a sound that Alice recognized. It was the sound of someone taking an extra breath for what came next.

"Clara Anne told me that Tony died while climbing a fourteen-thousand-foot peak in Colorado—doing something he loved." Teresa barely lifted both hands off the table, and then pressed them flat so that the table jiggled.

Alice felt the familiar cocktail of grief and resentment bubbling up in her chest, recalling Clara Anne saying on the night her brother died, "At least Tony was hiking, doing what he loved."

Alice closed her eyes. She saw the green trike and then slowly she opened her eyes and held her face in her hand, holding tight so that the trembling would not lead to a gush of tears. Even after five years, the tears came in waves from the depth of her chest. She didn't hate the way the tears made her feel, but they numbed her, and she didn't want that today.

Teresa said, "When Bobby died, I took no comfort in knowing he'd died riding that trike around and around the garage. He'd gotten up at dawn on the last day of his life to ride that trike. Bobby loved that green trike."

"I remember," Alice said and played with the eggs. "And I remember how Tony would do anything Bobby did, even nap."

"I couldn't forgive myself, Alice. But finally, after fits and starts it came to me that forgiveness means giving up every last shred of hope for a different past." She rested her chin then in her left hand and stared out the window. The two of them stayed silent for some time.

"Maybe those two little boys were just talking back there on the bed while we played bridge," Teresa said. She began to eat like someone who had a healthy appetite.

"And so, tell me about finding your mother," she said. "Come on Alice, Clara Anne told me."

Alice had not expected this switch in topic, and she felt as if her emotions were being twisted like an old dish rag. She resented her mother for the intrusion.

Teresa said, "Listen, Alice, I knew your mother left you. Either you told me or Blossom. We all talked about each other. For Pete's sake, we knew when Blossom—good Catholic girl and all that—went on the pill."

Alice took a bite, finished, and said, "Finding her was exciting. She was working and living at a school in Philadelphia. And she was a writer. But she'd kept her children a secret from everyone in her life. So, being found was hard for her. I think she liked blind people."

"Why would she like blind people?" Teresa was still eating but stopped to break into a big smile.

Alice put her fork down and shook her head as if emptying it, then mimicked Teresa's wide smile and felt like a girl.

Teresa said, "I'll go first. I'll tell you what I knew. Okay? Your father, who, by the way I never once saw, got custody of you kids. Five or six of you. He put you on a boat—I guess a ship—and took off for Corpus Christi and then got you up to the garden spot known as Albuquerque. And you kids were told not to speak of your mother. Zip it. Sounded like a fairy tale to me, what with a wicked stepmother and all, who by the way I never saw once either."

"They didn't like Matthew."

"Everyone likes Matthew. Okay, fast forward to finding her," Teresa said and went back to eating.

"I got on my high horse with my father and demanded the divorce papers. You know how it was—no one had copies back then."

"So, when was this?"

"Well, Clara Anne was a brand-new baby."

Teresa said, "Wow. Hormones got ahold of you, you think?"

They laughed in sync.

"I guess I let it go after that because it was years later when I went to New York with Matthew and went to the library that I found enough to go on. I found the name of an uncle I didn't know I had."

"Back up—you finally went to New York with Matthew?"

Alice nodded and felt a bit like her teenage daughters lounging on their beds, talking on the phone—on and on.

"Well, I happened on a way to find this uncle. I mean, for years if we went someplace, I'd get the phone book and look for my mother's name. I got nowhere with that. This uncle was a rector in the Episcopal church and I found him with some help. And my mother...she was alive, working at a school for the blind in Philadelphia."

"Ah, blind people. I see," Teresa said, and they both smiled before Teresa added, "So, just living a life without you?"

Now, Alice closed her eyes. She saw her mother in her backyard on Indiana Street admiring the cottonwood trees. On that visit, her mother's face showed disappointment when she thought no one was watching her. When Alice stepped out back to join her, Ruby had said, "Sorrow taking wing." Alice didn't tell Teresa that part.

"So, you met her?"

"Yes, Clara and I brought her to Albuquerque for a visit, and she stayed with Clara. She told us that it was too late to apologize." Alice grimaced. "She said she got over it."

"Shit," Teresa said. "Maybe she just got on with it."

"Clara Anne did some research later and discovered she had remarried. It didn't last. She never told us about that."

Teresa leaned back in the booth and sighed. "I nearly got married again," she said and held her finger and thumb apart about an inch and went on, "Came this close."

"What happened?"

"I was lonely, and he came along and was fun. It was nice for a while. He had a house on the Jersey shore and lots of family. Italians! I knew he wanted his own family, but I was thirty-five, so it was silly. He liked to say, 'Let's see what happens.'"

"I have to laugh," Alice said.

"Go ahead. Please do." They both giggled then, and Alice

felt good about it.

Still smiling, Teresa said, "New Jersey diners are our confessionals."

"What's his name?"

"Michael, of course. Back in the day, every Italian family had one Michael."

"What happened to him?"

"Lives down the shore full time. Lotta kids and some grandkids too. He got on with it."

Alice said she needed to find the ladies' room, and when she returned, Teresa took her turn. After they had settled back in their booth, Erma came by with her pots of coffee. She offered to pour them a fresh cup from the pot with the orange handle. But Alice opted for a Diet Coke and Teresa nodded in agreement.

"Two diet sodas," Erma said and left them to it.

"Good; we got all that out of our systems. So, what all do you and your daughter have planned tomorrow in Brooklyn?"

Alice sat back in the booth and then began, "Clara Anne has done lots of research about my mother's childhood in Brooklyn. So, we're going to visit my grandfather's church and we will go see the brownstone my mother grew up in. In her letters, she wrote a lot about her childhood. It was without a doubt the happiest part of her life."

"Good for you and how kind of you to come out to help with those grandsons next week when they are out of school. Hope you rested up. Matthew didn't want to come along? To help?"

There was that smile again, and Alice wished for a cigarette. Or maybe it was just the companionship of women sitting around a kitchen table that she was missing. But she had Teresa and this morning. Erma returned with the sodas and said, "Old friends?"

Alice felt her eyes flood and her lip tremble. Erma set the sodas down and squeezed Teresa's shoulder before moving on.

"Matthew? He loves New York and believe me, he wanted to be here to see Clara Anne, but we own a shop...paint and window coverings. It's called Cover All's."

"Don't tell me. Wallpaper?"

"Yes; it's making a comeback, you know."

They both got a good laugh out of that. And then Alice asked, because she felt she should, if Bob was here in New Jersey.

Teresa fluttered her hands like a bird taking flight and said, "I don't even know if he's alive. But I'm betting that if he is, he's in Florida. Do you remember that camper pickup we had? God, how he loved that camper. He remarried soon as we got a divorce. I had to go to Reno."

They sat in silence neither of them minded, and then Teresa said, "So, spill it. I want to hear about the old neighborhood. Start with Blossom. Do you remember how she used to stand on her front porch and yell at those boys to come home for dinner? I hear one of her boys became a priest. Don't tell me, let me guess which one. The second boy, the one who was the spitting image of Kirk?"

Alice nodded, and they went on to cover all the neighbors on Indiana Street, house by house, and included a few on Illinois. Teresa asked about the woman, Paula, who had lived behind her. She and Teresa had sometimes stood out at their back cinderblock wall and talked and smoked. Teresa said, "You know, Paula wrote me once after her husband left her to go to Washington and work for Kennedy. He actually took their kids with him. How was that possible? Those kids were little."

Alice shook her head in little bursts and said, "Well, she moved soon after that. Never heard another thing about her. She didn't like us much."

"Can't imagine why," Teresa said.

They'd started with the late breakfast crowd and Alice saw that now the lunch crowd had thinned out. By the time the two of them left the diner, Alice felt full up with memories.

She thought she'd like a town where you could wander into a diner and stay hours, and it made her happy for her daughter.

"We needed that," Teresa said and added, "Just like back in the day."

"But then we all rushed back to our houses to clean," Alice said.

"Yeah, we kept house, for pity's sake. That's all we did. Over and over."

When Teresa pulled up at the curb outside Clara Anne's yellow Colonial, she said again, "Pretty house." She stopped the engine and said, "Here's my advice for you. I'm sure that people have told you that losing a son gets easier with time. That's crap. You'll see that it just stays the same and you just live with it. Ignore them."

Clara Anne hummed a little song as she finished up at the kitchen sink on Saturday morning. Alice saw it was a diversion tactic her daughter was using to grab her oldest son unaware and attempt a goodbye hug and kiss. He was eight. He slipped through her arms and, acting as if he was making a break for it, slid out the screen door. It was a game. He used the sleeve of his baseball jersey to wipe off a kiss that had not landed.

Clara Anne had made all the arrangements for their day in Brooklyn. Her husband would tend to their three boys, keeping a close eye on the five-year-old who liked to wander off.

Matthew had called the night before to remind Alice which lane to be in once they got on the bridge. "I'm pretty sure that you can get on the upper deck coming and going but watch for signs. The Verrazzano-Narrows is a double-decker. You will need to look to the south to see the Atlantic. You'll be looking at open ocean."

He was not finished telling her about the bridge. "Longest suspension bridge in the whole world when it was finished in

1964. Just imagine that." He said all that before she could get her say in.

"Well, it gets damn rough before you get to open ocean," Alice said.

He had sent her to New Jersey with handwritten instructions to get from Morristown, where Clara Anne lived, to the New Jersey Turnpike, across Staten Island to the Verrazzano-Narrows Bridge to Brooklyn.

It sounded like a long trip.

Now, forty minutes into their drive, Clara Anne pulled her shoulders up against her neck, flicked her bangs off her forehead, and ran her tongue over her lips. "Look, there's the towers up ahead. Shit, we're already on the bridge, Mom. This thing is a monster."

Alice hadn't realized there was any doubt that they were now suspended. She had felt the exact moment the land had slipped away.

Clara Anne's ruby red Honda Civic took the bumps as if it had a grudge against making the trip.

"Top deck. Good job," Alice said.

Clara Anne took her eyes off the road long enough to glance overhead at the blue sky and said, "I wouldn't want an entire bridge over my head. All those cars." She ran her tongue over her lips again and said, "God help me if we have to do that on the way back."

The bridge threw a shadow on the water, and Alice watched the image. She felt the bridge tremble. Her daughter was trembling too, but she took the second lane in with ease. She was doing exactly what her father had told them to do.

The humming sound the Honda made was loud even with the windows closed. It sounded to Alice as if their tires had taken flight, as if they had no traction. Alice reached across and put her hand on her daughter's back and left it there.

They had reached the midspan and were starting down the other side.

"It made me happy to see Teresa yesterday," Alice said as she studied her daughter. "Thank you for all this." And now she patted Clara Anne's shoulder. Alice never touched her daughters now without thinking how Ruby had a way of putting her hand on her sleeve and then removing it quickly as if that tiny bit of a touch had been enough, as if she had thought it was something mothers were supposed to do.

"Three hours at the Colony Diner, Mom?"

Alice removed her hand from her daughter's shoulder and made the gesture of talking hands and Clara Anne grinned and said, "I can picture you there."

Alice studied the open water. She would have liked to roll down her window and take a big gulp of sea air, but thought it might be too much distraction for her daughter. The humming was enough. "It'll be your first glimpse of the Atlantic," Matthew had said the night before on the phone. She hadn't corrected him. He didn't remember much of anything about her childhood, not the way she now remembered his—all those dear Oliver stories of trips west and picnics in the mountains. But she remembered the Narrows and decided passing over it was easier than passing through. And then she looked over at her daughter and said, "We are going to have a good time."

"Once we get off this damn giant swing," Clara Anne said and squirmed.

One of the things Clara Anne had picked up quickly in New Jersey was the knack for cursing. It had shocked Alice when she first heard the word "fuck" coming out of her daughter's mouth. Clara Anne pushed her bangs back and said, "I want you to know this is not a narrow spot to cross. Somebody just wanted credit for building the longest fucking suspension bridge ever."

Alice felt inclined to agree. But then Clara Anne whistled, and Alice saw the archway ahead, signaling the end of the bridge.

"There! Right there, Third Avenue straight ahead," Alice said. "We can coast the rest of the way now, kiddo."

"I can't feel my legs, Mom. They've gone numb."

"Should we pull over?" Alice asked. "According to the map, we can take a right anytime to run into Seventh Avenue."

"No, I'm sailing now. Don't you worry, Mom."

"It's pretty," Clara Anne said as they drove up Seventh Avenue. "I didn't think there'd be big trees and forsythia growing wild in Brooklyn. It must feel good to know that this is where you're from."

When they came to the corner of Seventh and Carroll Street, Clara Anne crinkled her eyes and said, "Shit. Look at me driving to Brooklyn. This is it." She turned and pulled into a small parking lot behind a fenced-in playground. "There's the preschool, just like Pastor Beal told me."

The pastor came to the side door of the church when they rang the bronze doorbell buzzer. It made the door quiver. He opened both of his arms wide and said, "Alice Anne, come into your grandfather's church." And to Clara Anne he said, "Welcome, let's take a seat in the parlor."

Alice was still wondering how he had known her middle name when the scent of the parlor hit her and made her eyes water. This place smelled every bit of one hundred years old. The pastor motioned for them to take seats in the two wing-back chairs. They were upholstered in red velvet and looked itchy. A simple ladder-back chair sat waiting for the pastor, but instead he pulled the piano bench over close to them, dragging along the elaborate, fringed piano shawl. "Silly old thing," he said, and Alice liked him very much.

Across the room, a closet door stood open. Neatly labeled bank boxes were stacked five feet high. Pastor Beal looked back over his shoulder at the display and said, "A history of Reverend James McNall Farrar from the day he was called to the Old First." Now he clapped his hands as if he were starting up a band and said, "The past and the future."

He leaned forward and said, "It was your grandfather's reputation that called me here to the Old First. Tell me, Alice

Anne, what you already know about Reverend Farrar so that I'll know where to begin."

"Very little. Clara Anne is a research librarian." Alice thought he might have almost clapped his hands together again, but instead he raised his eyebrows as a gesture for her to continue. "She found out about the church when she was looking on an old map for my mother's childhood home on President Street. Finding that home led her here to the church and to you. At first, we were afraid that the home and church would be gone."

"Still here—here to stay," he said, and then Alice saw he was waiting for her to speak.

"Ruby, my mother, was the youngest child in the Farrar family. And I'm the youngest in my family. We lived in a home on Argyle Road."

The pastor nodded as if he knew this—the way he knew her full name. No one called her by her full name. Sometimes she forgot it.

"I have made a copy of your mother's baptismal record for you. Reverend Farrar baptized her and the two brothers just older than her here in the Old First. The other three Farrar sons were baptized before the family moved here from Pennsylvania."

"I did not know that," she said, and the man searched for her eyes in a way that men did not often do.

"I was born in Brooklyn at Kings County Hospital, but my parents got divorced, and the family broke up." Alice said this quickly. "My father took the six of us to New Mexico. I was five."

She'd wanted to tell him that her father had tried to erase Ruby from their life—had concocted a story that her mother had left them. But now Pastor Beal interrupted her thoughts and said, "I see. Yes, you said in your letter that you undertook a search for your mother and that eventually you and your sisters and brother were reunited with her."

Alice nodded.

It had gotten easier after she'd buried both her parents.

She didn't feel guilty about it being easier, either. "My parents are dead," she'd say to people who were talking about family. It required nothing more. Her father had died first in 1970, never knowing a single thing about how she'd found her mother. And after Ruby died in 1974, it seemed like she had a normal family. There was no shame in dead parents.

But with this man, she felt she owed something like an explanation. "My father left my mother here in Brooklyn. Afterwards, we children never knew her whereabouts. There were lots of secrets," Alice said to soften the story. She also wanted to tell him that her mother never came looking for her, but she stopped because the pastor didn't seem to want any more.

"But you found her, and she told you stories about her father?" This was less question than certainty and so Alice nodded. Her thoughts had gone so many places since she had sat down in the scratchy chair, and she needed a moment to gather them.

The pastor scooted his bench back a bit to include Clara Anne in what he had to say.

"Reverend Farrar stood six feet tall and weighed 250 pounds. A Princeton grad. Doctor of Divinity. When he died, children dropped rose petals on the road in front of this church, so that the wheels of the hearse should not touch anything but flowers."

It was the accumulation of the swaying bridge, the smell of mildew, and the absence of so much in her life that brought on the tears.

The pastor got up slowly and bent to take both of Alice's hands and said, "Alice Anne, I see mourner's tears flowing like seed pearls. Please, not on this day providence has given us."

He sat back down on his bench, and now he gave himself time to gather his thoughts.

"I want you to know this one thing, Alice Anne. Never once in my life did I dream that I would be sitting here speaking with the granddaughter of Reverend Farrar. A Farrar child. I could not have been so greedy as to pray for this day. It is my pure joy." He nodded at himself.

Alice felt in that moment as if she was a child spinning around in sunlight.

And then he jumped up and said, "Would you like to see Reverend Farrar's study? I find his presence strongest there. When I climb that ladder to his study...well, you'll see."

Alice and Clara Anne followed the pastor into the sanctuary where he pointed out the two Tiffany windows and explained that the organ was an 1891 Roosevelt pipe organ. "Our organist will be here soon to practice. She'll shake the rafters and we can only hope we will be up the ladder to the study by then."

He marched them up the carpeted steps to the dark balcony and then opened a door to a room with low-hanging eaves. "Duck," he said and then he pointed at the ladder. Alice had not expected a real wooden ladder.

"It's new. One of the first things I saw to when I was called to this church."

April light poured through the hole in the roof where the ladder was propped. "I'll go first and will help you ladies up. The last step takes a bit of practice. I've seen little indication that people ventured up here after Reverend Farrar retired." The pastor took three steps up before Alice took the first step on the ladder.

"He was losing his eyesight, you know, and that is why he retired to New Jersey."

Alice hadn't known that. But she wondered if that was why her mother had learned to read braille.

"My mother taught braille at a school for blind children in Philadelphia. That is where she was living when I found her."

"Braille is a gift beyond measure to a sightless child," he said and took her hand in a firm grip so that she could make it up through the opening in the floor of the study.

Alice felt pride in her mother in that moment, but she also could feel Clara Anne's eyes on her back. As a child, Clara Anne had complained that Ruby, her newfound grandmother, never smiled at her. Robin, who was nearly a teenager when she met her grandmother, tried to explain to her little sister that since Ruby worked with the blind, she didn't need to smile much.

"The blind children don't know the difference if she smiles or not." It was a kind thing for a sister to say. But Alice's children had known Grandmother Janie their whole lives and knew what a smile meant. Alice knew too.

Clara Anne took Pastor Beal's hand and made a graceful twirl as she stepped off the ladder into the study. "This is amazing," she said and then said it two more times. "Look at that pigeon-hole desk. Look Mom, each little compartment has a label. This one says morning glory seeds. Remember, your mother said they were her father's favorite flower."

Some stenciling remained at the top of one of the walls and bits of wallpaper hung from the ceiling. The pastor must have seen Alice looking at all this because he reached up and pulled down a piece of the paper, tore it off, and said, "A keepsake."

"May I have another piece for my sister, Clara?"

That was all it took for the pastor to leap into the air to grab another strip of the paper.

There were three narrow windows in the room, which were laced with wires. While Clara Anne sat at the desk and continued to explore the compartments, Pastor Beal motioned for Alice to join him at the windows. "One block over—right there—is President Street," he said.

Alice said, "857 President Street" and sighed. "Mother wrote stories about that home. She said that from the second story parlor window, she could see the silhouette of this church steeple when the sun sat behind it."

"I think maybe, Alice Anne, that your mother went on to have a great deal of sorrow in her life, but it seems to me that she was a happy child who went on to have happy memories of her childhood."

And then the grudge Alice nursed on and off was gone.

"If you don't look down at the cars and all, but rather just look straight out, you will be looking directly into the past. Even the gas lampposts are there. Alice Anne, I believe that sometimes we can see a memory of a beloved memory."

He left her standing there at the windows, freezing the moment, because she knew her mother had stood here at this very spot when she was just a girl.

He stepped over to a bookshelf and took out a book, dusted it, and handed it to Clara Anne. "A book for your library by your great grandfather," he said. Clara Anne held it to her chest. He said, "Now, what do you say we walk over to President Street and then grab a bite at a genuine New York deli?"

Over lunch, the pastor suggested that he take them next to Green-Wood cemetery where Reverend Farrar and his wife were buried. Alice saw the shape of Clara Anne's face change and the pastor must have seen it too. But he did not know that Clara Anne had not wanted her brother to be buried in a dry, weedy cemetery.

"I could not bear for him to be trapped in a cemetery," she'd told her sisters and parents. No one in the family had disagreed with her, although Alice had hated the scattering.

The pastor was skilled in the ways of kindness and pulled Clara Anne back by saying slowly, "Green-Wood is a garden. And I'd like you and your mother to see her sister Faith's grave under the rose arbor."

Alice tilted her head at the man, in the manner of a sparrow passing judgment before flying off into the hills. She knew it was an arrogant gesture. But her mother had said nothing about Faith.

"Her grave is always well-tended. I'm told someone named Irene prunes the roses each spring." He stopped there to give the two women a moment and then said, "Alice Anne, I recall you saying you grew up on Argyle Road. That is in Flatbush, and I believe we have time for a drive-by. I'll drive and then bring you back here."

Clara Anne nodded. "I'm new at bridges and want to be across that one before dark."

"I understand," he said. "But let me tell you, the Verrazzano is lit at night by a necklace of thousands of lights. It gives off a pearly glow. Someday you must see that."

They drove slowly down Argyle Road and stopped in front of Alice's first home. Clara Anne said, "Mom, do you remember living there?"

"I do, yes."

The Victorian house was set back from the street, and shade covered the spring grass.

"Mom, look at that wreath. I swear those are real flowers." Clara Anne had told Alice that her neighbors changed the wreaths on their front door with the change of season. She had gone out in early February and bought a Valentine-themed wreath for her front door. "Just because," Clara Anne told her.

Alice looked at the next-door house that shared the driveway with her old home and said, "I'm pretty sure those neighbors had a big dog that was blind."

"Did your mother tell you stories about this home too?" Pastor Beal asked.

Ruby hadn't and so Alice just shook her head and said, "I told my mother that I remembered my fourth birthday party on our front lawn. We were playing games—all my sisters and my brother. My mother said that was not possible."

As they drove through the Gothic gate into Green-Wood Cemetery, Pastor Beal said, "Leonard Bernstein was buried here last year. But I am not sure where."

"It's a maze," Clara Anne said.

"Yes, you can easily get lost. Some people come here and do that on purpose. Alice, your Uncle Dales is also buried here beside his mother."

Alice thought he was going to ask her where her mother had been buried, but he did not. He didn't pry. Alice said, "My mother adored her brothers Jimmy and Eddie. And she wrote often about Dales." The beautiful black sheep, Alice remembered, and thought her mother had loved him too.

The pastor pointed to a small parking spot and said, "Let's leave the car here and we will walk over hill and dale."

Clara Anne got out of the car first and headed in the direction he pointed, leaving them to make their way up the hill slowly. Pastor Beal stopped several times, once at three tiny graves with identical stones that only recorded a name and date. The one with the earliest date had a crow and an ox carved on it; the second a frog and an ox; and the last a wolf and a lamb. Pastor Beal brushed his hand across the top of each headstone.

Clara Anne called out, "Mom, come see." She was looking over the stretch of the Farrar family graves.

Pastor Beal leaned up against Reverend Farrar's headstone. The stone matched his wife's. A lilac bush, not yet in bloom, grew behind the markers. It seemed to Alice that their stones had not weathered as much as others.

"Over there under that cherry tree—that is where your Uncle Richard is buried." He walked over, brushed off the white blossoms from the headstone, and read aloud the inscription, which was fading away. "Buttons and Bows," he said with the hint of a smile in his voice.

Alice said, "My mother wrote a book about him, and dedicated it to a blind girl who lived at the school for many years. Her parents had abandoned her there. More than anything, my mother wanted to be known as a writer."

"She was a very good writer," Clara Anne said. "She also wrote mysteries. I've tracked down copies from all over the country, in vintage bookstores. The mysteries are all dedicated to someone named Kate."

Alice left the two of them there and walked over to the rose arbor, which was set off from the Farrar graves. A climbing rosebush had woven itself into the arbor. It shaded the grave. Birds were at work in the vines, and it seemed to Alice that they were not bothered in the least by the intrusion. They just carried on with their nest building.

"Those roses are peach colored," he said, but he was studying the birds and said, "I wonder if descendants of these birds return to this spot year in, year out to build their palaces." And when neither of the women seemed to notice what he had said about the birds, he added, "Not all mysteries need to be solved."

The grave was small like the three Alice and Pastor Beal had stopped at. The headstone was white limestone. Clara Anne kneeled and read the engraving aloud.

"Faith Farrar del Palacio
Precious Daughter
1924"

"I never knew you," Alice said to herself because it was the title to the book her mother had written about her baby brother, Richard.

"She has the Farrar name," Alice said and knew the sound of her voice carried that old grudge.

"Alice Anne, you too are a Farrar. You've always been. You just didn't know it."

Alice and Clara Anne arrived back at Clara Anne's house at dusk. Clara Anne's husband had set out frozen hamburger patties and was planning to grill. But Alice suggested they go to the diner. Her treat. The boys asked if they could sit at the counter and Alice said, "I don't see why not," and reminded herself to smile.

As they climbed into the minivan, Clara Anne told her husband that the Verrazzano-Narrows Bridge was one long bridge. Alice knew her daughter would not curse in front of her boys.

From the third row in the van, Clara Anne's oldest son said, "My teacher told me that falcons nest on bridges in New York. Those birds are one of the fastest birds in the whole entire world. They can go two hundred miles an hour. They are en-dangered."

"Interesting. I did not know that," Alice said.

"Now you know," the youngest boy said and made the entire family laugh so hard that the van rocked.

When Alice crawled into bed that night, she tried to close her eyes and sleep, but she couldn't settle her mind. She got up and went to the dormer window, stared out to the street, and then pulled up the sash. It was old and had been painted over, probably many times, but she worked it loose. If she lived here, she'd always sleep under an open window. Alice got back in bed and closed her eyes, thinking that if she could get a whiff of the grass out front that she could return to the birthday party on the lawn of her childhood home; could see her mother in the green and black lace gown again.

And then the tiny little buttons that ran down the back of the gown began to sparkle as her mother twirled, and when she stopped, she gave Alice a sneaky smile. She was beautiful.

But they were not on the lawn. Her mother had been right about that. There had been no birthday party for her on Argyle Road. It was only a moment frozen in time with the voices of her brother and sisters that had never happened. The twirling had in fact happened in her mother's bedroom. She was so very sick, and Alice was scared she would die and leave them. There was a strong smell of cloves and it made Alice's eyes burn. But still her mother twirled, trying only to make Alice smile. And with her eyes closed and her mind finally settled, Alice gave in to the smile.

"And now I know," she said as she began to drift into sleep. It felt like a benediction.

ACKNOWLEDGMENTS

I've always said that to truly know my mother, you had to know her deprivation. This novel is my mother's story. I hope that I've gotten the facts as she came to understand them right, but more importantly I hope that in my fiction I've arrived at her truth. I'm thankful for the opportunity I had to drive her across the Verrazzano-Narrows Bridge to Brooklyn, where she rediscovered her childhood home. I want to thank my many writing teachers and coaches from my first teachers—Dr. Robert Ready and Dr. Laura Winters—to my writing coach, Doug Kurtz, who pushed and pulled me to make this a better book. As always, I am indebted to my first reader, Teddy Jones, who read every word in this novel over and over again, and to my critique partner, Candace Simar. Working with my collaborators, Nick, Kyle, Alex, Colleen, Dan, Ronaldo, and Cameron, at Atmosphere Press on my debut novel, *Blind Eye*, and on this novel has given me back the joy of writing. I am grateful to have found New York romantic artist, Jen Toth, whose art emboldens mine. A big thank you to my enthusiastic publicists, Krista Soukup and Janell Madison of Blue Cottage Agency, and to indie bookstores, especially Garcia Street Books in Santa Fe, New Mexico, who together make it possible for my work to find readers. And from the bottom of my heart, I want to thank my sisters, Claudia Russo and Alice Dillon, who have trusted me with this story of our mother. And finally, a sweet thank you to my daughters, Hayley Purdy and Evayn Lundquist, and my husband, Dennis Burns, who in 1990 traveled with me to Park Slope in Brooklyn to find my mother's past and since then listened to my many attempts to tell her story. Without all of you, there would be no *Across the Narrows*.

ABOUT ATMOSPHERE PRESS

Founded in 2015, Atmosphere Press was built on the principles of Honesty, Transparency, Professionalism, Kindness, and Making Your Book Awesome. As an ethical and author-friendly hybrid press, we stay true to that founding mission today.

If you're a reader, enter our giveaway for a free book here:

SCAN TO ENTER
BOOK GIVEAWAY

If you're a writer, submit your manuscript for consideration here:

SCAN TO SUBMIT
MANUSCRIPT

And always feel free to visit Atmosphere Press and our authors online at atmospherepress.com. See you there soon!

ABOUT THE AUTHOR

A finalist for the 2023 Spur Award for contemporary fiction for her debut novel, *Blind Eye*, **MARTHA BURNS** earned a Doctor of Letters with distinction from Drew University and won the Faulkner-Wisdom Gold Medal for short story. After having lived and worked in Hawaii, New Jersey, California, and Switzerland, Martha and her husband returned to live in their home state of New Mexico.

MarthaBurnsWriter.com